Help us Rate this book...
Put your initials on the
Left side and your rating
on the right side.
1 = Didn't care for
2 = It was O.K.
3 = It was great

8/19

**DATE DUE**

| | | |
|---|---|---|
| SEP 2 4 2019 | | |
| | | |
| | | |
| | | |
| | | |
| | | |
| | | |
| | | |
| | | |
| | | |
| | | |
| | | |
| | | |
| | | |
| | | |
| | | |
| | | PRINTED IN U.S.A. |

m l c    1 ② 3
_____ 1 2 3
_____ 1 2 3
_____ 1 2 3
_____ 1 2 3
_____ 1 2 3
_____ 1 2 3
_____ 1 2 3
_____ 1 2 3
_____ 1 2 3
_____ 1 2 3
_____ 1 2 3
_____ 1 2 3
_____ 1 2 3
_____ 1 2 3

22.49
CF

# PAINTING HOME

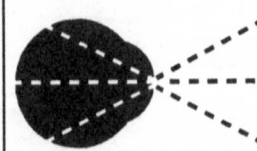

# PAINTING HOME

## ERIKA JOLMA

**THORNDIKE PRESS**
A part of Gale, a Cengage Company

Farmington Hills, Mich • San Francisco • New York • Waterville, Maine
Meriden, Conn • Mason, Ohio • Chicago

Thorndike Press, a part of Gale, a Cengage Company.

LIBRARY OF CONGRESS CIP DATA ON FILE.
CATALOGUING IN PUBLICATION FOR THIS BOOK
IS AVAILABLE FROM THE LIBRARY OF CONGRESS

ISBN-13: 978-1-4328-6751-5 (hardcover alk. paper)

Published in 2019 by arrangement with Harbourlight Books, a division of Pelican Ventures, LLC

Printed in the United States of America
1 2 3 4 5 6 7 23 22 21 20 19

To my grandmother, Kerttu
and her sister, my Great Aunt Soili,
who shared their stories about growing
up in Finland during the war.

# 1

*April, 1940*
*Ylivieska, Finland*

More boys. Just what she needed in her life.

They stood in the train station — four of them to be exact — ready to fill her house with muddy boot prints and raucous laughter.

Anna double-checked the hand-printed slip of paper to make sure she had the right name. She did. She had memorized the name on the slip of paper as soon as her father brought it home from the city offices last night.

R-A-N-T-A. Family of six. Arriving on the 4:20 train from Karelia.

Anna stared at the strangers across the crowded room and stifled disappointment. She had been hoping for a family with daughters — girls to share late-night giggles and afternoon jaunts through the wildflower fields behind their farmhouse. Girls to help with the endless laundry, cooking, and cleaning. Girls to teach her all of the things she didn't know because she had been blessed with six brothers.

But God evidently had a sense of humor — there was no mistaking the fact that their new houseguests were all of the male variety. Well, except for the mother who stood next to their family's lone trunk, looking at her sons out of the corner of her eye with a frown that seemed to plead with them not to do anything to draw attention to themselves.

The boys failed miserably. Every one of them was tall and handsome, with mussed blond hair and gorgeous smiles that would make the girls in Kalajoki swoon.

Every girl except for her, of course. She had learned to resist the charms of the male species.

Anna peered through the crowd to assess the strangers who would now be like family. Mr. Ranta — tall, thin, and graying — stood in the corner of the tiled waiting room, one arm placed protectively around a woman who was his polar opposite in stature — short and plump, with a firmly set chin, and a no-nonsense smile. In his other hand, he carefully grasped the yellow placard that identified them as the Rantas.

Behind them stood the gangly teenage boys. She scanned one blond head after another, until her gaze settled on the oldest Ranta boy. He was probably eighteen or nineteen, twenty at most, yet he stood straight and proud in his navy wool Finnish Army Corps dress uniform.

A soldier.

Catching her breath, Anna forced herself not to sigh. Not only did she suddenly have four more boys to take care of, but one of them was one of Finland's finest. And he was staggeringly good-looking too — from the tips of his Army-issue boots to his crystal-blue eyes.

Anna stomped her boot down hard on her own foot, angry with herself for letting her mind wander. She had enough to deal with right now without adding a handsome soldier to the mix. With her art and plans to immigrate, she simply could not be thinking of Soldier Boy as anything other than the charity case he was.

Raising her head, Anna made her way through the crowded room, doing her best not to stare at the rows of yellow signs, each printed with a name and a number, held by pairs of trembling hands and hovering below frightened eyes. She sighed loudly, allowing the images of tear-stained cheeks, dusty children, and travel-weary adults to sear into her memory.

Maybe someday she would paint this scene.

Show the world what the Russians had done.

But not today.

Today she would smile, laugh, and forget that her family was forced to give away half of their too-small farmhouse to people they'd never met.

Indefinitely.

Anna's footsteps echoed across the tiled floor of the train station. *Indefinitely.* This would put a damper on her life plans. How would she apply for a visa, move to the United States, and go to art school now that the Rantas would be living with them? She couldn't leave her mother alone with all these boys to feed.

Four steps, three steps, two . . . Anna wiped her moist palms on the sides of her dark green wool jacket and pasted on a smile. "Hello! I am Anna Ojala. We will be your host family."

"Good day, Miss Ojala," Mr. Ranta said, as Mrs. Ranta lunged to take Anna's hands into hers as if clinging to a lifeline.

"Welcome. I trust you had a pleasant journey?"

Mr. Ranta shrugged his shoulders. "As nice as it could be."

Soldier Boy nudged his father aside and held out a tentative hand. "I'm Matti."

Anna tried to smile back, but those blue eyes and perfect smile made it hard for her to concentrate. *Don't even think about it.* "My father has his flatbed wagon hitched up outside, so if we can find our way through this crowd, we'll load up your belongings. It's an hour's ride to our village." Anna stared at the Rantas' dusty trunk in an effort not to look at Matti.

Mrs. Ranta saved Anna from her own awkwardness. "Thank you. Boys, please bring the trunk."

"Yes, ma'am," four voices echoed in chorus.

Anna turned toward the door and waved for them to follow, a tiny part of her hoping that Matti watched as she walked away.

This was unexpected. Matti took a deep breath and tried to get a handle on his emotions. He had spent the last week despising the idea of Kalajoki, assuming he would hate everything about the tiny village where his family had been relocated.

He'd expected endless land and a backwoods farmhouse full of people who had no

11

idea what was going on in the world. He'd predicted three weeks of boredom and restlessness stuck way up north. But he certainly hadn't anticipated the beautiful strawberry blonde.

He watched Anna out of the corner of his eye as the wagon jerked and jostled down Main Street. She'd busied herself brushing straw off the wagon bed with the toe of her boot while idly chatting with his parents. She was making a valiant effort to be hospitable, but her fiery green eyes betrayed a raging storm of emotion. That would be hard to tame.

Oh, but he'd like to try. He grabbed a brown linen blanket out of a basket on the floor and handed it to his mother who already shivered in the wind. "It's very cold here."

"Yes, very." His mama's lip quivered as she spoke.

Matti helped her wrap her shoulders tightly before grabbing a blanket for himself. He leaned back against the side rail of the flatbed and tried to get comfortable. It might be cold, but this was a definite upgrade from the smoke-filled train car. At least he was in the fresh air. Matti turned his attention back to Anna.

Every few seconds, a wavy strand of silken

hair fell into her eyes, and she reached up absentmindedly to brush it away, only to have it fall down a few seconds later.

Matti chuckled quietly as she struggled to tame the wayward strand.

Her gaze darted up.

He opened his mouth to say something, but no words came out. He had to get hold of himself or he'd regret his total ineptness for a long time. "Where exactly is your farm, Miss Ojala?"

"We live in Kalajoki. It's about twenty kilometers from here."

"Oh . . . OK." *Way to make an impression, Matti, with the squeaky, shaky voice.*

"I didn't know you boys were already off duty after the Winter War."

"We aren't," Matti said. "They gave me a three-week pass to help my family relocate." He stared at her, his mouth opening and closing as he tried to think of something else to say. Was he entirely incapable of holding a decent conversation with this girl?

"And what do you do in the army, Mr. Ranta?"

"Matti's a sergeant, and a good one!" Mrs. Ranta chimed in.

Anna stared at him and heat rose to his cheeks.

"I was conscripted on my eighteenth

birthday, and they put me in the infantry right next to all of the other boys who had no idea what they were doing with a rifle."

She smiled — just a little — her green eyes sparkling.

Much better. He could stare at those beautiful eyes all day, even if he was stuck up here in Kalajoki. "When I get back to Helsinki in a few weeks, I suspect I'll be doing glamorous things like pot scrubbing, barracks cleaning, and maybe even some trench digging."

"Well, we could use a glamorous pot scrubber around the farm." Anna said, a tiny glimmer of laughter twinkling across her face.

Matti held up his hand in mock salute and gave her a smile. "At your service."

Anna smiled weakly.

"So, Anna Ojala, what do you do with your time?" Matti asked.

"I'm an artist."

He grinned at her, doing his best to portray confidence.

She glared.

So the confidence would not impress her. Maybe he could try honesty? "In truth, I love art. I mean, artists. I mean . . ."

She burst out laughing. So much for being smooth.

"You love artists? Any particular ones, or just those who like to do art in general?"

"I like artists in general, I think." He smiled widely, for the first time all week. What was it about this woman? She was beautiful, but it was more than that. She seemed kind and funny and smart. He could get used to this relocation. At the thought, Matti's face twisted into a scowl. No, he would never get used to this relocation. He frowned and turned to watch the passing scenery as the playful banter of the moment drifted away. For a moment, he'd almost forgotten Karelia was no longer Finnish. And his family was now homeless.

Anna's soft voice interrupted his thoughts. "I'm sorry, Matti. I'm sure this is not easy for you." Her lips clenched tightly.

Matti bit his lip, his heart softening. No, this wasn't what he had hoped for — but that wasn't Anna's fault. He couldn't blame her for the actions of corrupt politicians. He looked down and quickly brushed the rest of the straw off his jacket before returning his gaze to her. "It's not your fault, Anna."

Anna's soft smile quickly faded.

Matti pulled the blanket tighter around his neck and leaned back.

A cloud crossed over those green eyes.

15

Could it be that this farmer's daughter from Kalajoki understood what so many others had missed? Could he finally have an ally in this entire mess? For the first time in weeks, things were looking . . . hopeful. Sure, his life was a mess and his country was at war, but maybe, just maybe, there was someone in the world who would understand him and be willing to stand for what was right.

# 2

*Kalajoki, Finland*

Matti reached over and mussed his youngest brother's head as they walked down the dusty road in front of the Ojala farmhouse. "You hear that, Beni? Miss Ojala here has six brothers."

Beni looked expectantly at Anna.

"It's true," Anna said. "My brothers set up a makeshift soccer field over there in the middle of the cow pasture." She pointed out over a decrepit fence to a field of brown grass. "They even made goals out of old logs and fishing net. They will be glad to have more players." Anna looked at Matti to gauge if her babbling annoyed him.

He seemed almost interested. Anna pushed thoughts of him out of her mind. No man would be interested in her — not if he knew.

"And I'm sure you play captain of the winning team?" Matti smiled, the twinkle in his eye showing the serious conversation from before had been pushed aside.

Anna shook her head. "If you had ever seen me play, you would be asking me to stay as far from the field as possible."

"What? No soccer?" Matti raised his eyebrows.

"Let's just say that last time I tried to play, my brother Aabel had to fish the ball out of the creek over there."

"That bad?" Matti laughed.

The sound echoed through Anna's mind and wiggled its way into her heart. His laugh sounded nice.

She continued the tour of their farm. She turned her attention to the fields that surrounded them and willed herself to focus on the rows of plants, one after another — anything but Matti's blue eyes and movie-star smile.

"What are all these crops?" Mr. Ranta joined the group.

For a moment, Anna shifted her attention from Matti. "Flax. The fields will be full of brilliant blue flowers in a few weeks."

"Beautiful." Matti turned his gaze toward her.

Anna closed her eyes. The tenor of his voice made her heart tremble. Was this really happening? She had just started to emerge from the pain of the last year, to start to hope again, to dream. She didn't need to be distracted by this. "We grow flax and make linen, mostly for our own clothing and towels, but occasionally we sell some to old Mr. Niemi. He owns the mercantile in town."

Should she ask the Rantas what they thought about the war? No, that felt too personal. Instead, she sighed and stared off at the fields. She wished she had a sketchbook with her so she could capture the moment. Or escape the moment. *What's wrong with me, Lord? You gave me the role of helping these refugees — and all I can think about is getting away.*

Anna peeked through squinted eyes at Matti, who slid a piece of straw into his mouth and chewed pensively. With his cap propped on his knee, his blond hair blew every direction in the wind.

Anna's heartbeat picked up. She inhaled deeply, the chilly spring air filling her lungs with the fragrance of fresh pine mixed with the musky scent of cattle and sheep. Sweetness mixed with bitterness, like her true feelings about home.

She both loved and hated this place. She loved the comfort and warmth that came with being loved, cherished, and cared for, but she hated the stifling burden of wanting so much more than a simple farmhouse on a tiny plot of land in middle-of-nowhere Finland. She could never settle down here. Even this handsome and charming soldier wouldn't change her mind.

Especially after what had happened with Henrik.

Anna shuddered and swallowed a wave of emotion. It was best not to think about him right now. Or ever.

The group turned and walked down the long, narrow dirt road that led up to the Ojala farmhouse. Anna glanced up at the familiar scenery. What did their guests think of their new temporary home? The sides of the drive were lined with blackberry and blueberry bushes, each beginning to flower with the promise of summer fruit. Behind them stood her mother's famed garden, brown and derelict. Soon it would be bursting with fresh vegetables and greens.

Anna walked slowly, buying her parents a few last moments of peace before . . . well, before their house was overtaken.

"We decided that all of the boys — my brothers too — will sleep in the barn." She pointed to the wood-hewn barn that stood across the field from the farmhouse. "It should be nice and warm — we just rebuilt it a few weeks ago because the old roof crumbled under the winter's heavy snow."

"That will be wonderful, won't it, boys?" Mrs. Ranta asked. "Just look how lovely it is."

A bit of pride swelled in her. Her brothers had spent weeks cutting down pines from the family's back fifty acres, carefully choosing trees perfect in size and color and creating a final look both functional and beautiful.

"Oh, and look, it has your family crest above the barn door." Mrs. Ranta pointed.

Anna had carefully painted the wooden sign that hung above the front door of the barn, using oil paints to inscribe the Ojala name before embellishing it with rows of leaves and flowers. She had given it to her parents as a parting gift of sorts. Back when she thought she would be leaving for America this summer. "Thank you. I made it myself."

"Anna is an artist," Matti chimed in with a crooked smile.

Anna looked away. If she was to survive the coming days with her heart intact, she'd have to stay as far away from Matti Ranta as possible. She stared at her shoes before looking up and pointing to the tiny, dilapidated building in front of them. "Over there is the outhouse and next to the barn is the sauna. It looks as if my mother lit the stove so you can have a sauna after supper if you'd like."

"That would be nice." Mrs. Ranta stared off into the windblown fields.

Anna averted her gaze toward her parents' tiny farmhouse. "I think it's about time for supper. Shall we head inside?" She shuddered, wrapped her coat tighter around her waist to fend off the chill in the air, and started to make her way inside. If she allowed herself to think of what she had hoped this summer would bring, she would melt into a pool of despair. She had no choice but to put on a smile, do her chores, and smile at her guests. And make sure Matti never found out about Henrick.

# 3

*Moscow, Russia*

He wouldn't make it.

Dr. Alexandrov's words were optimistic, but Tanya could see the trepidation in his expression even as he reassured her that there was still a glimmer of hope.

Nicolai — her wonderful Nicolai — would not survive. The impact of the hard truth had wiggled its way down into her gut the instant their friend Alek had run into the house screaming there had been an accident.

She had raced out onto the street in front of their Moscow tenement to find her husband lying on the hard-packed dirt road. Blood gushed out of his mouth and pooled underneath his pale face, which had twisted into a grimace of pain. She vomited violently right there on the road, choking on her own tears as she screamed for someone to fetch the doctor.

The neighbors helped carry Nicolai up to their tenement. She laid him out on their cot before using her favorite purple wool sweater to try to ward off the bleeding, as if by giving up something that was precious to her, God would return the favor by allowing her to keep Nicolai.

Even then that was futile.

Tanya looked from Nicolai's grey-tinged lips to Dr. Alexandrov's pale face. Disbelief washed through her soul.

A crowd of friends and neighbors, now squeezed into her apartment, gaped as Dr. Alexandrov dug through his black leather satchel. He pulled out a pair of blunt scissors and carefully cut away Nicolai's shirt, exposing the focal point of his injuries.

Alek, Nicolai's best friend, gasped before vomiting onto the floor next to the bed. He steadied himself against Tanya's kitchen table.

"Go!" Tanya shouted to the nervous onlookers, waving them out the door. She wanted to be alone with Nicolai.

Her friends filed out, one by one, glancing back with pity-filled looks and tear-stained cheeks. Kneeling at the end of the cot, she ran her fingers over Nicolai's rough, unshaven face, tracing a line from his shaggy brown hair down to his quivering lips. Still beautiful to her. Dirty, bloodstained, but handsome as a man could ever be. And he was hers. He had been for eleven nearly perfect months.

Swallowing the lump in her throat and wiping desperate tears from her face, Tanya leaned down and kissed Nicolai's lips. She smoothed his hair out of his eyes, wishing he would open them, if only for a minute. But he didn't. She lay her head next to his, holding her breath to hear each and every heartbeat.

She kissed him on the temple, on the cheek, on his hands, and her salty tears dripped onto his skin before she gently wiped them away. Finally, she lay back on their shared pillow, closed her eyes, and hummed to drown out the sounds of Dr. Alexandrov working. She soaked up the scent of him, the feel of him next to her.

"I've . . . I've done all I can do." Dr. Alexandrov's words broke her silent vigil.

Tanya turned away, willing herself not to look into the doctor's eyes. She couldn't bear to see the dark shadows of concern. Of knowing.

"Will . . . he be all right?" Tanya looked at the floor. *Please God. Make the doctor's answer different than what I expect.*

Dr. Alexandrov pressed his lips together.

"I don't think so, Mrs. Egerov. Can I call someone to come be with you?"

"There's no one to call."

"What about Mr. Pederov?"

Tanya shook her head slowly. "I just want to be alone with him."

"OK. I'll be back first thing in the morning to check on you. If he wakes up or there is any change, send someone to get me right away."

Tanya stayed where she was, stroking Nicolai's hair.

He slept, his breaths coming out as wheezy gasps. She stayed as his skin turned from pink to white to a death-tinged grey and his breaths grew further and further apart. Then one last desperate shudder echoed into silence. His body turned from warm to stiff to cold and lifeless.

Her tears pooled onto his still chest, and every fragment of her hope floated away on those blood-soaked sheets.

What did a woman do when her husband died in her bed? What she was supposed to do now? "Why, Nicolai?" she yelled.

As if he could hear her.

Last night she had managed to be calm, steady even. But now that it was all over, she wavered between utter despair and relentless anger.

She was angry at the driver of the car that struck him. Angry at Dr. Alexandrov for not saving Nicolai. Angry at Nicolai for leaving her in a country where a poor, lonely widow had little hope for any kind of future.

She wasn't sure where to go or who to call. Should she fetch the doctor? He had said he'd come by first thing this morning to check on them, so he would probably be here any minute. Or maybe she should call the police? The morgue? She had no idea how to handle this sort of thing. But she couldn't bear to stay in that tiny apartment with Nicolai's body for much longer.

Tanya choked back a sob and flopped into one of the rickety chairs. She needed to get hold of someone to help with the body, obviously. And her neighbors — she wasn't really close to any of them, but they had all seen the accident and would most likely come knocking soon to check. She needed to plan a funeral. And clean up the sheets. And figure out how to pay the rent.

But she couldn't do any of that.

She wanted to run away and pretend none of this had happened. Surely his death was all one horrible nightmare and she would soon wake. The only man she'd ever love wasn't lying dead in the bed they had so happily shared.

# 4

*Kalajoki, Finland*

Anna just wanted to escape to her room with a good book. Forced conversation over forced smiles with the occasional helping of forced throat clearing was not how she wanted to spend her evening. Or any evening, for that matter.

Cringing, she wondered for the tenth time that night how her life had come to this. *Why, God? Everything I have worked so hard for has been postponed. And a blue-eyed boy in a Finnish Army Corps uniform is sitting across my table to remind me of . . . everything.* Her argument with God was interrupted by yet another long and awkward silence.

It would be a long summer.

Anna spread the butter onto her dark brown *limpua* bread as if it took careful concentration. Keeping her gaze away from Matti's blue ones took an immense amount of willpower. She would have to get a handle on her emotions if she was to live in the same place as him.

"How are you settling in?" Anna's mother broke the silence.

"We . . . we are fine. We appreciate your kind hospitality," Mrs. Ranta said.

"And is everything to your liking?"

"It is just lovely." Mrs. Ranta sat up straight in her chair and looked around the room. "We're doing quite well, all things considered."

Matti spoke up, his words full of fire. "Quite well? They stole everything from us! Everything."

"Matti, not now." Mr. Ranta looked at his son with pleading eyes.

"But we can't just sit back and pretend everything is all right . . ." His voice trailed off. He straightened in his chair, pushed his food away, and looked around the table, his fiery gaze eventually landing on Anna.

What did he want her to do? Smile as if he wasn't ranting about war and politics at their dinner table? No, he wouldn't find an ally in her.

"I'm sorry, but I'm not feeling well. Please excuse me." And with that, he slammed back from the table and stalked out the front door.

Anna stared at the still trembling door. That was . . . rude. Her soldier boy needed to learn some manners. She shook her head. No, *that* soldier boy needed to learn some manners.

He wasn't her soldier boy. And he never would be.

Matti swung through the rickety front door and headed down the porch steps, glancing back just long enough to see a table full of angry looks.

Angry, pitying looks.

He made his way out of the Ojala farmhouse and into the icy-cold night air. Walking down the narrow gravel road, he glanced back, hoping to catch of glimpse of Anna in one of the lighted farmhouse windows. No one in sight.

She was probably laughing, chatting about knitting socks, and eating pie as if nothing had happened.

As if his family hadn't just lost everything.

Watching his parents eat a strange supper around a strange table with strangers was just too much for him. He had not fought in the war — had not lost Johan — for this.

Matti let out a shudder. Looking around in the moonlight, he found a smooth stone and chucked a rock into the distance, grunt-

31

ing his displeasure as he leaned against the fence. He picked up another rock, this time letting out a sob as he slammed the rock into the road. His shoulders trembling, he sank to the ground, and for the first time all week, allowed himself to cry.

How had his life come to this? Homeless, purposeless . . . friendless? He still couldn't believe that Johan was dead. Or that his parents' house and fish packing plant was in Russian hands. Or that he was up here in the middle-of-nowhere Kalajoki making small talk with a bunch of farmers when all he wanted to do was hop on the next train down to Lake Lodoga and show those Russians what he thought of their peace treaty.

Either that or grab Anna Ojala and kiss her breathless.

He exhaled deeply and whispered a prayer. *Lord, let me get back there and fight. I can't handle more of this . . . nothingness . . . up here.*

Matti scrunched up his face as he remembered the look on Anna's face as he'd raced out of the house. It reminded him of the look his fourth grade teacher gave him when he'd brought one of the family's newborn piglets to school. Shock that quickly turned to disgust.

He picked up another rock and threw it

into the road, watching it bounce and tumble, leaving a trail of bumps and scratches in the mud. He clearly had a lot to learn when it came to girls. Especially girls like Anna Ojala.

He closed his eyes and pictured her at the train station yesterday, so soft and sweet and totally enticing that he'd felt the need to restrain himself from pulling her closer into his arms, from inhaling the scent of those golden waves. He'd known right away that she was just about perfect for . . . well, that was enough of that.

With his little outburst at dinner tonight, he had ruined any chance of Anna ever being more to him than a kind benefactor's daughter. Which was probably better anyway.

He wouldn't be here for long, and he needed to focus on fighting, winning, and retrieving Karelia from those blasted Russians. He didn't need to be thinking about a green-eyed girl with rosebud lips and the potential to make his heart hammer as it did right now.

# 5

*Moscow, Russia*

Had Nicolai only been gone for three days?

His face was already starting to fade in Tanya's mind, washed away by the dark images that had filled her last hours. First the funeral, then the reception, then having to endure the pity of a thousand shaky smiles.

And now Nicolai's great Aunt Katya insisted that Tanya couldn't be left alone, that she must have constant supervision lest she . . . what? Melt into a puddle of tears on the floor? She'd already done that several times. And even with people around to pull her off the floor, desperation and loneliness filled her.

Tanya looked around her apartment, squinting in the early morning light, willing her eyes to stay away from the neatly made bed, the place where Nicolai had breathed his last breath. No, she would never be able to sleep there again. She'd spent the last three nights in a hard, wooden chair, crying more than sleeping, moaning more than thinking.

"Tanya, why don't you come over here and I'll make you some tea." Aunt Katya's soft voice startled her.

"No, thank you." Tanya sounded distant, even to herself.

"All right, well, I need to talk to you. I need to run to my house to grab a few of my belongings, since it seems I will be staying a bit longer than expected. I would like for you to come with me."

Tanya stared at her, unblinking.

"Tanya? Are you all right?"

"I think . . . I will stay here."

"All right." Aunt Katya seemed lost for a moment. "I suppose I'll go quickly and be back in about an hour. Nicolai's Uncle Boris will be returning with me. We would like to talk to you about your plans." She waved around the tiny apartment Tanya had shared with Nicolai.

Uncle Boris? Why would Uncle Boris care what she did next? It wasn't really his business, was it?

"Tanya?" Katya grabbed her by the shoulders and looked sternly into her eyes. "Tanya, we have to make some decisions. Your rent is due soon and you can't stay here without Nicolai."

The words echoed through Tanya's head, reminding her of all she had lost.

"Are you all right, dear?" Katya's voice was soft, but hurried.

"I . . . yes. I understand." Tanya sank into a chair and tipped her head to her chest. Of course she wasn't all right. She would never be again.

"That's good, dear. You just sit right there and take a little rest, and I'll be back soon." Katya was kind and gentle, but seemed relieved to have a break.

Who wouldn't want to leave this place of desperation, of hopelessness?

Katya quietly shut the door and panic rose in Tanya's throat. She would have to move away from her apartment and live with someone else. But who? Her parents were gone and Aunt Katya and Uncle Boris must be a thousand years old. Her friends were all either moving away or moving in with family because of the war.

Tanya stared at the door and closed her eyes. She had to think. Pressing her fingertips into her temples, she did her best to focus. She couldn't wait here for Aunt Katya to make decisions for her. Living with Uncle Boris and Aunt Katya simply wasn't an option.

What about . . . Tanya concentrated on the possibilities. There was Alek. He would take her in. But he lived in a one-room studio with his wife and newborn son. And her cousin Ida would maybe allow it for a short stint, but her husband was off at the war and she had six kids to feed. *No. No. No.* Tanya swallowed the panic that welled up in her throat.

Was there anyone left for her?

"What if?" An idea planted itself in her mind and wouldn't let go. Did she dare? She certainly couldn't live on her own in Moscow. Aunt Katya wouldn't allow it, but what if?

In a flurry of desperate tears, she grabbed Nicolai's old leather satchel and started filling it with the few things that mattered to her — the quilt she had carefully stitched together in the months before their wedding as a gift for Nicolai and the photograph they'd splurged to have taken on their honeymoon just eleven months ago. Stuffing her treasures into the satchel, she laced on her only pair of decent boots and dumped every ruble they owned into the pocket of her threadbare wool coat.

She knelt next to the bed where Nicolai had died and grabbed his well-worn Bible. She clutched it to her chest. She didn't believe in God anymore, but Nicolai had loved this book. "Goodbye, my love. I will treasure these months for always," she whispered.

Her heart squeezed. She had to do this. She had to go before Katya got back. Before rational thought could change her mind, she kissed her palm and blew her last hope of love into the air, grabbed Nicolai's treasured violin from its spot next to the hearth, and headed out the door into the still-chilly morning air.

Tanya navigated the misty streets toward Komsomolskaya Square. If anyone saw her walking down the street making loud hiccupping sobs and doing nothing to wipe the tears streaming down her face, they'd probably put her into the insane asylum.

Hanging her head low, she kept walking, driven by a pain she would never truly escape. She clung white-knuckled to her satchel and hardly noticed the sun as it peeked over the tops of the buildings, signifying a new day.

Her first day on her own.

Tanya spotted the yellow spires of the Leningradsky Station and reminded herself to hold her emotions in check. She made a beeline for the front doors, not glimpsing backward at the sights and sounds of the city where she grew up. The city she had loved deeply and now, lost fully. She was done with Moscow. There was nobody and nothing left for her here.

Studying the board above the ticket counter, she read the list of cities, rolling them around on her tongue. Which one would hold opportunity and hope for a lonely young widow? Leningrad. Pscov. Murmansk. She had never been to any of them, had never even considered leaving home. Until home left her.

She willed herself to make a choice before she changed her mind and went back to her apartment. Taking a deep breath, she asked the ticket clerk which train left the soonest and paid her fare.

Leningrad, it was.

# 6

## Leningrad, Russia

Tanya eyed the intricately carved fresco that stood above the main doors of the Moscovsky Rail Station in Leningrad. The men and women carved into the images looked so strong and happy. Maybe that was a sign that she, too, would find strength and happiness on the streets of Leningrad?

Probably not. Not when her heart ached so heavily for the only man she would ever love.

Tanya leaned back into the leather seat in the waiting room, frozen and unsure. She scowled at the smiling faces on the fresco. What did a stone statue know about life anyway? Turning back to the train platform, she watched the shifting shadows of bustling passengers dance across the pink-tinged tiles.

Were any of them like her? Alone. Unsure. Lost. Everyone else seemed to know exactly what they were doing and where they were going, as evidenced by the almost frantic rush on the platform. No one took time to glance backward at the lonely figure sitting in the waiting room with tears streaming down her face.

Her impulsive nature had always been her greatest weakness. Even as a child, her mother had constantly reminded her to think before she jumped in headfirst. Which hadn't stopped her from trading her mother's entire supply of red currant jelly for a copy of *The Romance of an Empress* when she was in the seventh grade.

Who cared about eating when there was a romantic novel to read? At least, Tanya felt that at the time. Two weeks of nonstop chores later, she had realized that perhaps the library was a better place to find books.

Nicolai had tempered her impulsiveness a little bit.

All right, a lot.

Nicolai had been her rock when the rest of her world fell apart. First her father — carried away by navy-clad police officers claiming he was a Bolshevik sympathizer. Then her poor mother, dead from pneumonia weeks before Tanya had received word that her father had died in a prison camp. Tanya had been devastated. But through it all, Nicolai, her Nicolai, stood by her, held her, and loved her. Yes, without Nicolai, she would've been lost.

As she was right now.

Now, he was gone too. And Tanya was entirely alone in the world, sitting in a train station with the anguish of indecision and loss covering her heart with a black blanket of regret. If only Nicolai had been around this morning to talk her out of hopping on a crazy train to nowhere.

*Impulsivity mixed with grief do not a great decision make.* She should stitch that on a sampler someday to remind herself to never do something this stupid again.

She pushed out of the chair, grabbed her satchel and Nic's violin, and walked over to the ticket counter. How much was a ticket back to Moscow? Maybe she should go home and chalk this crazy adventure up to blind grief. No one would blame her.

Bile rose from her stomach as she gagged down a torrent of tears. No, she couldn't go back to Moscow. Not to an empty apartment and a life without Nicolai.

But could she survive here? Did she have the strength to start over?

Pinching her lips between her teeth, she turned toward the smiling stone figures over the door and started walking.

"I don't have a choice but to find out," she whispered under her breath as she used the hem of her coat to wipe her tear-soaked cheeks.

One foot after another, the echoes of each step resounding across the cavernous room, she made her way to the front doors of the station. Pausing underneath the golden beams that framed the doorways, Tanya turned back toward the intricately carved walls of the station.

Stepping into the road in front of the station, she shivered. The air was cold as the sun set behind the buildings in Vostanniya Square. She looked to both sides to get her bearings, clutching her stomach as it growled loudly.

"Here we go."

She started down the street, not sure of what to do. Maybe she should find herself something to eat? Her stomach turned to acid at the mere thought of food, just as it had every time she'd tried to eat since Nicolai died. But she must survive. And the first step was sustenance. Stepping into a tiny café at the edge of the square, she found a small table by the window and scooted into her seat.

"*Privet!* Do you want bread?"

The cheery waitress grated against Tanya's

dark mood.

"Yes." Tanya inhaled the rich aroma of cooking kolbasa and potatoes as her stomach clenched. "And a helping of whatever you have on special."

It smelled just like home. Cringing, Tanya reminded herself that if she kept thinking about Nicolai, she'd never make it through this meal. Much less, the rest of her life.

"I'll put the order in." The waitress's smile disappeared as she jotted down the order.

Tanya turned toward the window, somberly studying the crowds of people as they hurried by. At least she had something to distract her from thoughts of Nicolai. A group of women made their way down the street, hauling baskets of produce on their shoulders. Their children ignored their grim faces as they scrambled between their legs playing a game of hide and seek as they followed their mothers down the street.

A regiment of soldiers strolled by in uniform, grim-faced and focused as they marched in rows down the street, their rifles strapped to their backs.

Tanya scrunched up her face and tried to remember the maps she had studied in school. Was Leningrad closer to Germany than Moscow? She thought so. Why hadn't she taken a train to Siberia and gotten far,

far away from the threat of war? Siberia would've been safer.

And less civilized. In Siberia, they probably slept in tents and ate raw meat from tigers. At least in Leningrad she could find herself a quaint café that served human food like kolbasa and potatoes.

Glancing at the ticking clock on the wall, she realized it was already too late to find permanent housing tonight. She'd have to stay in a hotel and look for something more long-term tomorrow.

She waved at the waitress and beckoned her over.

"Do you need something, Miss?" The waitress's eyes twitched toward two men sitting at a table on the other side of the restaurant.

"Yes. Do you happen to know of an inexpensive hotel where I can find a room around here?"

The waitress harrumphed. "Not around here. The hotels around the square cater to travelers. You won't find a place for less than 150 rubles."

Tanya winced. One hundred and fifty rubles. That was a lot. But where else would she sleep? She quelled a wave of longing for her tiny apartment back in Moscow and reminded herself that this was her life now.

"All right. Where's the closest one?"

The waitress pointed down the road, gave her quick directions, and then explained that lower-rent boardinghouses could be found down by the Neva River. She just had to head east and walk two or three miles.

"Thank you."

"You're welcome." The waitress glanced at the men at the other table before turning back to her, her mouth opening and closing as if she seemed to be contemplating telling her something. "Around the square, people are more friendly toward outsiders. Once you get out of this area, you might want to keep your words to a minimum."

"Outsiders?"

But the waitress had already walked away to help another customer.

Five minutes later, she returned with a gray metal tray balanced on her left shoulder. "One order of kolbasa stew." She set the tray down, unloading a large yellow glass of lukewarm water, a small loaf of simple white bread, and a heaping bowl of kolbasa stew, laden with onions, garlic, and potatoes.

Tanya's stomach clenched as the aroma hit her nostrils, and she impulsively covered her nose. Tanya looked up at the waitress who now stared at her with empty eyes. "What did you mean about me being an outsider? I'm from Moscow."

The waitress glanced into the back of the restaurant. "Just be careful. People around Leningrad aren't exactly open to people from elsewhere."

Tanya forced herself to smile and once again thanked the waitress as she hurried off. She took a bite and swallowed before her stomach could revolt. She was no outsider. She couldn't worry about the words of a silly waitress who didn't know anything about her situation. Tanya forced another bite and another until her stomach was full, her resolve growing with each bite. She could do this. She would make it here in Leningrad.

Nicolai had always said she was strong. She just had to trust herself. And take one tiny step after another.

# 7

*Leningrad, Russia*
It had to be before five in the morning.

Tanya flung herself onto her stomach and sank into the soft sheets, willing herself to get back to sleep. She needed to rest.

*Dear Lord, help me to . . .*

She stopped her prayer abruptly. She didn't do that anymore. She had given up on God after losing her parents.

Nicolai had begged her to reconsider her stance.

"My mom spent half her life on her knees and a lot of good that did her."

"It did do her a lot of good, Tawnie. She's in heaven, rejoicing with Him now."

Tanya had frowned, making it all too clear that it was a closed subject between them.

After that, Nicolai had taken to praying for her — out loud and seemingly all the time — that she would find her Savior again.

Tanya stifled another sob. Would the pain

of losing Nicolai — her parents — ever dull? If loving felt like this, she would never love again. Not a man, not a friend, and not the God who had allowed all of this to happen. Tanya didn't need anyone but herself anymore. She would make it on her own.

Rolling out of bed, she slipped on yesterday's clothes and splashed cold water on her face, hoping her red-rimmed eyes weren't too noticeable. She headed downstairs, hardly noticing the ornate lobby of the famed Hotel Astoria in her quest for coffee and breakfast. Finding a small café in the lobby, she purchased a small folding map of the city along with a cup of coffee and a carrot Piroshky. She found a spot on a soft leather chair in the lobby and forced down her food while she mapped out her plan for the day. First up on the agenda: Push everything from the last few days out of her mind so she'd be able to function like a normal adult. There was time for grieving later. Today, she had to start her new life and she couldn't afford to spend the day wallowing.

The waitress said that there were lower-rent boarding houses a few miles down the road along the Nava River. She traced her finger east on the map and carefully circled the places where boardinghouses were

49

marked. Maybe she'd find a nice place with a private room that included breakfast.

Tanya took a big bite of piroshky and allowed herself to daydream. What if the proprietor needed help in the kitchen? Or with the office administration? At the right place, she could get a job and a place to stay in one fell swoop.

Suddenly anxious to get going, Tanya brushed the crumbs from her dress and headed back up to her room to clean up. All she had to do was put one foot in front of the other and she'd make it through the next few hours.

Scrubbing her face with water from the basin by the sink, Tanya straightened out the wrinkles on her skirt before packing her satchel. She laced her boots, using the tiny cloth that the hotelier had laid by the sink to scrape off yesterday's travel grime from her soles.

Once presentable, she stepped out onto the road, careful to avoid the muddy sidewalk with her shiny, clean boots and headed in the general direction that the waitress had pointed out. She kept her head down and walked in a straight line, not daring to make eye contact with anyone on the streets.

A few miles later, she came across her first boardinghouse. It was a large, cream-painted house situated off the road on a patch of carefully groomed grass. Planters filled with green plants that looked ready to burst into bloom hung from each window, giving the house a homey feel. The sign on the road proclaimed "Sanatoria Belyakov, established 1913."

She marched up the walk and knocked loudly on the door. A plump woman wearing a patchwork apron answered with a tentative smile, holding a steaming wooden spoon dripping with gravy.

"May I help you?"

"Yes Madám, I'm Tanya Egerov." The woman's smile disappeared and was instantly replaced by a stern frown. Had she said something wrong? "I'm looking for a place to stay."

"We don't have any rooms available." The woman's voice was clipped, angry.

"May I inquire how much a room would cost were there one available?"

"950 rubles a month."

Tanya winced. 950 rubles a month was out of her price range. She was hoping for more like 450. "Thank you." She smiled shakily and willed herself not to cry until she was out of view.

Tanya blew out a deep breath and drew a giant X on her map over the tiny scrawled letters that said *Sanatoria Belyakov*. One down, thousands to go. Tanya tried to cheer herself up by dreaming of the room she would soon have to herself. A place where she could refresh, rejuvenate, grieve. There had to be hundreds of other boardinghouses in Leningrad. She checked her map and headed toward Sanatoria Chzov, which according to her map was around the next bend.

Another tentative knock and another rejection followed. This pattern continued for most of the day, until Tanya's map held eleven giant X's over her circles of hope.

What was wrong with this city? Or, maybe she should be wondering what was wrong with her?

Tanya glanced up at the sun, which was already sinking behind the buildings on Ulica Ryleeva. Her heart felt heavy. What now? Should she head back toward the Hotel Astoria? It was pricey, but one more night couldn't hurt.

Yes. She would head back and sink into clean cotton sheets and give herself some time to rest. And think. And cry. And maybe sleep away the shame of the day.

Because tomorrow was a new day. And she was certain to have better luck then.

# 8

*Kalajoki, Finland*

Anna stacked every blanket she could find into her arms and braced herself as she stepped into the cool night air. A cold front was coming in and the boys sleeping in the barn would need all the warmth they could get.

Shivering in the cold, Anna considered the last few days.

Matti had been able to rein in his anger a little, but he certainly hadn't been a cheerful guest. Instead, he had been stoic through meals and had all but avoided the evenings around the card table with the rest of the boys. He had made it clear he couldn't wait to get away. Away from both Kalajoki and her.

That was fine with her. It wasn't as though they were best friends or anything. They hardly knew each other and had yet to have a real conversation. The fact that her heart seemed to dance into her throat every time he walked into the room — well, that was just a girlish crush.

"Hello?" She rapped on the barn door, hoping that one of the younger boys would answer the door and relieve her of her load. She didn't need a run-in with Mr. Tall, Handsome, and Brooding tonight.

No one answered.

"Hello?" She carefully balanced the blankets on her hip as she nudged the door open with her shoulder, her ears tuning in to angry voices echoing from the hayloft.

"We have to fight. For our country. It's only right." That voice belonged to her very own knight-in-shining-army uniform.

"But I'm not old enough to be conscripted, Matti. I'm only fifteen." Was that her brother Arvo talking? Anna groaned at the thought.

"We all have to do our part, Arvo. If you're not old enough for conscription, I know a place to get false papers. I'm taking Patri down before I head out next week."

Anna hovered behind the rafters, afraid to move forward into the light and even more terrified of what she was hearing. What were they talking about? The Ranta boys had just escaped a hostile takeover of their home by a horrible enemy. And now Matti was trying to convince them to join the army? Risk their lives in battle?

Anna slinked back against the wall, anger welling up in her chest. At least now she knew the truth. Sure, Matti Ranta was handsome and charming and made her stomach flip flop, but he was also crazy. So crazy that he seemed to think it was a good idea to drag innocent, fifteen-year-old boys into a war. Her brother, of all people! She had heard enough.

She slammed into the room, glaring up into the loft at Matti as she threw down the pile of blankets on a table next to the ladder. She crossed her arms and stared at her brothers as if imploring them to speak first.

"Hello Anna." Fifteen-year-old Arvo looked as guilty as he had the day he'd crashed Daddy's sleigh into the snow bank while trying to race the Korkonen brothers home.

"Hello, Arvo. What are you guys doing?"

"Just talking," Matti chimed in, as smooth as ever. That man must have icy water from the Kalajoki River running through his veins.

"About?"

Matti's facial muscles tensed.

"Anna. We were talking about the war. I was just explaining we all have to do our part to take back our homeland. There are ways for strong, fighting men to help our country regardless of their age."

Anna nearly choked on her spite. How dare he bring her brothers, her innocent and much-too-young brothers, into this war? "I'd appreciate it if you kept your sentiments to yourself, especially when it comes to breaking the law and encouraging my brothers to do the same. We took your family into our home and I cannot stand for you to repay us with . . . this!" She stormed out, her final words clipped, as if she said them through a locked jaw.

She raced out of the barn, wishing with every step there was some way for her to grab her brothers and fold them into the warmth of her parents' farmhouse where they would be safe. Even if it took every bit of her strength, she would make sure her brothers never had to face what Henrick had.

She raced into the house, flung herself onto her bed, and buried her head into her pillow, wishing she could forget all about terrible peace treaties and violent wars.

That and the fact that the coldest man in all of Finland was living right there in her barn.

■ ■ ■ ■

So much for getting on Anna's good side.

What was wrong with him? Strike that. What was wrong with Anna? She was beautiful and charming and witty and fun, but the girl sure didn't understand war. Or him.

He shuddered, wrapping the worn wool blanket Anna had practically thrown at him around his shoulders. He settled into the hayloft to sleep and thought about the nights he had spent huddled in snowdrifts with shells exploding all around him. Horrible nights he'd spent praying in fear, wondering whether he would die from a Russian bullet or freeze to death. He thought of the friends he had lost — of Johan who had been shot down on the front less than two days after the war started. He hated war as much as Anna did. But he understood it so much better.

Anna might have understood the realities of sacrifice and work, but she didn't know how it felt to lose friends. She hadn't watched her parents' faces as everything they'd ever known or loved was ripped away from them. She hadn't seen what Russian occupation had done to Karelia. And she didn't understand how it felt to board a train and look back at beloved hills and valleys for possibly the last time.

No, Anna didn't understand anything about this war. But he wouldn't be the one to explain it to her, not after the little fit she threw.

Well, at least his family was safe. He would only have to manage Anna's narrow-minded drama for two more weeks. Then he could go back to the front and forget all about her.

As if that were even possible.

# 9

*Kalajoki, Finland*

Even after a good night's sleep, Anna was so seething mad that she could hardly paint, which was the one activity that calmed her emotions.

She grabbed her paintbrush off of the easel and dipped it into fiery red paint, allowing a slash of red to cover the orange that she had already thrown across the canvas.

How could he do that? He had no right to drag her brothers or anyone into this war. Sure, she felt sorry that he'd lost his home and friends and was headed off into an unknown country to fight a ruthless enemy. But that wasn't her problem. Couldn't he see that dragging her brothers off to fight in Russia would cause more heartbreak and pain?

Of course, he didn't see it that way. He was all gung-ho about some brand of patriotism that they must have been selling by the flaskful in Helsinki. He was angry. And he wanted to fight.

She squeezed a few drops of green paint onto her palette and did her best to calm down the scene she was painting. Closing her eyes, she tried to picture a distant meadow — somewhere in South America or Africa maybe. Somewhere wildflowers grew without worry of frost and the sunrise brought warmth instead of just light. Somewhere peaceful and warm and far from here where angry, war-mongering soldiers tried to drag her brothers off into cold trenches.

She banged her hand against the table next to her, instantly regretting her impulsivity as a splattering of red paint leapt up and covered her face with flecks of paint.

She rushed to the kitchen to grab a towel to clean up the mess and ran smack dab into Matti. She couldn't escape the man.

He grabbed her by the shoulders. "Anna." Her name came out huskily.

"Let go of me." Anna ducked out of his grasp, trying to give herself space from those eyes that repelled and summoned her at the same time.

"I'm sorry, Anna. I know I made you angry and that wasn't right of me. I just . . . you can't understand what I've seen." Matti trailed off, as if there was more but he wasn't sure he could say it.

She waited.

"I'm just sorry. Down in Karelia, men are dying. People are being forced out of their homes and, well, I lost . . . a few months ago." His voice was pinched. "I lost my best friend. They never found his body. There's just something in me that feels the need to fight for Finland."

An image of Henrick's face flashed into her mind and her heart softened a little. If anyone understood what it was like to lose someone, she did. "I think I do understand, Matti."

"How? How could you understand what it was like?" He stared at her with eyes that shimmered like ice on the lake in January. Dark and cold.

"My fiancé . . . Henrick. He was a pilot. He flew one of the Bristol Bulldogs."

Those icy eyes widened.

Anna took a deep breath and continued. "He was shot down last fall."

A cloud of regret inched across his face. "Oh, Anna. I'm so sorry. I didn't know."

"I didn't tell you." She flashed what she hoped was a convincing smile, hoping he wouldn't ask her more. She couldn't let him find out that Henrick's death was her fault.

Matti sighed deeply. "I just can't let their sacrifices be in vain."

Anna bit her lip. "But Matti, not our brothers. They are too young."

"I know. I should never have involved them." Matti frowned. "I regretted bringing that up as soon as I'd said it. If I promise I will go tell him right now that they can't fight until they are conscripted at eighteen, will you forgive me?"

Anna paused. If she could get him to promise that, at least she wouldn't have to worry about Arvo going to Helsinki. "Do you promise?"

"I promise."

"And you'll stop warmongering out in the barn?"

"What exactly do you mean by warmongering?" His tentative smile cut through the tension that had filled the room a few minutes before.

"I mean . . ." she trailed off. She couldn't exactly tell him not to talk about the war at all, not when so much depended on it. "I mean, let the boys come to their own conclusions about the war. Tell them the facts, but don't try to convince them."

Matti let out a deep breath.

She had to admit that her soldier boy was a tiny bit cute when he smiled like that. Just a little bit.

"What if we were to start over?" He flashed that heart-stopping smile once again.

Anna stuck out her hand as if meeting him for the first time. "I'm Anna Ojala. I love to paint and read and I'm chairwoman of the Junior War Support Committee here in Kalajoki. You know, helping keep our boys safe on the front and all that." She stood as tall as she could and saluted him.

"Nice to meet you Anna. I'm Matti. And I have a complaint to make to the Kalajoki Junior War Support Committee." He leaned against the counter and tugged off his muddy black boot, revealing a black wool sock with a gaping hole in the toe. "You see, Anna Ojala, the socks that I received in my care kit were defective. In fact, I wonder if the women who knitted these forgot to finish off the toe section."

Anna grinned, stepping forward and pulling his sock off of his foot for a closer inspection. Running her hands up and down the length of it, she stretched it between her hands. "In my expert opinion, this is some fine workmanship. In fact, I can clearly see from the way the stitching has torn that the wearer is clearly to blame for any defect."

"And what makes you so sure of this, Miss

Chairman?" His easy-going grin made her want to burst out laughing, but she bit her lip to keep a straight face. She was still mad, after all.

"Well, it's quite evident from my inspection that whoever has been wearing these socks has been using them incorrectly. Socks are meant to be worn on your feet, Soldier Boy. Didn't they teach you that at basic training?"

That smile.

Her heart went limp. She'd had a hard time resisting him when he was brooding, forlorn, and upset. But this Matti? The fun, teasing, and earnest Matti? She kind of liked him, as much as she hated to admit it.

His voice turned serious. "I — I wish we'd met under different circumstances, Anna Ojala."

Anna stared into those crystal-blue eyes, the ice having melted. She let the emotions wash over her. Goodness, he *was* handsome. And kind, and funny when he wasn't in one of those moods. Scowling at her own silliness, Anna turned away so she could collect her thoughts. She didn't want or need a boyfriend. She was perfectly capable and happy to forge her own path in life. She could forgive him, of course, it was the Christian thing to do, but that didn't mean she had to get carried away with him.

Biting her lip, Anna regained her composure. The last thing she needed or wanted was to get involved with Matti Ranta, which was probably a good thing since he wasn't offering. Instead, he leaned against the counter all suave and handsome with a crooked grin. Probably enjoying this.

Anna glanced down at her hands, now caked with dried red paint. She would be picking paint off of her skin for days. She scrunched her nose. Why was she thinking about painting right now anyway? Oh, yes, to distract herself from that heart-stopping smile and those sparkling blue eyes fastened onto her.

"I have to run back to the barn. I made a promise to this girl that I'd have a little chat with her brother about the merits of staying at home and helping Finland by harvesting a bumper crop of flax. But shall we resume this conversation tonight after dinner? Perhaps over a hand of cards?"

Anna closed her eyes, relieved for a moment to catch her breath. "Talk to you later, Soldier Boy."

He winked at her and then walked out of the room.

She turned back to her painting and groaned. It was shaping up to be a lovely scene — a brilliant, albeit angry-looking, sunset was the backdrop for a picture-perfect landscape. Sighing, Anna closed her eyes and tried to drum up the familiar longing she often got after painting — the longing to paint herself into the picture and run away to some exotic scene she imagined.

Only today she couldn't do it. Instead, all she could see was herself, wrapped in the arms of a handsome, blue-eyed soldier right here in Finland.

A thought that made her stomach flip upside-down.

# 10

*Kalajoki, Finland*

"What is the matter with me, Kaino? His family moves into my house as refugees and a week later, I can't stop thinking about him."

Anna flung herself backward into a pile of hay in her father's hayloft and let her body sink into the itchy pile. Frowning, she allowed herself a few moments to let it all sink in.

After Henrick, she had sworn she would never again allow herself to feel like this for a man. Yet here she was, doing it again. Only this time it was worse. Every time Matti came near she got all sweaty and fluttery. She pictured the large words she had scrawled across the pages of her journal just last week.

*Forget about getting married. Make your own plans. You don't need a husband anyway.*

Good advice. Advice that Anna should

probably heed right now, because she wasn't about to give up her plans to move to America for anyone.

Even Matti Ranta.

"I've never seen you like this, Anna. Your Soldier Boy must be handsome."

"Yes, Kaino. Handsome. And stubborn and pig-headed and dead set on fighting in a war that will do nothing but bring pain and destruction to Finland."

"And tall and blond and walks with a smooth swagger, as if he just knows what he wants and how he'll get it?"

"That's about right. How did you guess?"

"I'm pretty sure he's swaggering toward us right now."

Anna shot up onto her elbows, quickly brushing yellow strands of hay off of her dress. She turned toward the direction Kaino stared.

Matti walked straight toward them, wearing a pair of military-issue khakis and a white shirt, looking as dreamy as ever.

She moaned.

Kaino laughed. "He *is* handsome, Anna."

She tucked that wayward strand of hair behind her ear. *For the ten thousandth time, you're not looking for romance. Not now, not ever.* She pasted an all-business smile onto her face and vowed to be calm and collected around Matti.

"Hello, Matti. This is my friend Kaino Korkonen."

Kaino stood, tossed her long, blonde braid behind her shoulder, and leapt down out of the hayloft before doing a quick curtsy. She held out a slender hand. "It's good to meet you, Matti. I've heard a lot about you."

Anna glared at Kaino, blushing. Matti now knew she had been talking about him. As if this situation could get any more awkward.

"Hello, Kaino. It's a pleasure to meet you." Matti shook her hand and then turned to Anna. "Your brothers are taking me out to the river to go fishing, and I was wondering if you would like to come along."

Anna's mouth dropped open as she tried to think of an excuse that wouldn't sound as desperate as she felt. As nice as it would be to spend the afternoon by the water, her fragile emotions couldn't withstand an afternoon with Matti. Especially if just being around him for two minutes made her feel all giggly and irrational. "I can't. My mom needs me in the kitchen."

"I already asked her. She said you could come along as long as you promised to bring back some fish for her to fry up for dinner."

She quickly turned to Kaino, pleading with her eyes. "Kaino was just telling me that we hadn't had much time together recently so I would hate to leave . . ."

Kaino interrupted before Anna could finish. "I'll come with you guys. Let me just run home and grab my fishing pole. My mom would love some fish for dinner tonight."

"Great," Matti shouted, already turning to head back to the barn to grab poles and bait. "Come on, Anna! Your mom said she was packing us a picnic lunch to eat while we fish."

Less than an hour later, Anna sat wrapped in a hand-knitted afghan in the shade of an old spruce tree next to the Kalajoki River. She pulled the blanket tighter and shivered in the cool spring air. Anna tried not to stare at Matti, standing less than twenty meters away with a fishing pole leaning against his knee.

At least they would have plenty of fish stored up and canned for next winter. And they'd need it, too, since it was looking as though the Rantas would be staying with them for much longer than any of them had previously expected.

There hadn't been any retractions to the peace treaty. No one was admitting a mistake or calling for all Finns to return to Karelia as Anna had hoped. Instead, the news was full of tragic stories about families like the Rantas losing everything. With each passing day, it became clearer. Finland would get sucked into this war. That or half of her population would be left homeless.

Anna turned her gaze toward Matti and her heart ached for him. He had lost so much. And he had so much more to lose. Anna was a bit proud of him.

Standing there all strong and confident by the water, stubbornly dead set on fighting, Matti was passionate. She would give him that. And honest and kind and . . . well, his blue eyes were so light that they almost looked violet. His pale skin almost glowed in the early afternoon sunlight. His blond hair was mostly straight but curled a tiny bit above his ears. Would his commanding officer require him to cut it so it wouldn't curl out from under his uniform cap?

He carefully strung a herring head onto his hook, explaining to her brothers that fresh fish heads and guts were the very best bait when it came to catching the biggest trout.

"Eww!" they all screamed, but then followed Matti's lead and strung their own hooks with a variety of fish entrails. No one seemed to ever doubt a word Matti said.

Except for her, of course. Fish guts. Gross.

Anna turned her head toward Kaino, who dozed on the blanket, her unused fishing pole propped against a tree. A lot of help Kaino was today.

She must look pretty silly sitting on the blanket staring at them while they fished. She was a perfectly capable woman . . . who was scared away from the water by a few fish heads. Standing, Anna buttoned her coat, grabbed her pole, and found a spot far enough away from the boys so she wouldn't have to smell their fish guts. She dug a chunk of dried herring out her dad's bait bag and strung her hook with civilized bait before dropping her line, hoping that maybe the peace and quiet of the river would clear her racing mind. It did nothing of the sort.

She quickly went through her mental list of the reasons she didn't want a man like Matti. He was a down-home Finnish country boy who planned on living his whole life here. He wanted to settle down, have a family. He wanted to fight for home and country and all that.

She had different plans. Bigger plans.

She wouldn't stay in Finland. Not where war had stolen everything she had dreamed of. No, she would move to the United States and go to art school. She would get a great job and settle down in a cozy house some- where and . . . well, there was no room in that plan for a man like Matti. Even one who made her heart race with a crooked smile.

"Catch anything, Anna?" Matti's calm voice interrupted her racing thoughts.

"Nope. Not a thing."

He held up a string with seven beautiful trout. "Well, we caught more than enough for dinner tonight, plus several to can for winter."

Anna tried to smile, slightly annoyed that his fish guts were actually working. No wonder he was so confident. It seemed as if he was always right about everything.

"Mom will be happy to have fresh fish for dinner."

"Yes. I'm sure . . ." The conversation trailed off, neither of them knowing what to say or how to say it.

The air seemed to flicker whenever Matti was next to her . . . as if the bright lights from the aurora were flashing around them, in and out through their conversation. She couldn't breathe when he was around. He turned toward her, giving her that heart-melting smile she had come to know as Matti's gentle hello.

"Anna." He plopped down beside her in the damp grass, careful not to get tangled up in her unmoving line. The trickle of the river seemed to go silent. As if time stood still for them, for their conversation.

She waited for him to finish his thought, the cool breeze making her wonder if summer would ever come to Kalajoki. Certainly not today.

"I know you don't like this war. I know you don't like anything about it. And if I'm being honest, I don't either. But I've always felt it was my duty to fight. To fight for Finland, for my family. Until . . ."

"Until what, Matti?"

"Until you. Now I wonder if it's all worth it."

Anna's heart sped. What might it be like to be in his arms? To be safe, protected, loved. She should get up and run far away. But she couldn't.

Not when she had never felt like this before.

# 11

*Kalajoki, Finland*

Anna sat up tall in the pew and tried to focus on what the pastor was saying instead of on Matti who sat beside her, close enough to hear his every breath. Of course, it didn't help that every time she looked over at him, he winked as though he knew exactly what he was doing.

It was driving her crazy.

Actually, having a handsome, blue-eyed soldier sitting next to her felt pretty great. Straightening out the skirt on her blue flowered dress, Anna traced the words on the cover of her Bible, trying to concentrate on the pastor's words.

"Bear one another's burdens and thus fulfill the law of Christ."

Anna smiled. She couldn't have picked a more fitting verse herself. Nearly everyone in town had taken in someone from Karelia in the last few weeks.

"It's easy to assume that simply by feeding the hungry and providing a home for the homeless that we are doing enough to bear each other's burdens. But we aren't. It's a great start, but it's not enough."

"Read Galations 6:1. It talks about redemption and restoration. That's right. It's not enough to simply bear each other's physical burdens. Instead, we must stand by one another to bear our emotional and spiritual burdens as well. This means walking beside one another in a way that's meaningful and real. And being willing to stand up for what's right, even if it costs us."

Anna stared at the hastily scribbled notes she had taken on her bulletin.

*Stand up for what's right, no matter the cost.*

That's what Matti was dead set on doing, wasn't it? He was angry, but it was justifiable anger. He knew there were some things worth fighting for, and the oppression of the people of Karelia was one of them.

Anna sighed. He was willing to fight and even die for his brothers in need. She was so focused on her own plans, her own life, that she had dismissed his as warmongering. Some friend she was.

Pastor Laiho continued, "In Proverbs 17:17, it says 'A friend loves at all times and a brother is born for adversity.' I think we often pay attention to the part about friends loving at all times and overlook the part about adversity. It's only through adversity that true brotherhood and sisterhood in Christ is formed."

Her cheeks flushed. For her whole life, she had put a blockade around her heart, convinced that she didn't need anyone else in order to reach her goals. When adversity poured in — and it had recently — she'd wanted to throw a tantrum instead of reaching out and deepening her relationships. And in doing so, she also missed out on the opportunity to form deeper relationships — brotherhoods and sisterhoods in Christ.

Was she ready to open up and let someone in? To share the load of the adversity that they all were facing? To share her own spiritual and emotional burdens with someone else?

Glancing at the handsome soldier sitting beside her, she allowed a smile to creep onto her face. It felt terrifying to even consider they could ever have something more than friendship, but it also felt so right.

Maybe it was time to open up that tightly blockaded heart.

Matti wandered out into the courtyard,

wondering how he would get Anna away from Mrs. Aalto who had just loudly invited the entire Ojala and Ranta families over for supper. He only had five more days here in Kalajoki and he didn't want to waste his entire Sunday afternoon at a potluck with one of the elders.

Stepping beside Anna, he unbuttoned the top button of his navy dress uniform and stuffed his hands into his pockets. Nothing but a casual Sunday afternoon. He smiled at Mrs. Aalto and politely introduced himself before turning his attention toward Anna.

"I'm wondering if I could ask my kind benefactor one more indulgence before I ship out to Helsinki. This poor soldier has yet to see Kalajoki — could I impose on you to skip the family dinner and show me the sights instead?"

The relief on Anna's face made her eyes sparkle.

And the smile on her face made his heart almost stop. Goodness, she was beautiful. He'd been trying all morning not to look at her for fear that he wouldn't be able to concentrate on anything else. And his fears were confirmed. She had his undivided attention.

Stepping aside so she could pass, he

glanced back toward the old, whitewashed church. So, this tiny building was where Anna had grown up, said her first prayers, and learned her first Bible stories. A beautiful church — old, but maintained with flowers blooming throughout the grounds and oversized stained glass windows framing the front doors. Just like a thousand other Lutheran churches in Finland. Only this one was different. This one was Anna's.

Matti squelched the temptation to reach out and take her hand. Instead, he hooked his elbow through hers as they strolled down the lane away from the milling congregants.

Anna pointed out the old red barn sitting a block away from the church. "When I was a little girl, Kaino and I used to run over to that barn after Sunday School and hide in the hayloft until our parents came looking for us. One Sunday, my mom must have assumed I had gone home with Kaino's family and Kaino's parents assumed we went home with ours, because they left us there. For a couple of hours, it was fun. But then we started to get hungry and came out to find the churchyard empty. It was a long hike home in the cold. We learned our lesson."

Matti chuckled and then pulled her toward

the barn.

"I'll need a tour of the place where Anna Ojala got herself into trouble."

"Who, me?" Anna looked at him with wide, innocent eyes. "I've never been in trouble in my entire life."

Matti's laughter echoed across the straw-strewn path as he pulled her inside, careful to avoid the rusty tools littering the floor. Sinking down on a hay bale, Matti turned to Anna. "Mmm. You smell like blueberries and sunshine." Had he just said that?

She smiled widely. "You try making blueberry pancakes for ten teenage boys without getting blueberry juice all over you."

"I just might. I can cook a mean pancake, if I do say so myself."

"Oh, really?" Anna looked up at him with quizzical eyes. "I have a hard time believing that my rough and tough soldier boy would stoop to women's work like making pancakes."

"Am I hearing you ask for a pancake cook-off? I'll whip up a batch of my top-secret batter and griddle them hot and golden. Women's work, ha! I could beat any woman, any day."

"It's on, soldier. Looks as if we're having pancakes for dinner tonight."

"Prepare to lose."

Anna reached over and brushed the hair off of his forehead. Then a blush rose to her cheeks.

That did it. He wanted to kiss her.

She was beautiful. With her hair curling softly over her shoulders like that, she looked almost like the porcelain doll his mom had displayed on her bureau.

"So, Matti, did you want to spend the day taking a tour of this ratty old barn or did you want to see the rest of the town?"

"Right now, this barn is looking pretty nice. That trough over there has probably seen better days, but those horse stalls, well, those are quite the works of art. As far as horse stalls are concerned, of course."

She laughed, stood, and led him toward the back of the barn where an old tractor sat up on blocks of wood. "And this beautiful instrument, Sergeant Ranta, is the answer to all of your agricultural needs. It cuts. It hauls. It even bales. That is, if you can get it started."

"Well, I do have a lot of agricultural needs."

Was there any chance Anna could ever love him? On his first night in Kalajoki, Anna's brothers had warned him not to even think about the possibility. Sure, she was beautiful and kind and smart, but she was also the woman who thought she could sail across the Atlantic Ocean by herself and settle in a new country. She had no intention of ever settling down in Finland, of living the simple life he craved.

Did he dare try to change her mind? To show her that he was someone she could trust? Maybe even love? Looking into those grass-green eyes, so alive that they almost glowed, Matti wasn't sure it was possible. But he wanted to try. "So, what are you thinking, Anna Ojala?"

"I'm thinking that I'm sorry."

"Sorry?"

"Yes, I've been too hard on you. I realized at church this morning that you don't want to fight because you love war, but because you want to help your brothers in need. I respect that."

Matti looked at her and blinked several times. This was new. "Thank you, Anna. I know I'm not always the easiest to be around, but I do want what's best. For all of us."

"I know you do." Anna wrapped her arm into his, breaking the tension with a soft smile. "I'm still having a hard time getting over some of the things that happened last year. But let's just say my eyes are starting to open."

"That's good to hear. Want to talk about it?" He closed his eyes and prayed she'd feel comfortable enough to tell him what was really going on in her heart.

She looped her arm through his. "Why don't we head down the street, and I can show you all of the other places where Kaino managed to wreak havoc?"

He sighed. Maybe she wouldn't open up to him.

"So, a few years ago, Kaino decided she would marry Johannes Rahkamo. The problem was that Johannes Rahkamo saw her as his kid sister, not as future wife material."

"And so?"

"And so she came up with a plan. We knew Johannes brought milk and butter down to the market every Wednesday morning, and so we hid right over there behind those posts in front of the store. When Johannes started walking in, Kaino was going to dive out behind the post and pretend she had fallen. The whole damsel in distress act."

Matti loved the way Anna talked with her hands, gesturing wildly as she explained every detail.

"We saw Johannes' wagon pull up and oh, Matti. You would've died laughing. Kaino arranged her hair just so and put on this pouty face just like a real actress in one of the romantic movies."

"An actress?"

"Yes, you know, batting her lashes and cooing. Kaino was a regular movie star as she stumbled off of the porch and fell flat on her face right there on the road. Immediately, she looked up toward Johannes's wagon with big, batting eyes."

"And?"

"And Mr. Rahkamo stepped off the step and ran to her aid. Johannes had been sick that day and so his father had taken their goods into town." Anna burst out laughing, clearly enjoying the memory as much as Matti had enjoyed the story.

"Did Kaino ever catch Johannes's attention?"

"I guess. After that day, she insisted on visiting the Rahkamo family so she could say thanks to Mr. Rahkamo for his kind aid when she'd "injured herself" in the fall. While we were out at the farm, Kaino did her whole act again, batting her eyelashes and cooing all over Johannes. It was pathetic, really."

"Pathetic? Sounds adorable to me."

"No, completely pathetic."

"I just can't picture it. I think I'll need a demonstration. Let's see it, Miss Actress.

Let's see your best damsel-in-love impersonation."

Anna batted her eyes furiously and pursed her lips into a dainty pout. "Oh, Sergeant Ranta, I do believe this road is a bit rough for my liking. Could you be a dear and escort me to the café? I do think I'm in need of some refreshment."

"Will do, milady." Matti grabbed her elbow and pulled her close, grateful for an excuse to have her on his arm. "So, where is this Johannes character now?"

Anna's gaze drifted away. "He's in Helsinki. He was conscripted last year. He joined the fifth army and fought in Karelia and got shot in the shoulder in February. He's in a hospital in Helsinki, hoping to save use of his arm so he can fight again. And Kaino is here making plans for a summer wedding if he can get some time off."

"So, looks as if both you and Kaino will be pining away for men in uniform next fall."

"Kaino, maybe. Not me." Anna shot him a wicked grin.

Matti pushed his lip out into an exaggerated pout. "You won't be pining away for me even a little?"

Anna grinned. "Maybe just a little, soldier boy."

"Good. Let's go grab a cup of coffee and you can fill me in on all the ways you'll miss me when I go. Then we can make mushy plans to write long, tear-stained letters every day."

As they walked down the street, Matti couldn't help but wonder if she was his own "future wife material."

She was everything he ever wanted.

But the timing was all wrong.

# 12

*Leningrad, Russia*

Tanya fingered the coins in her pocket, listening to the quiet jingle as she gazed across the park and over the Neva River. She tried her best not to think about what she would do when those last few coins were gone.

Her money was running out quickly. As was her hope.

Even as she willed her grief to stay hidden and not to crash down on her, the crushing pain of regret, disappointment, and loss overwhelmed her spirit. After three days of searching for a decent place to live, she had finally plunked down her last four hundred rubles to buy two months at the Azov Sanatoria, a grungy hovel in the worst part of town that she wouldn't have considered if she hadn't been beyond desperate.

A despicable place, really. The Azoz family lived on the first floor in what Tanya would have considered squalor had she never seen the attic rooms they rented out to forlorn boarders. A tiny, low-ceilinged attic room that they dared called "boarding space" stood just up a rickety staircase from the owner's living quarters. In that room, they had placed fifteen stained and wobbly cots into rows with less than six inches of space between them. And, for a mere two hundred rubles a month, an unlucky lodger could rent one of those cots and all the space underneath to store their possessions.

Oh, and rent included round-the-clock access to the Azoz family's sole outhouse.

The Azoz Sanatoria with its rats and dirt and grime was the only barrier standing between Tanya and the streets, but her time there was quickly running out.

With a deep sigh, Tanya wondered what would've happened if she had stayed in Moscow. She didn't have many friends left — the war had scattered them — but she did have a few. Surely living with Uncle Boris and Aunt Katya would have been better than this. At least they tolerated her. Unlike the people here in Leningrad who seemed to detest her.

With a scowl, Tanya remembered her latest attempt to find a job. She had waited outside the office of a plant that manufactured ammunition for the war. Surely, they would have a need for workers right now.

"Excuse me, sir. I'm Tanya Egerov." She'd thrust out her hand in cheerful greeting as the plant manager came up the walkway toward the building. "I'm fresh off the train from Moscow, and I'm here to inquire about a job. I can read. I can type. I can file. I would make a great office manager."

The man scowled and rolled his eyes. "Not hiring. Not now, not ever." His words were tinged with acid, as if she carried a disease that threatened to overtake his shiny, clean office. "Now get out!"

Times were tough, but why was everyone being so mean about it? They acted as if she was asking them to hand over their businesses and the keys to their houses as well. Would it really hurt if she typed or filed for them?

Every single person she'd talked to about a job in the last three weeks had scoffed at her.

It was high time for a pity party. Shoveling the coins out of her threadbare pocket, she ran her fingers over each coin. She missed Nicolai. He had been her rock for as long as she could remember — and now when she needed him most, he was gone.

"Oh, Nicolai, why did you do this to me?"

She screamed the question out loud, her voice echoing over the water. Tears came, flooding down her cheeks and onto her sweater, and for the first time in weeks, she allowed them.

She needed a good cry. And then a good kick in the pants.

Choking back a last blubbering sob, Tanya wiped her tears and stood. Time to figure things out. She had to get a job or she wouldn't survive.

Staring at those last few coins in her hand, she made some mental calculations. She had enough to buy herself two, maybe three loaves of bread. Maybe, if she was really careful and allowed herself just a few bites every day, she could make that last for a week or two. Maybe. It was better than nothing.

Tanya hoisted up off of the park bench and walked back toward the sanatoria, stopping at the corner bakery to buy one small loaf. Taking in a deep breath, she breathed heavily in the yeasty air, hoping a waft of baking bread would satisfy her rumbling stomach. Anything to quell the temptation to rip open the bag and devour the whole loaf in one sitting.

She tore off a tiny bite and savored her meal for the day. Warm. Chewy. Moist. She kept it in her mouth as long as possible, chewing slowly with her eyes closed. "Mmm. . . ."

The shop keeper stared at her with concerned eyes. Had she really just moaned out loud while taking a bite of bread? She hurried out the bakery door and down the street to the Azoz Sanatoria, where she would at least have a modicum of privacy as she enjoyed her feast. Racing up the stairs, Tanya plunked down on her cot, kicking a stray tin cup away from her foot. She hugged Nicolai's satchel to her stomach as she sank onto the creaking frame.

At least she still had Nicolai's satchel and violin.

The other residents stored their possessions — old boots, books, cups, and photos — under their cots, but not her. She didn't dare lose her last few fragments of Nicolai. She carried the old satchel with her wedding quilt and his violin everywhere she went. It was exhausting, but she wouldn't lose the few last remnants she possessed.

Maybe a nap would settle the hunger pains?

Hobbling feet and bubbly laughter echoed up the creaking stairs. By the sound of it, her next-door neighbor — if one could call the person who slept on the cot next to her a neighbor — Feodora Yezhof was home.

Tanya had been trying to avoid Feodora ever since she'd moved into the boarding house, doing her best to steer clear of the woman with a foul mouth, boisterous laughter, and vodka-tinged breath. The other residents seemed to like her although she was constantly drunk and loud, but Tanya couldn't see why. Five minutes with her in the room often sent Tanya scurrying outside for peace and quiet.

Feodora burst into the room and scanned the cots, scoping out who was home and who wasn't. Her eyes settled on Tanya and she grinned wildly, showing the gap between her crooked front teeth.

"You! You've been here three weeks and have hardly said a word." Stumbling over, Feodora fell onto her own cot, holding a paper bag that smelled of fresh bread.

Tanya groaned. Could this day get any worse?

Tanya tucked the rest of the loaf she was hoarding under her pillow and forcing a smile. "Hello. I'm Tanya."

Feodora winced as if Tanya had told her she had the plague. Why did everyone hate her so much?

"I'm from Moscow."

"I know. Your accent gives you away."

Her lips parted. Was that why Feodora winced? Did people in Leningrad hate her because she was from the capitol? Stalin's regime came from Moscow, and in the last ten years, their government had wreaked terror on the people of Russia. Good men had been killed for no reason, and the country had been thrown into chaos and war. The people of Leningrad were notoriously freethinking, and most didn't hesitate to admit that they hated Stalin.

Could it be that the people here hated her by association?

"I'm from right here in Leningrad," Feodora continued.

"Do you have family?" Tanya asked, already knowing the answer. Anyone who had a family wouldn't be living in the Azoz Sanatoria.

"Nope. My husband was sent to the gulag back in '34 and I haven't seen him since . . ." Her voice drifted off, causing Tanya to shudder. She'd heard about the gulag, a forced labor camp where opponents of Stalin's economic policy were sent and often tortured. There was little hope Feodora's husband was still alive, and even if he was, there was no hope of him getting out of prison.

Feodora tore open the bag and ripped

hefty chunks off of the loaf, stuffing them into her mouth and chewing loudly.

Tanya turned her head away, unable to watch.

"Do you want some?" Feodora ripped the loaf in half and held out a steaming hunk. "I have a whole loaf. It'll go stale by tomorrow."

"I couldn't." The instant the words slipped out, she wished she could grab them and stuff them back into her mouth. What was she thinking turning down an offering of bread? She was hungry and Feodora was offering, yet a tiny bubble of pride stuck in her throat, blocking her from the one thing she needed to survive.

"No, I insist." Feodora set it gingerly in Tanya's lap. "Eat up!"

Tears stung her eyes. Could this really be happening? Her first kind interlude in weeks, and from the most unlikely of places. Feodora, the boardinghouse drunk, the woman she had avoided for weeks was giving her bread. "Thank you Lord for something to eat," Tanya's heart prayed out of habit. She'd almost forgotten she didn't believe in God anymore. "Thank you, Feodora. This really means a lot."

"You look half-starved the way you're downing that."

Tanya let out a sob. All semblance of pride now gone, she might as well spill it. "I'm out of money! I thought I'd find a job by now, but . . ." Tanya trailed off, swallowing a huge chunk of bread while eyeing the dirty pitcher of water that sat on the table at the edge of the room. Grabbing her own tin cup, she stood to pour a drink.

Feodora sighed loudly, the cloudy look in her eyes revealing her own sadness and fear. "It's a tough time in Leningrad, Tanya."

How had she been so stupid? Most of the country hated Stalin after the great purge. Why had she been so naïve to think she could waltz into town and land a great job to start over?

Feodora took a deep breath and looked Tanya in the eye. "There are jobs out there for girls like us, Tanya. You have to know where to look."

A glimmer of hope?

"Oh, please, I will do anything. Tell me what to do!"

"I'm not talking about an office job."

Tanya stared at her expectantly. Did she mean a factory job? She could do that too. Sure, it would be boring . . . Oh. That kind of job.

She slumped back onto her bed and dropped her cup, the clattering of tin on the hard floor drowning out the thoughts racing through her mind. She could never do that. Not ever. "Oh, Feodora, I couldn't. I can't."

"I said the same thing once." Her eyes were distant, pensive, as if she relived the choice she'd made years ago.

Tanya gave her new friend a once over. Frizzy blonde hair hung loosely over her shoulders, framing a pale face that was probably beautiful at one time. But now, with dull, gray eyes and sagging cheeks, she simply looked tired. Old.

Tanya bit her bottom lip. She didn't want to judge Feodora — especially since she was the only friend she had — but she had to wonder how anyone could stoop that low. Tanya reached out to Feodora and gave her a tentative smile. "Thanks for the bread, friend."

And as she turned around to sleep, Tanya told herself that even if she were about to be thrown onto the streets where she would starve to death, she would never, ever do that.

Never.

# 13

*Kalajoki, Finland*

"Your brothers already set up the picnic," Kaino hollered over her shoulder.

Anna tightened her jacket and walked through the meadow, trying not to trample any of the tiny white valkovuokko that were blooming everywhere around her.

Kalajoki was beautiful this time of year.

Wildflowers peeked out of the soil, exposing their soft petals to the still-chilly arctic air. They bloomed in clusters amongst the edges of the tall, towering pine trees that made up the forest that bordered their farm. Up ahead, where two of her brothers had set out a large, hand-knitted afghan for their picnic, the Kalajoki River glimmered a deep navy blue.

Anna and Kaino sank down on the blanket, each grabbing a handful of frozen blueberries from the bowl that sat in the middle. Mmm. In a few months, they would have fresh blueberries again. Still, nothing could beat a picnic on the Kalajoki River in early summer. Well, actually, something could beat it. A picnic on the Kalajoki River with her soldier boy sitting beside her.

Anna glanced back down the trail and wondered if Matti was coming at all. When they'd left, he had been caught up in a lively discussion about the war with her father. He had tersely told them to go on ahead and he would meet them down here.

Would he come?

Anna distracted herself by pulling a tin of roast chicken and some limpua out of the basket, setting it out beside the blueberries and the basket of *pipparkakuts* she had baked this morning. Grabbing one of the spicy cookies, Anna took a huge bite, hoping the cardamom-tinged goodness would distract her.

Arvo picked up a soccer ball and tossed it to Kaino, who ran onto the field, screaming at him to kick it to her. Before long, the Ranta boys and her brothers had teamed up and played an intense game with Kaino serving as the goalie. Anna watched warily, briefly considering joining in on the game until a flash of red caught her eye.

"Hi!" Matti panted as he jogged down the path wearing a red jacket over khaki pants and a T-shirt. An extra blanket hugged his shoulder.

"Hello." Anna fought to keep herself from staring at him. The way this shirt clung to his muscular chest left her stomach tingling in a way that it never had before.

He gestured toward Kaino and her brothers. "Looks like an intense game."

"That it does. Which is why I'm sitting here with only a basket of cookies to keep me company. Want one?"

"Did you make them?"

"Yes."

He grabbed three out of the basket and sat beside her.

Anna took a deep breath to compose herself. Three minutes into their day, he was already giving her that look that told her he wanted to kiss her — and if she was being honest, she would've been happy to oblige. In fact, if her brothers weren't ten feet away . . .

Seriously, this man drove her crazy.

"I had an interesting talk with your father. He thinks that even though Karelia is still in Russian hands, the government will wait a few months and feel out this peace treaty before marching back down to Lake Lagoda."

"And, what do you think about that?"

Fire flashed in his eyes. "I think our government is stalling."

Anna bit her lip.

He looked at her with wide eyes. "I just can't believe anyone thinks they can hand Karelia to Russia on a silver platter without fighting back."

"Some would believe that Karelia is a small price to pay for peace. And if we can get ourselves over the hump and find new housing for all of the refugees, we won't be that bad off."

Matti's eyes flashed. "Do you really think that, Anna?"

"I . . . don't know what I think, Matti."

"You don't know? Karelia is my home, my heritage. My family has run our fish-packing plant there for five generations. And now it's just gone."

"I'm not sure what I think about the war, Matti. I'm still figuring it out. But I do know that I will support you and pray for you no matter what happens." She stood. Things were getting a bit too intense for her liking. Time for a distraction. "Let's agree to disagree for now. Do you want to go for a walk?"

His eyes brightened as he leapt up to follow her.

"We're going for a walk," she yelled toward

the crew playing near the river. She grabbed Matti's hand and dashed down the path before anyone could get the idea to come along.

As soon as they were out of view, Matti flung his arm around her shoulder and leaned in to whisper in her ear. "Now this, Miss Ojala, was a smart idea."

"I'm just full of them, Sergeant Ranta."

"I'm starting to see that. So, where are we headed?"

"There's a field of wildflowers just around that next bend. It's gorgeous this time of year." Gorgeous and romantic and . . . what was she thinking? There were enough sparks flying between her and Matti as it was — taking him to a field full of wildflowers on a beautiful spring day . . . well, that sounded like a recipe for romance.

Either that, or a recipe for disaster.

# 14

*Kalajoki, Finland*
One more day.

The words echoed in her mind, taunting her as she carefully buttoned the wooden buttons on her best dress. He had asked her if he could take her out to dinner to say goodbye.

She shivered, pulling her red, hand-knitted cardigan over her shoulders. Who knew if she'd see him again? After what had happened with Henrik, she was well aware that life was tenuous. And even if they did see each other, it wasn't as if they were, well . . . anything.

Her heart began to pound. Could he be her boyfriend? They had only just met and he was leaving for who knew how long. But he could be. Yes, she was willing to admit it that he could be. "Don't even think like that right now," she whispered to her reflection in the dingy mirror on her dresser.

A soft knock sounded on her bedroom door.

Anna turned around. "Hi, Mama." She allowed her mom to smooth out her hair.

"Matti is waiting for you in the parlor."

Anna pursed her lips together, willing herself to keep it together and hold her emotions in check for one last night.

"Anna. . . ." Mama's voice trailed off.

"It's all right." Anna put on her bravest face. "I'm all right."

She slipped her practical black pumps over bare feet and pinched her cheeks to bring some redness, some cheeriness. She glanced in the mirror one more time, measured herself, liking what she saw. No stockings, but at least she looked somewhat presentable. Tucking that wayward strand behind her ear, she turned and sauntered into the parlor. "Hi, Matti."

He leaned over and whispered into her ear. "You look beautiful, Anna."

She turned and waved goodbye to her parents, who stood by the stove with barely contained smiles.

"I'll have her home by ten, sir. And don't worry. Your little girl will have the best of care."

"Have her home by nine, sergeant." Her father smiled.

"Yes, sir!" Matti gave a mock salute and lead Anna out the door. "I thought about taking the horses, but it's so lovely out, would you be up for a walk?"

"Why, of course, soldier boy, as long as you keep your eye out for horse poo. I'd hate to stink at dinner."

"I do not need a stinky date." Matti tentatively looped his arm through hers. "I'm so glad we met, Anna Ojala. And just in the nick of time — you with your big plans to go to America. You would've had those Yanks lining up for you."

Anna's laugher came out jingling and melodic, just how she felt when Matti was around. As if music burst around her, inviting her to sashay through a meadow, or something sappy and romantic like that. Rolling her eyes at her poetic thoughts, she couldn't help but giggle again.

No one had ever made her stomach flutter like this before. Even talk about going to America didn't bother her tonight. In fact, the only thing that bothered her was that niggling reminder that he was leaving tomorrow. And she may never see him again.

"So, where are you taking me?"

"Well, considering the fact that there's only one restaurant in Kalajoki, I'm sure it will come as a surprise to you that I'm taking you to Iida *Merenelävät.*"

"I knew it. I figured it out as soon as you turned onto *Pääkatu* Street."

"Brilliant detective skills."

While sauntering up the lane to the tiny house that served as both Iida Niskala's home and business, Anna explained that Iida had recently moved the tables out of the center of the room to make room for a dance floor. She said it was her effort to boost morale in town, although she thought it was perhaps more of an excuse for Iida to dance. Rumor had it she had been an amazing dancer when she was younger.

Regardless, anyone could see that Kalajoki needed a morale boost. The mixture of defeated soldiers on leave and peace treaty refugees certainly hadn't brought Christmas in May.

Iida led them to a corner table.

Matti pulled out a chair for Anna before sitting down on his own and unbuttoning the top button of his uniform. He raised one corner of his mouth in a forced smile. "Can I tempt you with a soda?"

"That'd be great." Luxuries like American soda were a rare treat in Anna's world — in fact, she had only tried the soda once in her life.

Iida hurried off with their drink orders.

Anna turned her attention back to Matti. "Are you scared to go?" The words slipped out before she had the chance to censor them.

"Yes and no. I'm not scared to fight. I know it will be hard — cold, miserable, and terrifying — but I also know it's right. We can't lose Lake Lagoda and the rest of Karelia. But I don't want to leave my family. Or . . . you."

Anna choked back a lump. Was it possible that he felt that same flutter of hope when he thought of her? Maybe they had a chance to be something more than . . . well, more than whatever it was they were right now.

Matti broke through her teetering emotions with a handsome grin. "Would you care to dance?"

Oh, goodness, she wasn't exactly a graceful dancer. She'd square danced with Kaino on sunny lakeside afternoons but never in public. And never with a man. What if she fell all over herself? Or worse, stomped all over his toes? She wasn't exactly known for her grace and rhythm. Anna let out a soft sigh and looked at Matti. Those big blue eyes. That soft smile. How could she say no to him?

She couldn't. She grabbed his hand and led him onto the dance floor. Turning, she gazed into his face, handsome even in the dim light, and did her best to act as though she knew what she was doing. Holding up her palms with a shrug, she allowed him to wrap his hands around her waist.

"So, Miss War Committee Sock Making Queen," he whispered. "How are you feeling about everything?"

Anna drop her gaze, suddenly self-conscious about her bare legs. They had spent all winter knitting socks for the soldiers, which left very little time and supplies for making her own unmentionables. What if she brushed against Matti with her bare legs? How embarrassing.

He pulled her closer, yanking her out of her reverie. He didn't seem to care about her bare legs. Or that the music was scratchy. Or even about her inability to dance with any semblance of coordination.

No, tonight, her solider boy didn't seem to care about anything but her.

He hummed softly in her ear along with the saxophone solo playing on the record. Matti's soft humming soothed her, relaxed her. Soft as the whisper of a thousand promises — a lifetime of gentle moments, stolen kisses, simple yet strong love. Promises she wasn't sure could ever come to be.

"You're a good dancer, Matti. I think I

need lessons."

Matti beamed. "My mom taught me. She said it would come in useful someday. I guess it has."

"Well, maybe I should have her teach me. Then you can come back and I can really show you how it's done."

He pulled her to his side, spun her around the floor so quickly her feet left the ground.

"Ahh!" She clung to his shoulders, trying to maintain some semblance of balance and grace. "I hope I don't stomp on your toe."

"Wouldn't be the first time."

Anna punched him in the arm. "Not fair. You drag me out onto the dance floor and then insult me?"

He spun her around in a circle, dipping her backward before pulling her up to him, his face so close his warm and sweet breath caressed her.

"Nice move. You'd think you planned that."

"Maybe I did." He gave her that schoolboy smile — the one that made her insides melt and her guard drop. She searched his eyes, wondering if his emotions matched hers, looking for a sign that this was real, that it would last.

Instead she saw her brother Aabel.

She skittered backward and smoothed her

skirt, frowning at Aabel as he walked up behind Matti. "Aabel. What are you doing here?" This was supposed to be her night. Hers and Matti's. Why in the world would her brother be in the restaurant?

"I'm sorry Anna. Matti." Aabel's words rushed out, the strain in his voice punching Anna in the stomach. "But a message came for Matti. It was marked urgent so Mama had me race down here." He held out a small cream telegraph page, his hand trembling.

Matti grabbed and unfolded the thin paper, frowning as he read the page. He looked up at her, his eyes dark. "Anna. I'm so sorry, but I have to go. They're calling our unit back to Helsinki a day early."

"Early?" The word stuck in her throat. "But you have one more night."

"No, it doesn't look like it. It looks as if they want me on the last train out tonight." He glanced at his watch and closed his eyes. "It leaves in less than an hour. I need to go now."

Anna slumped against the wall as Matti walked over to their table and slipped his arms into his navy jacket. He left money on the white tablecloth and then turned back to Anna.

"I'll escort her home, Matti. You go

ahead." Her brother stepped beside her, placing his hand on her shoulder.

"Anna. I'm so sorry." Matti wrapped his arm around her in an awkward side-hug. Just minutes ago, he had almost kissed her. Now he hardly touched her.

So much for Matti as a boyfriend.

Anna swallowed hard. Would she ever see him again?

"Anna?" His voice sounded pinched now. "I didn't want to leave like this, but I don't have a choice. Will you promise to write?"

She took a deep breath, bit her lip, and willed herself not to cry.

He turned and ran out the door, seemingly desperate to make the last train out of town. More like the last train out of her life.

Trying not to cry, she hooked her arm into her brother's elbow and began to walk home. Had the last three weeks been nothing more than a misguided dream?

Or the biggest mistake of her life.

# 15

*Leningrad, Russia*

It was gone. All gone.

No money, no food, and only a few days left in the boardinghouse before she would be out on the streets. What would she do?

The only plan she could think of was to sell Nicolai's precious violin. Feodora had suggested it a few days ago when she'd noticed Tanya hoarding a stale loaf of bread, trying to make it last her as long as possible. Tanya had considered it — really, she had — but how could she sell Nicolai's treasure to settle her own stomach?

She couldn't. The thought made her sick. Literally.

Tanya jumped out of bed and raced down the stairs, desperate for fresh air to quell her nausea. What was wrong with her? Over the last few days, the nausea had been relentless, sending her scurrying for the tiny grass patch behind the boarding house at the most inopportune times.

Vomit erupted from her insides. Her shoulders heaved as she bent over the grass at the edge of the muddy sidewalk. Her very last bite of bread, wasted.

She'd never been sick like this before. Probably the stress of her situation or the lack of food.

Unless . . . no. She staggered against a nearby tree. It couldn't be that. Could it?

Tanya thought back to last May. She remembered a long stroll with Nicolai on a sunny afternoon. Blooming geraniums created a fairyland path through the abandoned park. The air bubbled with the scent of ginger and apricot. A romantic scent of young love, of hope, of new beginnings surrounded them.

He had smiled at her so hopefully, so earnestly that Tanya hadn't been able to resist him. Kissing him passionately right then and there, she grabbed his hand and hurried him back to their apartment. If only she had taken the time to savor that hungry passion in his eyes, the loving tenderness of his touch. If only she had known that their time making babies would be short lived, gone before it really even started.

Tanya hadn't gotten pregnant that day, or in the months that followed. But giddy with young love, they kept trying, praying, making it a newlywed game to guess which time would be the time. The time when everything would fall into place. The day when she would feel life.

Tanya couldn't help but smile, her thoughts solemn. Wouldn't that be ironic if after all those months of trying, she was pregnant now? Her fingers touched her flat stomach. Now that Nicolai was gone. Now that she was alone, with no food, no home, no one to share in the joy, the laughter or the hope that came with a baby?

Tanya tried to remember when she'd last had her monthly. She hadn't had one in Leningrad. It had been five weeks at least. Maybe longer.

Back when she'd started trying with Nicolai, she'd gone to the library and checked out a book on pregnancy and childcare. She had read the book, carefully making mental notes of the signs and symptoms of pregnancy so that if she get pregnant, she'd know.

Nausea. Yes.

Sore breasts. Yes.

Constant fatigue. Yes.

Inability to think rationally and cohesively about life in general. Yes, yes, yes. Tanya covered her mouth, trying to quell another

113

wave of nausea. The signs fit. Could it be? She again ran her hand along her stomach, a wave of maternal love pouring over her.

"I think I'm having a baby," she whispered out loud to the empty street. "I'm having Nicolai's baby."

She trembled against the brick wall of the boarding house. If she really was pregnant then she had to do something fast. She was already half-starved. She had already re-signed herself to the fate of starvation, but if she was pregnant, everything changed. She couldn't let Nicolai's baby die. Not without a fight. Not that she even knew how to fight now.

It was despairingly clear that no one would hire her. She'd tried that route. She gazed up at the sky. Tiny white clouds floated through a blue as clear as Nicolai's eyes. So peaceful. So beautiful. So out of tune with the struggle that waged in her heart hundreds of meters below.

Nicolai's violin sat propped against the wall next to her feet. His one remaining earthly treasure. It wasn't worth much, but it would buy her a few more weeks in the boarding house and a few loaves of bread.

Maybe it was time? Nicolai had loved that violin so much. Tanya remembered quiet evenings in their tiny apartment. They would light a fire and she would make tea. Nicolai would sit on the hearth and play slow, sad songs. Tanya closed her eyes and strained her ears, hoping to catch a whisper of one of the mournful, drawn-out notes Nicolai had loved to play.

Nicolai's music would be a perfect backdrop for the life she was now living, yet she had no one to play it for her. And his beautiful violin was just collecting dust. Tanya straightened her tattered dress, resolved to do what she had to do. There was no room for sentimentality in what would possibly make the difference between life and death for her baby. For Nicolai's baby.

Plus, if Nicolai were alive, he would've given anything — even his prized violin — to save this baby.

Steadying herself against the wall — oh, dear, she was weak — Tanya picked up her satchel and Nicolai's violin and headed down the street to the old music shop. She would do this before she changed her mind.

Her baby's survival depended on it.

# 16

*Leningrad, Russia*

Oh, the bread tasted good.

Tearing off a chunk bigger than her fist, Tanya stuffed it into her mouth, the crumbs falling on her skirt as she savored the feel of food. It had been too long.

She hadn't gotten what she'd hoped for Nicolai's violin, but she'd still earned enough to survive for a few more weeks. And now, she celebrated. She was almost certain a tiny heartbeat pulsed in her belly. She went all-out for this party, too, allowing herself an entire demi-loaf of potato bread in one sitting.

Feodora turned toward her on her cot and mumbled, "Someone's having a feast today!"

"Yeah. I finally sold Nicolai's violin. Bought me six more weeks in this place and I still have enough money for food. Maybe by then I'll find a job somewhere. Someone has to be hiring poor widows from Moscow." She threw up a thin smile.

Feodora looked at her sadly. She wasn't buying her false peppiness. "Good for you, Tanya. I hope you find something great."

She hoped so too, but she could tell from Feodora's distant look that she didn't have much faith in Tanya's prospects. Tearing off another precious chunk of bread, Tanya held it out to Feodora. As many times as Feodora had shared with her, she must do the same. "Want some?"

"No, thank you." Feodora poured a clear liquid from a bottle into her tin cup and took a giant swig. "I'm on a liquid diet today."

If Tanya had a kopeck for every five Feodora spent on vodka, she wouldn't be in this predicament. Of course, Tanya realized, if she did what Feodora did every day to earn money, perhaps she'd need vodka too. "Are you sure you don't want some bread to wash it down?"

"Are you sure you don't want some vodka to wash your bread down?" Feodora cackled. She knew Tanya didn't drink, but that never stopped her from trying. "I'm glad for you. I know it's been rough. I'm glad you at least have some hope."

Tanya looked down. Should she tell Feodora her news? She would find out soon enough, right? Why not have a friend to help her through. "Um, Feodora, I think . . . I'm pregnant."

Feodora's eyes grew wide. "Oh, no!"

Not exactly the response she'd hoped for.

Forcing a smile, Tanya swallowed the lump in her throat. "It's a good thing, I think. It's Nicolai's baby. I want her." Something inside told her the baby she carried was a girl.

Feodora turned her head slightly, looking at Tanya out of the corners of distant eyes. "But right now, Tawnie? When the city is bracing itself for war and you have no way to support yourself, much less a baby?"

"She's Nicolai's baby. I'll figure out a way. I have to."

Feodora shook her head slowly. She slipped off her shoes, shoved them under her cot, and sank onto the creaking frame. "I hope you do, Tawnie. I really hope you do."

No one had called her Tawnie since her mother and Nicolai had died. Somehow it felt all right coming from Feodoram her strange but loyal friend.

Tanya took another bite of bread and settled into her cot for a nap. Would she really be able to keep herself alive until the baby was born? And what about after that? Would she be able to keep her little girl alive? She wished for a moment that she still prayed. Because if she did, she'd beg God to show her a way — any way — to keep herself and her baby alive.

Any way but Feodora's way.

## 17

*Helsinki, Finland*

"Want some coffee?" Marko Jokinen grabbed the pot and sniffed, wincing as he poured the steaming liquid into a chipped, white tin cup.

Matti gritted his teeth and scowled. "Is it as bitter as normal?"

Marko took a tentative sip and grimaced. "Probably more. But hey, at least it will match your mood."

Matti poured himself a cup. He added a hefty pour of milk and silently wished for sugar. Maybe that would sweeten his coffee and his attitude. He glared at Marko over his cup. "Do you know what we're doing today?"

Marko moved to the wall where their unit posted the weekly agenda. He slumped back into his seat. "Looks like more timber and brush clearing."

"Wonderful. Our country's best trained

soldiers are rushed to the front in order to spend their days clearing land for refugees who shouldn't even be refugees."

"Look on the bright side. At least on Rapid Resettlement Duty, you don't have to trek through landmines with bullets whizzing around your ears to pick up the pile of letters you get every day."

Matti glared.

Mail availability didn't exactly make up for their Corps being assigned by the Ministry of Defense's Rapid Resettlement Act. Or that he had been pulled away from Anna early in order to prepare tent cities for the flood of Karelian people who needed somewhere to live. They said it was the Corps' opportunity to help those in need.

More like pouring salt in a wound.

Matti tossed his cup in the mess sink and headed outside. He grabbed a rake and a pick-axe and ran to join the rest of the men for their morning huddle.

"Ranta!" A voice boomed loudly above the din of quiet chatter, startling Matti.

"Sir?" Just his luck. Singled out before the day even began.

"I'm moving you to Takala's company. They've been assigned to assist with increased productivity at the Tuomela Fish Packing Plant. We have new people to feed.

121

I know your father owns a similar plant, so I figured you'd be able to lend some expertise."

Fish packing expertise. That he had. If it meant spending a day out of the hot sun, he was game. Stepping away from his former crew, Matti walked over to introduce himself. "Sergeant Ranta, sir!"

"Lieutenant Pauli Takala." The company commander shook his hand firmly, looking down on him with a cocky half smile. Charming, that one. He'd have to remember to never introduce him to Anna.

"Glad to meet you."

"Shall we go, boys?" Takala turned toward the lot where they'd parked their trucks, smacking one of the other soldiers on his back. "That is, if Sergeant Uotila here can hack working today. After the night he had last night, who knows."

Sergeant Uotila turned to him with tired eyes and grinned. "I can hack it, boss. Just give me a little something to take the edge off."

One of the men looked behind him at the commanding officers and then quietly tugged something out of his front jacket pocket and handed it to Uotila. Uotila kept an eye behind him and took a swig before tucking it back into his jacket pocket.

Was that a flask? Matti had heard that Takala's company was a bit wild, but drinking on duty, well, that seemed a bit much. Shaking his head, Matti ran to catch up with the group.

Hopping onto the back of the dark green open-backed truck assigned to their company, Matti braced himself for the ride. The Soviet bombings in November had caused quite a bit of damage to the roads around town, so he'd learned to hold on tight when riding in the back of a flat bed.

Squishing in next to him, another tall, blond, movie-star-looking soldier leaned over and smiled. "Hiya, newbie, I'm Ahti Ilmarinen, but people call me Käärme."

"Käärme . . . snake . . . because you're so, um, thin?"

"Nope, because I'm so smooth with the ladies."

The other guys in the company laughed, slapped Käärme on the back, and guffawed like a bunch of kids at a lakeside reunion. Not like soldiers with a job to do.

Matti bit his lip hard, reminding himself that making enemies of the men in his company would just make his life miserable. Still . . .

Ahti — Käärme — whatever his name was — turned toward Matti. "Takala and I went to high school together so when it came time for our conscription, his dad made sure to pull some strings to make sure I got into his company. His dad is high up in the Ministry of Defense, personal assistant to the assistant director or something like that. Which makes this the best company to be in, my friend. You just got lucky."

Lucky? Lucky would be fighting for Karelia, advancing toward the front, or strategizing a way to take back what was theirs. Not sitting on the back of a flatbed truck with a bunch of yahoos talking about vodka and women. Oh, and fish packing. Perhaps he should turn the conversation back to that.

"So, Takala, what exactly is our assignment at the plant today?"

Takala looked up with glazed eyes. He pulled a folded slip of paper out of his pocket, quickly read over their instructions, and then looked up at the men. "All right, men, listen up. The government is worried that we'll run out of food this winter. Lake Lagoda has always been a significant source of herring, and now that it's in Soviet hands, they're worried we won't be able to feed the population, especially the refugees."

"Why don't we take back Lake Lagoda then?" The angry words slipped out before

124

Matti remembered to keep his emotions in check.

Takala's face jerked up, his cool blue eyes turning icy at the angry words. "Sergeant Ranta, I know you're from Karelia and you're angry about the loss of your home, but there is no place for angry outbursts in our company. We do what we are ordered."

Matti flattened his smile and sealed his lips shut. Takala's company had more of a reputation for following women than orders. "Yes, sir!"

"We've been assigned to assist the Tuomela plant's owners in coming up with a plan to get more herring canned and packaged before winter. Whether that means helping with the fisheries or with the canning process, I'm not sure."

Great. The work Matti learned to hate when he was twelve. A lot of good it was doing him being a decorated veteran in the great Army of the Isthmus.

"Ranta." Takala's voice nearly drowned in the wind, so Matti leaned closer to hear. "Since you grew up packing fish, I'll need you to meet with the foreman first thing to observe what they're doing well and what could be improved upon. We need to help them increase production."

"Käärme and Uotila, I want you to go

with Ranta. You, College." Takala pointed to a small, wiry soldier in the corner who had kept to himself the entire ride. "You'll come with me to look at the plant's production records."

"Will do." College looked up over his glasses and shook his head.

Matti wondered what type of college he attended and how he'd managed to go to school in the middle of wartime. College educated soldiers were uncommon in the lower ranks of the Finnish army because most men were conscripted on their eighteenth birthday. Still, it would be nice to have someone on their squad who could lead them in an academic sort of way.

Takala continued to give instructions to the company, giving each man an assignment and a specific objective.

Matti had to hand it to Takala. He might be a flask-toting, girl-chasing playboy, but he was actually a strong leader in his company. Matti couldn't help but like the guy.

"Does everyone understand their objective?" Takala finished up. "Meet here at 1800 to head back to base. Drinks tonight at Suomenlinna are on me. I hear the piano player there is a real ladies' magnet, so maybe some of you yeehaws can find a decent date at the bar."

Käärme whooped and Uotila grinned as he flung his legs over the side of the flatbed and started walking toward the plant.

I came .........ped and Uncle .......... to
............... over the side ......... tietled
and started rubbing to ...... its nose.

# 18

*Leningrad, Russia*

Tanya swallowed hard and looked down at the green satin dress that she had borrowed from Feodora. It sagged in all the wrong places and clung exactly where she didn't want it to, but considering her only other option was her threadbare calico, it would do.

Giving the stubborn neckline one last desperate tug upwards, Tanya stepped out of the ladies' room. She had a job to do, a paid job.

*It's just work. It's just work. It's just work.*

Her footsteps echoed across the hallway, being drowned out only by the music that cascaded out from the ballroom. Inside, thousands of officers in the great Red Army sipped vodka, ate delicious food, and chattered nervously, all realizing this could be their last big hurrah before Russia was thrown into imminent war.

Feodora had convinced her to do this.

OK, Feodora and her rumbling stomach.

Feodora had marched into the boarding house yesterday with a grin and a proclamation. "Tawnie, I have a perfect opportunity for you to make some money."

Tanya frowned and shook her head firmly. Hadn't she made it clear to Feodora that she wouldn't walk down that road?

"No, I promise Tawnie. It's not what you think. There's a big officer's ball downtown tomorrow night. They're throwing a party to reward the men who fought hard for the motherland up in Finland last winter. All of the guys want to show up with a beautiful woman on their arms . . . and, well, if beautiful women they want, then beautiful women they can have."

"Meaning?"

"Meaning you show up, you flirt a little, you smile big and make your officer feel as if he's the most handsome man in the room and you make two hundred fifty rubles."

"Two hundred fifty rubles!" That was enough money to buy her another month in the boarding house and several loaves of bread. "And I don't have to . . . uh . . ."

Feodora cut her off. "You don't have to . . . ummm, you know . . . with anyone, Tanya."

129

She considered the idea for several minutes. She was getting desperate. She was paid up for only a couple more weeks and the cash from the sale of Nicolai's violin was quickly dwindling. Two hundred fifty rubles would definitely help.

"Plus, Tawn, you'll start showing soon, which means no man will hire you . . . to do anything. You need to make money now when you still have your figure."

Tanya rubbed her still-flat stomach. Feodora was right. She couldn't ignore that she was pregnant and desperate. She had to do something, and if she could earn two hundred fifty rubles for a little flirting, well, she could do that.

For Nicolai's baby, she would do almost anything.

And so, the decision was made. Feodora flew into preparation mode. After sending a messenger down to the army base, she tugged a tattered cardboard box out from under her cot and explained to Tanya that she would have to look beautiful to be able to play the part.

The next few hours were spent forcing Tanya into lacy unmentionables and altering the dreadful green dress so that it at least stayed up on Tanya's slight frame. As they sewed, Feodora coached her on what to do, what to say, and how to say it so that she'd be perfectly worthy of her earnings the next night.

Tanya fell asleep heartsick. Out of habit, she had started to pray. *Lord? Is this really Your will? That I let an officer pay me to flirt with him?*

But no booming voice from heaven directed her, and no miraculous answer to her dilemma presented itself.

Of course it hadn't. She had given up on God. It wasn't as though He would listen to her now.

She kept with her plan. Had it only been this morning that she had wrapped her hair in rags and then dunked it in the basin to wet it? Sitting on her bunk, she let her hair air-dry while Feodora carefully rubbed pink rouge into her cheeks and blue cream eye shadow onto her eyelids. And then, just a few hours ago, she'd presented herself at the ballroom to one Lieutenant Andrei Pudovkin, officer in the great Red Army and her official date for the night.

She had to admit Lieutenant Pudovkin wasn't nearly as bad as she had expected.

No boorish comments or sweat-soaked shirt.

He was clearly a shy and uncomfortable

man who had absolutely no experience with women.

"Hi, soldier." She tried to saunter like Feodora had shown her, but her legs shook as she balanced on too-high shoes. Sidling up next to the Lieutenant, she brushed her hand against his shoulder.

"Hi, Miss Egerov." He forced an awkward smile.

"Tell me, Lieutenant Pudovkin, what heroic actions earned you a ticket to this gala?"

"You can call me Andrei. And I flew fourteen missions over Helsinki last winter," he whispered, clearly uncomfortable about the situation. He wasn't the only one.

Tanya did everything she could not to sprint out of the ballroom and back to the boardinghouse.

"And you, Sir Andrei, can call me Tanya." She drummed up her most flirtatious look, which probably ended up looking more like a forced grimace.

What would Nicolai think of her now? He would've laughed hilariously. And then he would've taken her into his arms and kissed her soundly.

But Nicolai was gone.

And Andrei clearly wasn't one to take girls into his arms. Not that she wanted him to.

"Want to grab something to eat?" Andrei offered his elbow and led her to the large buffet table laden with platters of delicacies. She had to bite her bottom lip to keep drool from dripping out of the corners of her mouth. Feodora had warned her to only eat if Lieutenant Pudovkin offered, and it had taken every bit of willpower to restrain herself from digging in.

Thank goodness, he offered! She was so delighted she could've kissed him . . . almost.

She piled her plate high with slices of ham, grapes, and bread with pate, careful not to overdo it. Wouldn't it be her luck to end up with a stomach ache tonight of all nights? No, she would eat reasonably.

Once she'd selected her food, she followed Andrei to a quiet table in the corner and waited as he pulled out her chair. Reminding herself that she had a job to do, she inched closer to him and gave her best smile. "This looks delicious, Lieutenant. But the meal wouldn't be complete without something to drink. Can I grab you a cup of coffee?"

Andrei cleared his throat. "Some vodka would be great."

Vodka. This could change things. And not for the better.

But he was paying her, so she had no choice but to oblige.

"It's all right, Tanya. It's a job," she whispered as she stood up. She reminded herself to swing her hips as she walked. She had practiced this walk at least twenty times for Feodora last night, and now she was grateful for the instruction.

What had she been so worried about? She could do this. A few hours of flirting and she'd have two hundred fifty rubles in her pocket. And a full stomach.

Returning with the vodka for Andrei and a glass of water for herself, Tanya set the drinks down at the table and took her own seat. Scooting as close to him as she could, she crossed her legs suggestively and looked into his eyes. "Shall we?"

"Looks delicious."

"Yes, it does." Tanya forced herself to eat slowly instead of inhaling the food so the lieutenant wouldn't guess it was the only meal she'd eaten in weeks. She finished her last bite.

Feodora strolled over to them, clinging flirtatiously to a dark-eyed officer who clearly enjoyed her attention.

"Hi, there, Miss Egerov! Lieutenant Pudovkin." As she talked, the strap on her red satin dress slipped off her shoulder, revealing creamy white skin. "Oh, my!" she looked up at her date with a wink. "Looks as if this dress is just aching to come off."

Tanya's mouth dropped open. Was her friend really that shameless?

The officer grinned. "Maybe I should take you out back and we can teach that naughty dress a lesson."

Feodora's mouth curved into a tiny circle and she giggled. "Oh, but Lieutenant, that would be so inappropriate — what with all of these people waiting for you to get your award." She beamed up at him and kissed him on the lips as though they were long lost lovers. She certainly was good at her job.

Shaking her head slowly, Tanya forced a smile at good old Andrei, the man willing to pay her to sit by him looking beautiful. He didn't seem to expect anything more.

What a relief.

"Care to dance, Lieutenant?" She'd already stood and pulled toward the dance floor.

"I'm not very good at it."

She did her best to keep her voice from cracking as sentences Feodora had practiced with her last night poured out of her mouth. "Don't lie to me. I know a smooth dancer when I see one. I bet you could dance me out of this room."

He smiled tentatively and shrugged. "Well, it looks as if I don't have a choice, do I?"

"That's the spirit." She pulled his arms around her waist, shuddering at her own audacity. Was she really acting like this? She pushed her warnings out of her mind and allowed her body to sink into his strong chest. If she closed her eyes, maybe she could pretend he was Nicolai.

Nope.

Nicolai would never have stomped on her toes. Plus, Nicolai smelled like hard work and lye soap. This man smelled like cologne. Better to keep her eyes wide open and pretend her heart wasn't still too bruised to think about Nicolai without crying.

Tanya rested her head against her new reality.

No, he wasn't Nicolai, but he also wasn't a monster. He had treated her kindly all night.

"Do you like the band?" she asked.

"Oh, yes. Everything about this night has been wonderful." He winked at her. Oh, goodness. She forced herself to giggle as he pulled her close, rubbing his cheek against her shoulder.

As the song ended, he leaned back, his arms resting on her lower back, his gaze slipping over her shoulder toward the back door.

"Want to go outside?"

Tanya swallowed hard. Feodora had promised her it would be dinner, dancing, flirting and a nice pay day before she headed home . . . not a trip outside to do who-knew-what. Her gaze drifted around the room, searching frantically for Feodora. No such luck. Feodora was probably outside doing who-knew-what with her own lieutenant.

Tanya looked up into Andrei's eyes and found desperation. If she said no, would he not pay her? She took a deep breath and forced herself to soften her clenched jaw, hoping to erase the panic from her face. Not worth the risk — she needed that money. Desperately. "Let's go, lieutenant."

She wouldn't sleep with him. But she could give him a tiny kiss behind the ballroom in exchange for his two hundred fifty rubles. Her feet didn't seem to agree with her as she followed him to the back doorway, each step heavier than the next. As though walking to her death. In a way, she was. Turning to him, she smiled and leaned in close. "I had fun with you tonight, Lieutenant. In fact, if you ever need a date again, you know who to call." Smooth and calm, she reminded herself. Stay smooth and calm.

He beamed.

He did remember he was paying her, didn't he? Licking her lips, she forced herself not to back away as he leaned in and kissed her, gently at first, then passionately. *Stay calm. This is just a job.* She must have succeeded. When he pulled back a minute later, he grinned as if she had handed him ten thousand rubles.

What had she done? She pinned her hands behind her back to keep them from trembling. "Thanks for inviting me here tonight, Andrei." She said the words softly, as if she really meant it. And part of her did. "We'd better get inside. I wouldn't want to miss you getting your award."

"No, we wouldn't want that," he said with a tinge of sadness to his tone.

Maybe Andrei had his own demons? For a moment, Tanya's heart ached for him, knowing all too well how it felt like to love and lose.

Swallowing a sob, she turned toward the ballroom, careful to swing her hips as Feodora had taught her. She looked exactly like the woman she had become.

Someone who sold her dignity for bread.

# 19

*Leningrad, Russia*

"So?" Feodora shook her awake by kicking the legs on her cot roughly.

"Go away, Fe!" Tanya closed her eyes and sank beneath her scratchy blanket, wishing she could just disappear under the covers and forget everything.

"Come on, Tawnie. It wasn't that bad, was it?"

"Yes!" Tanya bolted upward and threw a pillow at Feodora before she raced down the steps to relieve herself. "It was that bad." Downstairs, Tanya quickly used the outhouse but stopped herself in the muddy yard before returning inside.

The sun peeked out behind tiny white clouds, making a perfect backdrop for the bright yellow and orange leaves that had changed to their new fall color. The morning air cooled her skin, and a chill ran down her bare arms. Overhead, the shrill of an unfamiliar bird called. The breeze whispered of promises.

If only her mood matched the beauty of the day.

Tugging her sweater closer, Tanya yawned deeply. She was exhausted. Last night, she had tossed and turned for hours, stifling the realization that she would never again be the woman she had tried so hard to be. It was all lost now. Her innocence. Her resolve. And any hope for a different life.

"Lord, what have I done?" A reminiscent prayer sneaked into her heart before she had the chance to push it back. She could hardly pray to a God she didn't believe in, could she?

Pray, no. But she could think. What had she done? She'd sold her kisses for cash, that's what. What would Nicolai think of that? Well, he wasn't here now, was he? And the Tanya Egerov who grew up on Tverskya Street and went to mass every Sunday with her beloved husband wasn't either. That Tanya Egerov had stayed in her tiny apartment in Moscow next to her dead husband and her dreams.

The new Tanya was a bit more streetwise — enough to realize that if she didn't figure out a way to make money, she would die on the cold Leningrad streets — and her baby would die with her.

Was last night really that bad? Feodora's question came to her as if spoken by a tiny voice in the wind.

"No. It wasn't that bad," Tanya whispered back.

Swallowing the tinge of guilt that crept into her throat, Tanya patted her belly. She would do anything for this baby, even if it meant spending another evening with good old officer so-and-so. And if she was being entirely honest, waking up with a full belly and a pocket full of rubles hadn't exactly felt bad. Why should she suffer and starve for an archaic set of morals because she had once believed in a God whom she was no longer sure existed?

Regardless, she would have to stifle all of her emotions and do something to earn money if she wanted this baby to survive.

A plan formulated in her mind as she trudged up the stairs. If she could attend a few more officers' balls in the weeks to come, maybe she would have enough to ride out the remainder of her pregnancy in the Azoz Sanatoria. With bread to eat and a place to sleep, the baby at least had a chance at survival.

Tanya plopped down on Feodora's cot and forced a trembling smile. "So, Feodora, know of any other officer's balls coming up?"

Feodora studied her with probing eyes and pulled a flask out from under her pillow. Taking a big swig, she offered it to Tanya.

"Why not?" Tanya grabbed it and choked down a swig, wincing at the slow burn as it trickled down her throat.

"Are you sure, Tawnie?" Feodora clearly understood that a line had been crossed.

"I need the money. And if that means spending a few evenings pretending with an officer or two, I'm willing."

Feodora's eyes narrowed to tiny slits. Her mouth opened and shut several times before she finally whispered. "There's no going back. Ever."

Tanya's gaze shot up, widening as she realized what Feodora was thinking. "I don't want to . . ." She couldn't say the word.

Feodora shook her head. "And I hope you never have to. But sometimes it comes with the territory. Not all men are as understanding as Lieutenant Pudovkin."

"What if I just say I'm an escort, nothing more? They will respect my boundaries, won't they?"

"Sometimes, yes." Feodora looked as though she was about to cry.

Was Feodora talking about rape? These

were officers in the Red Army. They weren't raping the women whom they were inviting out on social occasions, were they?

Tanya looked up at Feodora with glistening eyes. "Fe, no . . .."

"Sometimes these things don't turn out like you would hope. I once thought I would earn enough money to survive by going out to nice dinners and sharing an occasional kiss. It didn't turn out as I had hoped."

Tanya clutched one hand into the other. Was it worth the risk? Maybe Feodora's experience wasn't typical. She would be extra careful.

"I'm not telling you not to do it, but I'm just telling you to think hard before you make any decisions."

"I don't have time to think hard, Fe. I'll start showing in a few months, so if I want to earn enough money to survive this pregnancy, I have to do it now."

Feodora's eyes flickered with an odd mixture of regret and hope. Clearly, she was trying to help Tanya. Who wanted to watch her friend starve to death? But Fe also seemed to feel guilty for leading her down this path.

Tanya was done with guilt. And hunger. "Come on, Feodora. Give me one more chance to show you that I can do this. You won't regret it. You are saving my life. No, you're saving my baby's life."

"OK." The word came out slowly, as if Feodora wanted with all of her being to say no. "Yes, I'll do it. Let me send a message to Lieutenant Dubrovskiy down at the base and let him know that I have a friend. He'll get the word out. I bet I can get you a date for tonight if you want one."

"Yes. I do." The words stuck in Tanya's mouth, filling her throat with acid. Feodora was right, there was no going back. Of course, if going back meant going back to the way she had lived the last few weeks, she wasn't sure she wanted to.

It didn't matter. Nothing mattered anymore.

# 20

*Leningrad, Russia*

"Message for Tanya Egerov!" A gruff voice yelled up the stairs, causing a chorus of groans to rise from various sleeping people on cots around the room.

"Don't you people have anything better to do than wallow on your cots all day?" Feodora was already on her second flask of vodka and more than willing to speak her mind.

"Such as go on so-called dates with soldiers like you and your little whore friend?" A condescending voice rose from the corner.

Tanya froze. Did her roommates think she was a prostitute like Feodora?

"I don't . . ." It was all Tanya could get to come out around the giant lump that formed in her throat.

"Sure you don't, honey." The woman who'd spoken looked at her with mocking eyes. "I'm sure that message waiting for you downstairs is just a note from the mayor asking you to tea."

Tanya stormed out the room, refusing to let them see her shame. Grabbing the folded message from the table by the door, she stepped outside into the cool afternoon air to read it.

*Lieutenant Petrov Ivanov requests your presence at the Rossiya Hotel for dinner and drinks. Please come dressed for dancing. Two hundred fifty rubles.*

She let out an audible groan. Wasn't this exactly what she had asked for? An opportunity to earn more money so that she could save up for this baby?

The door slammed behind her. Fedora.

"Don't mind them, Tawnie."

"A Lieutenant Ivanov wants me to meet him at the Rossiva tonight for dinner and drinks."

"Lieutentant Ivanov. I know of him. A nice man."

"And?"

"And I don't know anything else, Tawn. I've never gone out with him."

"Will I be all right, Fe?"

"I hope so."

"What do I do now?"

"You can't tell him no, or you'll never get another date again." Feodora glanced at her watch. "Come upstairs. We'll find you something to wear."

"But, what about them?" Tanya's gaze veered to the door.

"What about them? If you do this, you'll have to get used to the mean comments and the pitying stares. Comes with the territory. Some people don't understand what it's like."

Tanya shook her head, wishing that Nicolai was there to take her into his arms and tell her it would all be all right. A tear trickled down her cheek.

"Oh, Tawnie. I'm sorry." Feodora wrapped her into a hug. A whiff of vodka surrounded both of them. Pulling away, Feodora dragged Tanya upstairs. "But it's too late to back out now."

"So, you wore this green dress last night. What about this red one?" Feodora held up a red satin dress that had clearly seen better days. It was knee-length with black buttons up the front and a black satin sash that would cinch any loose fabric around Tanya's waist.

Tanya stepped behind the changing screen to try it on, looking longingly at the small stack of practical cotton dresses folded under her bunk. She would never be comfortable in red satin. Then again, she would never be comfortable going out on a date with Lieutenant so-and-so.

She buttoned the red dress up the front and adjusted the loose fabric where she could. Stepping out from behind the screen, she did a little twirl, and Feodora let out a low whistle. She reached over and unbuttoned the top button. "Let's show a little décolletage."

Tanya's hand instinctively flew up to cover her pale chest, but Feodora was right. If she did this, she needed to look the part. And act the part. "What should I do when I see him, Fe?"

"You smile your biggest, walk up to him, and plant a big one on his lips." She laughed hysterically, the vodka clearly telling her she was funnier than she was.

"Ha-ha."

"OK, so not on his lips, but a seductive little kiss on his cheek wouldn't hurt."

"I don't want seductive. I want to survive the night with some dignity intact."

"If you want to do that, you'll need to be a little seductive."

Tanya swallowed hard. What was she getting herself into? Maybe it would be better to die on the streets. Maybe. But the baby. This was her baby's only means of survival. She had no choice but to do this. "OK, Fe, seductive it is." Tanya's lips formed into a sultry pout and she stuck her hand on her hip, swinging it out wide.

Swaggering her hips as she walked down the stairs, she turned and blew a kiss at Feodora, and then made her way out into the cool evening air. She hailed a pedi cab and stepped in. With a deep sigh, she closed her eyes and tried to pretend she lived in a different world.

A world where good men didn't die as a result of senseless accidents, lonely widows had a means to provide for themselves, and pregnant women didn't have to sell kisses to officers in exchange for a loaf of bread.

# 21

Anna wrinkled her nose at the dingy basement and brought her hand up to her face, trying to brush away the tickle so she wouldn't sneeze.

Pastor Laiho had agreed to let her use the church's basement for her Junior War Committee meetings, but since the maintenance staff rarely ventured down there, it was up to her to make the room usable.

Looking around, this was a tall order. Concrete walls stood starkly around her with only rusty pipes to break the monotony of gray. The floor was also concrete, only it had been painted a dingy cream color. Whoever had come up with the idea of painting a floor cream had clearly not thought that through. Muddy stains marked the floor every few inches. She needed to go find some chairs. There wasn't a woman in her committee who would agree to sit on that floor. Good thing she had come twenty minutes early.

She inspected two dark closets looking for chairs before finally finding eight wooden ones. They would have to do. If more than eight people came, she'd stand. Dragging the chairs one-by-one into the meeting room, she arranged them in a circle around a small pine table. The table was in much better shape than the rest of the furniture. It actually even looked clean, so Anna placed a loaf of her Äiti's pulla on the table along with a knife and some linen napkins.

Nothing like making do.

A rustle startled her and she looked up to see Kaino, as well as their friend Mary scooting into two of the chairs. Last winter, Anna and Mary had knitted socks and packed boxes for soldiers.

"Hi, Anna. How are things?" Mary looked at her with sad eyes. Mary's father had been killed last winter by a Russian bullet.

"Good, Mary. And you?"

"Better. We still miss my father so much, but things are looking up now that Mr. An-nala and the boys are helping with the farm." Mary had grown up an only child, and so her father's death had nearly destroyed their family's farm. Mary and her mother weren't able to keep up on their own, but fortunately, the Annala family from Karelia had moved in just in time to help with the spring planting. Now they were helping with the fall harvest. A blessing in disguise.

Kind of like when the Rantas had moved in with them.

"I'm so glad, Mary. If you need more, I know that Mr. Ranta and the boys would be happy to help. We have more than enough men to share."

Everyone laughed.

Mary shook her head. "And Kaino? How's Johannes doing?" Mary's voice was pinched.

Tears sprang to Kaino's eyes. She missed her on-again, off-again boyfriend. It was enough to drive everyone around her crazy. Anna and Mary shared a commiserating look as Kaino launched into a sappy dissertation about the agony of being away from the only man she'd ever loved and the anguish of having to communicate by letters when he was stuck in a hospital somewhere in Helsinki. Kaino wouldn't rest easy until he was home safe in her arms. Oh, and until there was a shiny, gold ring on her finger.

Anna smiled. Sure, Kaino was a bit dramatic, but she was also her best friend and she meant well. "Maybe we can think of something to help Johannes and the boys this winter."

"I hear that most of the soldiers have been reassigned to help with the refugee crisis as part of the Rapid Resettlement Act." Their friend Paivi walked into the room and set a notebook on a chair.

"Yes, that's what I've heard." Anna hated the thought of so many refugees pouring into Helsinki. Not only because it would mean a tough winter, but also because she knew what it would tear Matti up. Anna couldn't imagine how he would react to seeing fresh reminders on every street corner. She glanced at her wristwatch. Five minutes more and they would get started.

Mary stood up and helped herself to some pulla, slathering her slice with the butter Anna had carefully churned this morning. At least they weren't under strict food rations yet. Anna had heard that flour and sugar and butter were practically non-existent in London. She couldn't imagine life without sugar or flour. What would they eat? With the way things were going, she might soon find out.

And if giving up her pulla would bring Matti and the other soldiers home quicker, she would do it in a heartbeat.

Two of her other committee members,

Soylï and Katarina walked in.

Anna looked at them with a smile. "Thank you for coming."

A few more stragglers trickled in.

Anna handed each a napkin with a slice of sweet, warm bread. "Shall we get started?" She brushed crumbs off of her skirt. Pulling her chair closer to the center, she prayed over their meeting and then pulled out a bag.

Balls of gray wool yarn and knitting needles fell out onto the floor. "I know we don't need socks for the soldiers right now, but I figured that some of the refugees could probably use something warm. Plus, sitting here with idle hands drives me crazy."

Kaino grabbed a ball of yarn and two needles and elbowed Anna in the side. "We haven't even decided what our next group effort is and you're already giving us jobs to do."

"Just doing my part to keep everyone warm and dry."

"Everyone? Or a certain blond-haired soldier?" Kaino teased.

Glaring, Anna looked around the room, not sure if any of the others knew about Matti. Or if she wanted them to know.

Mary looked up. "Anna?"

Anna puckered her lips and blew out a

frustrated breath. "All right, so I met someone. He's a soldier from Karelia and he's now working on Rapid Resettlement Duty in Helsinki."

"And his name is?" Katarina stood up to help herself to another slice of bread.

"Matti Ranta."

"Wait . . ." Wheels seemed to turn in Mary's head. "Isn't the refugee family that your family took in called Ranta?"

Anna looked down at her shoe and rubbed a speck of mud off the painted floor vigorously. "Yes, they are. I met him when his family moved in with us . . ."

". . . and within a week, she was head over heels in love with the guy." Kaino finished her sentence with a smug smile.

Anna frowned at her over her knitting needles. Head over heels in love? Not even close. "Shall we discuss what we came for?" Anna straightened her yarn and restored the conversation to a place that was a bit more comfortable.

"You mean how to help Matti Ranta stay warm this winter?" Kaino was taking this a bit too far.

Well, she wouldn't be telling Kaino anything ever again. "Maybe we could focus on refugees from Karelia this winter. I hear there are hundreds of thousands of them flooding Helsinki, and many have nowhere to live and very little to eat."

The conversation turned to a serious discussion about how they — just a ragtag group of poor farm girls from Kalajoki — could help.

"I have an idea." Mary's cheeks reddened as the group turned to her. "What if we were to collect foodstuffs and blankets for the refugees? Then we could package up the goods in boxes and ship them to the camps in Helsinki."

"But everyone here is trying to store up as much as they can to survive the winter with our own flood of refugees. Not many have food and clothes to spare." Katarina brought the voice of reason.

Anna's family had doubled their garden size and sent the boys out on countless fishing expeditions to make sure they'd have enough to feed both themselves and the Rantas over the winter. How could they ask the townspeople to give, when they hardly had enough for themselves?

"Well," Mary added, "we're all short on supplies right now, but we have so much more than most of the refugees. In fact, I read in the newspaper that we are best off. Relatively few refugees have made it all the way up here, and relatively little of our food is going to the front. We have more than most. I was talking to my mother, and she suggested that we could ask each family to give up five items — it could be five tins of pickled herring or five jars of applesauce or five pairs of socks. That way, everyone is sacrificing a little. A lot of little sacrifices can go a long way."

Anna's mind reeled with the possibility. She knew her family didn't have a tin of herring to spare, but she could probably convince everyone to miss one measly meal. It could make a huge difference. Anna looked around the room and saw her own concerns mirrored on the faces of the others.

Could they make this work?

Kaino's eyes brightened. "Maybe we make posters. Say something like 'Five to Keep Them Alive' and hang them all over town."

Excited murmurs picked up.

"I think this really could work," Mary said.

"I think we should do it." For the first time in weeks, Anna felt fulfilled. She was doing something worthwhile.

"Wait," Katrina said. "How would we get the supplies to Helsinki? Last winter, shipping cost almost more money than we could afford."

"I thought of that." Mary smiled. "What

if we were to load the boxes into the cargo compartment of the passenger train to Helsinki? I asked down at the train station, and it costs less to buy cargo space than it does to ship using the postal service. We would have to send someone to Helsinki to make sure everything gets offloaded and carted away as it should."

Anna's heart danced into her throat. Someone would go to Helsinki?

"But train tickets are expensive too." Katarina's eyes widened.

"I know. But still not as much as shipping. We can buy tickets on standby for only a few marks if there are open seats. We would just have to be flexible with our dates. And whoever goes would have to arrange to pack and haul several loads of supplies when she arrived."

Anna smiled at her friend. Clearly, she had been doing a lot of thinking as of late.

"And I think Kaino and Anna should be the ones to make the trip to Helsinki," Mary finished.

Anna's gaze snapped over to Mary. She had never been more than ten kilometers away from Kalajoki. Helsinki? If she went, could she see Matti?

"How would we pay for those tickets?" Kaino sounded so skeptical.

158

Anna had been wondering the same thing. She had money saved for her passage to America, but she simply couldn't spend it on a frivolous trip to the capitol. Or should she? For the refugees?

Mary grinned. "My mother told me she was willing to chip in cash from my father's death benefit if it would help the refugees. She said if we can raise the supplies, she'll pay for the train tickets."

The entire group erupted into applause.

Kaino and Anna exchanged a wary look. Was it possible?

Anna cleared her throat, unable to hide her smile. "Do you think we could have our collection done by the end of November? I'd love to have supplies collected so we could get them on a train down to Helsinki before Christmas. We would be like Saint Nicholas — taking the Christmas train to spread gifts and cheer to the refugees."

"I think we can do it if we all work together." Mary set her hands in her lap as if the decision was made.

"I like this plan. Thank you, Mary." Anna looked at her feet. Why didn't she feel as excited as she should? Was it that she didn't believe it would happen? Maybe she wasn't sure what she would find when she arrived in Helsinki. Or maybe she couldn't quite allow her heart to imagine what it would be like to see Matti again. If she let her thoughts go there, she'd be able to think of nothing else until December.

# 22

*Helsinki, Finland*

Tiny white snowflakes drifted down from gray skies, soaking Matti's hair and fur-lined collar. He had never minded snow until last winter, but after spending months shivering in frost-filled trenches, he wouldn't mind if he never saw a snowflake again.

Maybe when this war was over he'd marry Anna and move somewhere warm — like the French Riviera.

Bad idea. France was occupied by the Nazis, who were the only people in the world worse than the Russians.

Anyway, Anna seemed to want nothing to do with marrying him. But maybe he could change her mind?

Matti stomped his boots and brushed snow off of his jacket and then stepped inside the Army Corps barracks building. At least here there was a place to get away from the relentless cold. Hanging his coat on a hook near the door, he pulled off his navy-blue wool gloves and walked over to the fire roaring in a wood stove in the corner. He held his hands in front of the flames, allowing them to turn from cold, to burning, to numb.

Sinking down onto a hard sofa in the commons room, Matti closed his eyes as a wave of nostalgia enveloped him. What he wouldn't give to sink into the soft, velvety cushions of his mother's dark green sofa. Leaning against the pillows, he could almost feel the warmth of home and smell the aroma of hot, sugared pulla baking in the oven.

How he longed for home . . . or a freezing cold trench with a Molotov cocktail in his hands.

He twisted his mouth into a frown. How ironic it was that he wanted one or the other, but not this.

Matti pulled his small leather Bible out of his front pocket and flipped to Phillipians 4:4. "Rejoice in the Lord always, again I say rejoice." He ran his fingers along the verse he had read so many times, contemplating the words that had carried him through so much difficulty. He'd always believed God had a perfect plan in everything. Even in tough times, he'd reminded himself to rejoice. But now? Now that he was stuck in Helsinki sitting on scratchy olive drab linen while the Russians made themselves at home on his Äiti's green velvet sofa?

He hardly felt like rejoicing.

For the first time in his life, Matti questioned God's plan. Johan and others had died for . . . this? How could he rejoice in a God that allowed so much suffering?

Matti slammed the Bible shut and looked up toward the ceiling. *God, if You're real, show me that there is a purpose in all this.* He waved his hands around the room, not caring that people might see him and think he was acting crazy. *Because right now, I'm feeling like a lot of bad stuff has happened and nothing good has come out of it.* A crinkling in his front pocket reminded him that there was at least one good thing that had come out of this war.

Anna.

He pulled out her latest letter from his pocket and leaned back against the scratchy cushions. He reread the words that had almost made his heart stop earlier that day.

*Oh, Matti, I'm so excited to tell you about our "Five to Keep Them Alive" campaign. The Kalajoki Junior War Committee has asked everyone in town to donate five items to help the refugees. You should see how much we* have collected! We have dozens of boxes of hats, scarves, mittens and socks, piles of warm blankets and more than three hundred jars of preserves. It'll really bless needy families and I'm so grateful that our little town was able to do so much.

But here's the best part, soldier boy. The committee members have agreed to send Kaino and me on the train to Helsinki to deliver the supplies in person. Yes, that's right! Would you have time to spend a few days with a lonely farm girl from way up north?

Matti's face cracked into a grin. Did he have time? There was no one in the world he'd rather spend a few days with than Anna. He pulled out a pencil and began to draft a response.

Anna,

When I read that you were coming to Helsinki, I jumped up and down and did a little jig through the mess hall. The guys all thought I had trench fever, but after realizing that I had gotten a letter from you they realized I was just crazy.

I can't wait for you to come!

Please hurry. It's getting awfully lonely down here with only the snow and the guys to keep me company. Come quickly! And bring some sturdy socks (ones without holes) . . . it's cold here in Helsinki.

Tapping his pen against the table, he looked up and spotted Takala and Käärme coming toward him. He quickly folded the page and put it in his front pocket. The letter would have to wait. He would never hear the end of it from the guys if they knew he was being so flirty with a woman.

"There you are, Ranta." Takala stepped up behind him, grabbed his arm, and pulled him up into a standing position.

"Hello." Matti quickly saluted his captain. "Just trying to warm up before we head on out to the Suomenlinna. It's cold out there."

"I still don't have feeling in my hands after that ride back from the plant." Matti held up red, swollen fingers and waved them at the men.

"I know just the cure for cold, frozen fingers, Ranta." Käärme shook his head firmly. "Come with us tonight and I'll introduce you to my tried-and-true cure for just about any ailment, *glögg*."

The guys in Matti's old company had perfected their recipe for glögg on a cold night like this one. They had mixed wine and vodka with raisins, cardamom, and cinnamon until they'd said it reached perfection. One of the men had forced him to try a swig and he'd almost choked on it

165

before forcing himself to swallow.

*No, thank you.*

"I think I'll just stay in, tonight. Listen to the radio, get some sleep."

"Oh, no you won't." Takala moved behind him and pushed him toward the door. "Grab your coat, Ranta. You're coming with us."

Matti sighed visibly and grabbed his coat, buttoning it up to the top as the other guys grabbed their own parkas and cinched them tight.

"All right, it looks as if I'm going with you." He shrugged. It actually wasn't that bad. The guys in his company were wild, but they were good men. Men he would have to rely on if they ever marched into Karelia.

They opened the door and a snowy wind blew into the room, making Matti wish for a car. Or at least a horse. Slogging down the sidewalk in this weather wasn't exactly the most comfortable thing to do — even if it was only for a few blocks.

"So, Ranta, you were down at Lake Lagoda last winter, right?"

"Yes, sir. Army of the Isthmus, 4th Division, Second Corps."

"We were in the 8th Division, Third Corps under Major General Heinrichs." The three men rattled off numbers and ranks as if they were schoolboys doing arithmetic.

But Matti could hardly hear those numbers without thinking of Johan. *Keep it together.*

Takala plodded through the snow, his boots clumping loudly so that Matti could hardly hear his voice. "It was horrible, wasn't it?"

"Yes . . . it was."

Takala stopped in his tracks and turned toward Matti. "It's been really nice to have someone else who understands what it was like. You know, in our company, Sergeant Ranta. I was beginning to think I was one amongst hundreds of greenhorns."

Matti shifted his weight and took another step toward the street.

Takala squinted at him. "I'm glad you're here with us."

Matti shrugged. "Me, too. Even if you guys are dragging me out to the night club in a blizzard."

"Hey, we're just helping you warm up."

"That you are." Matti held open the door and brushed snow off his friend's shoulders as he walked inside. The music drowned out the loneliness that had almost overwhelmed him just an hour before.

For the first night in months, he was able

to forget all about the what-ifs surrounding his future with Anna and the war and just focus on the moment at hand.

For those couple of hours, it felt nice to forget.

# 23

*Leningrad, Russia*

Tanya paused on the sidewalk, allowing herself the luxury of stopping to listen to the violinist who strummed Russian folk songs to busy passers-by. With a frown, Tanya shook her head. It was downright blasphemous that Russian folk songs were being strummed on the streets of Leningrad today, on St. Nicolas's Day, of all days.

Tanya closed her eyes and allowed the violin music to transport her back to Christmases past. She pictured a brightly decorated tree that her Papa had hauled in from the woods behind their house on St. Nicolas's Day. That day they had feasted opulently on roasted pork, sauerkraut soup, and *koliadkis* fresh from the oven before sitting down in the candlelight to exchange small gifts.

A beautiful Christmas memory — one that was quickly stuffed into the recesses of

169

her mind, only to be treasured in solitude after the Bolsheviks banned Christmas. Oh, her Papa had been angry the day he'd heard the government mandate that New Year's trees would now be decorated instead of Christmas trees. And Russian folk songs would replace Christmas carols at holiday concerts and gatherings.

Standing there, listening to the folk music, Tanya chuckled when she thought about that mandate. Sure, the Bolsheviks thought they were stealing Christmas from Russia, but in reality, they were only making it more special. Stealing Christ's holy day from a nation of dedicated Catholics was akin to stealing Nazi tanks from an angry company of Germans.

After the ban, her parents made sure their Christmases were even more Christ-centered. They made sure their only daughter understood the true meaning of Christmas regardless of what the government claimed. And she understood.

She looked back at the violin player and briefly considered throwing a kopek into his worn case, but stopped herself. She had none to spare. Not if she was to survive the rest of the winter with a new baby.

Tanya swallowed a lump in her throat and did her best to push aside the clamoring memories of the last few weeks. Memories of flirtatious smiles, of awkward kisses, of . . .

She shuddered. She hadn't had a choice, had she?

The man had offered her five hundred rubles. Enough to pay for milk for her baby for months. Enough to pay for a roof over their heads. Enough to make sure her baby survived. Enough to send her out onto the streets with a slip of paper in hand today.

It had been worth it, hadn't it?

She turned the corner onto Sadovaya Street, peering in awe at the Church of the Savior on Blood that loomed ahead. Nicolai would've loved the place — the brightly colored onion-shaped domes towering over the dingy city streets, a bright spot in her field of vision. But she wasn't on a tour of Leningrad today.

She was on a mission.

Tanya walked a few more blocks toward the church and stopped to check the crudely drawn map Feodora had sketched for her this morning. Yes, this was it. Turning, Tanya looked warily down the street as the houses seemed to grow more run down and decrepit with each step.

This wasn't the nice part of town. But it wasn't the Azoz Sanatoria either. And it wasn't as if she had any hope of living in the nice part of town ever again. Not with what she did for a living.

Tanya pulled her coat collar tight and reminded herself that it was all for the baby. Nicolai's baby. And the heavy jingling in her pocket reminded her she was well-fed, well-clothed, and warm . . . thanks to her work.

The alternative was so much worse.

She stepped up to house number 423, removed her gloves, and knocked lightly.

"Coming!" A cheery voice called from inside.

Rubbing her hands together, Tanya surveyed her surroundings. Tall apartment buildings crowded the street, leaving no room for trees or bushes or even weeds to grow. Instead, a concrete jungle of sidewalks, paver-brick streets and crumbling houses spread for as far as she could see. An endless sea of grays and browns.

"Hello." The door creaked loudly as it opened before it settled at an unseemly angle, revealing a thin woman with wispy grey hair. She wore a peach-colored housedress and dull grey glasses.

"Hello. I'm Tanya Egerov. Feodora's friend. I'm here to look at your attic bedroom."

"Why, yes, hello Tanya. I'm Vera." The woman's gaze fell on Tanya's belly with a questioning look.

Tanya hung her head, feeling a sudden urge to explain her circumstances. "My husband died last summer."

Vera's eyes grew soft. "Oh, poor thing. Come on in!" She stepped aside, allowing Tanya to enter a tiny entryway with peeling pink and lilac flowered wallpaper on every wall. Tanya moved to the side of the foyer and waited to follow Vera's lead.

Vera hobbled through a tiny door to their right, stopping every few steps to rub a spot on her back as if each footfall pained her. She chatted busily as she led Tanya down a narrow, dark hallway. "When I ran into Feodora last week at the gastronom and she told me that she was staying in that awful Azoz Sanatroia, I immediately told her she had to move in here. My attic bedroom has been sitting empty since my Sergei enlisted. I just wish I had found her sooner. Do you know that Feodora's grandmama and I were best friends when we were girls?"

Tanya stared at Vera's crinkled lips and tried to keep up with the conversation. It was the first time anyone other than Feodora had paid her even a modicum of respect in weeks. She wasn't quite sure how to take it.

Vera continued. "Anyway, it's just awful what has happened to poor, sweet Feodora. I love her like she was my own child, you know. The granddaughter I never had. I'd always hoped she would fall in love with my Sergei and they would give me some great-grandbabies . . ." She turned a corner and headed up a dark, rickety staircase. "Of course, the war does funny things. Sergei enlisted in an officer's training program after his daddy was hauled off and hasn't been around here since. I live here all alone, you know." She rubbed her lower back again, cringing as she hobbled up the last few stairs. "You have a good friend in Feodora. I told her to go pack her things and move in here right now and she said she couldn't unless you could come with her. That girl is always looking out for others. Such a dear thing."

Tanya frowned, her view of Feodora clouded by images of her friend guzzling vodka and flirting with men in order to make a few rubles. She loved her, of course, but she had never seen the side of her that Vera described. "Yes, Feodora is wonderful."

"Anyway, I told Feodora that I wish I could just let you stay here for free, but I'm hardly making ends meet right now, what with the war and all." Vera swung open a thin wood door to reveal a tiny attic bedroom, complete with two twin beds with thick, flowered bedspreads, a wash pan and a tiny armoire in the corner. "So she said you two could pay five hundred rubles a month, which would go a long way in helping me pay my bills. I've been worried that I could lose this place. Do you think you could come up with that?" Vera looked at her hopefully, swinging her arm out into the room and pointing to the features.

Tanya smiled. It was the most beautiful room she had ever seen — clean and homey and private enough to nurse a baby without dozens of drunk revelers screaming obscenities. Gulping down her smile, Tanya considered the idea of paying two hundred fifty rubles a month — her share of the rent. She had enough in her pocket to pay her portion through the end of February, but after that, she'd have to start earning money again. Somehow.

Suddenly, the room felt stuffy and she leaned against the wall, trying to get hold of her emotions. Was there any hope of ever finding a respectable job?

Vera caught sight of her. "Oh, dear, are you all right?"

"Yes, I just got a bit queasy for a minute. I probably need to get off my feet."

Vera smiled. "Oh, come down and have tea with me, my dear. I don't have sugar, but I have plenty of honey and some cream." She led her down the stairs, looking back at Tanya every few moments.

With a sigh of relief, Tanya followed Vera and took one last glance at the room. Wouldn't it be wonderful to finally have peace and quiet and warmth? And since she had saved up some money, she could spend the next few months hanging out here with Vera, helping her with the house and resting to get ready for her new arrival.

This was perfect.

*Thank You, Lord, for providing.* She swallowed the prayer, reminding her stubborn heart that she didn't pray anymore.

Plus, God hadn't provided her this room, Feodora had. Feodora and Vera.

"Can I help you make tea?"

"No, dear, I can manage. You just sit down right here and put those feet up. You must be exhausted. I remember when I was eight months pregnant with my Lillya. My ankles were so swollen I could hardly get my boots on. I'd just lay here with my feet propped up on the table and pray that baby girl would come."

Tanya sank down onto the couch, resting for what felt like the first time in months. She looked around the tiny parlor. She stared at fading brown-and-gray pictures of happy children and happier times. An old wedding photo hung in an oval frame in the center of the wall. Tanya started to ask Vera about it but stopped herself.

She had enough to cry about without hearing the sob stories of others.

Vera hobbled into the room, a tray with china teacups and a steaming pot balancing on her frail wrists. Setting it down gingerly, she poured Tanya a glass and then poured her own cup before sitting and taking a tentative sip.

"So, my dear. Will this work for you and Feodora?"

"Yes. It's just lovely." Tanya meant it. Sure, the house was starting to fall apart, but that didn't matter. It was clean and safe.

But what if Vera found out what she and Feodora did for a living? They would end up on the streets.

Was it better to move into this wonderful house if she would lose it in a matter of months? Or would it be smarter to stay at the Azoz Sanitoria, where at least she knew her baby would have a roof over her head?

# 24

*Leningrad, Russia*

"She'll find out, Feodora."

"No, she won't. We'll be discreet."

Tanya glared at her friend. "You are never discreet. Not when you're drinking."

"Well, then I won't drink when Vera is home. We can't turn away from this opportunity. You can't stay here." Feodora pointed to Tanya's bulging belly and then at the dingy room at the Azoz Sanatoria, cringing as she scanned dilapidated cots and peeling walls.

She was right. Tanya would give almost anything to get away from here before the baby was born. There were more than twenty people crowded into this tiny room, most of them hard of luck. One peep from the baby and she'd be kicked out on the streets by a drunk, angry mob.

"But how will we earn the five hundred rubles a month without . . . you know?"

178

"We'll just have to cross that bridge when we get there." Feodora's face was steely with determination. "We have enough saved up to get us through February. Maybe by then the war will be over and someone will hire us to file or something."

"Maybe."

"In the meantime, I don't see any better options than us moving in with Vera, do you?"

Tanya sighed and looked at her swollen belly. She didn't really have a choice, did she? "No. I don't." Tanya clenched her jaw, the reality of her circumstance once again causing her heart to despair. "Can you promise not to tell Vera about what we do?"

"Promise!" Feodora grinned widely, reaching under her cot to grab a dingy knapsack. She started filling it with her few belongings.

"So you will leave that here?" Tanya pointed to her flask and the half-empty bottle of vodka lying on her friend's cot.

Feodora looked up with sad eyes and blew out a deep breath. "You know I can't do that." A tear trickled down her cheek. She quickly wiped it away.

Tanya looked at her friend, her heart softening. "It's all right, Fe. We'll figure it out. I'm just glad we have somewhere to get away from this."

The two stopped talking, focused instead on packing their possessions to leave the Azoz as soon as possible.

The boom of footsteps pounding up the stairs broke the awkward silence between the two friends.

Oleg Titov, one of the men who slept five cots down, burst into the room carrying a wrinkled stack of leaflets. Taking a moment to catch his breath, he huffed, "Stalin's guys just dropped these."

President Stalin employed a troop of fixed-wing planes that flew through the skies with the sole purpose of sending important messages to the people.

Feodora and Tanya each grabbed one of the pamphlets and started reading. "Be ready to protect the USSR from evil regimes! Learn to shoot accurately today!"

The pamphlet showed an angry looking solider pointing a gun at a looming monster holding a Nazi swastika and a Finn flag.

Tanya trembled. She had grown up under an oppressive regime, and her father had lost his life because of Stalin's great purge. The thought of a worse enemy taking over in Russia terrified her.

She looked up at Feodora, who was still reading. "Do you think it's true, Fe? Would

Hitler dare come to Russia?"

Feodora shook her head adamantly. "No way, Tanya. Hitler would be crushed the moment he crossed our border. Plus, I heard Molotov and Hitler are pals. In fact, Molotov is probably drinking a stein of beer at Hitler's hunting lodge as we speak."

Tanya glanced away and then grabbed another flier from Oleg. This one was a single page with a fierce-looking soldier standing at attention. Across the top, it read *Long live Red Army of workers and peasants, the true guard of the Soviet borders!* On the bottom it read, *We can all play a part in this great, patriotic battle.*

Tanya couldn't help but smile at this one.

It claimed that peasants like her — women who had no money to buy war bonds and no ability to fight — could also play a part in saving Russia, of making it better. But what could she do? Nudging Feodora with her elbow, she showed her the flier and then saluted her friend with a grin.

"Long live the Red Army, soldier!"

Feodora grabbed the flier and read it quickly before saluting back. "At ease, soldier!" She stood up on her cot, as if she were leading her troops into battle.

Oleg and the rest of the group rolled their eyes at them and turned to lay on their cots.

Tanya couldn't help but dissolve into a fit of giggles. Just imagine Feodora in the Red Army. She certainly would keep things interesting. "But really, Fe, how can we play a part? I can hardly buy myself bread."

Feodora grinned and winked. "I think we do plenty to boost the morale of the soldiers."

Tanya blanched. That wasn't exactly the contribution she had envisioned. Maybe knitting socks? Or collecting food stuffs? "No, Fe, what can we really do? Maybe I can knit some socks while I'm in my lying-in period?"

"Where will you get the money to buy yarn?"

Feodora was right. She was probably the lone person in all of Russia who had nothing to give to the war effort. She folded up the fliers in her hand and stuffed them into Nicolai's satchel along with her few earthly possessions. No, she wasn't much help to the war effort, but at least she was getting out of the Azoz Sanatoria.

Maybe her baby would someday make a great contribution to the world, to the motherland. That was, if her baby survived the next few months.

## 25

*Leningrad, Russia*

"Tea, my dear?" Vera called up the stairs to where Tanya was resting.

"I'd love some. Be right down!" Tanya called back as she hoisted herself off her bed and hobbled down the stairs.

"What about Feodora?" Vera asked.

"She went out for a while."

Feodora had actually spent the night at a hotel with a soldier last night, but Tanya wasn't about to tell Vera. So far, they'd managed to keep their work a secret from Vera, although Tanya suspected Vera knew more than she let on.

Running a clenched fist over her lower back, Tanya lowered herself into a threadbare chair in the corner of Vera's dusty living room while Vera poured tea into chipped china teacups. Tanya imagined that at one point, tea at Vera's house was a festive place — full of creamy teas, delicious pastries, and beautiful decorations.

Now they had plain tea and toast, but it was still wonderful to Tanya. After what she'd lived through a few months ago, she would never take something as simple as tea and toast for granted again.

"So, how are you getting situated, my dear?"

Tanya looked up absentmindedly and reminded herself to stay in the moment. "Oh, it's lovely here."

"And how are you feeling, you know, with the baby?"

"I've had some minor pains, but I'm fine. I have at least a month to go, so I'm trying not to think about it. No use getting nervous now."

Vera smiled, as if she understood perfectly. The room grew silent, a sentimental gaze settling across Vera's wrinkled features. Looking at the wall, Vera pointed to a tiny picture of a young, tow-headed girl with pig-tails and big white ribbons. "That's my Lillya. She was a lot like you." Vera's thin, frail voice seemed to come alive as she spoke about her daughter. "When she was a little girl, she desperately wanted to go to school, but the system only let boys go. Our neighbor boy had a big test coming up in Russian literature and so Lillya offered to help him study. When he brought home his test, she covered the answers with her hand so she could quiz herself. She got a perfect score."

Tanya laughed. "That does sound like me. I loved school when I was a girl."

Vera cracked a tentative smile. "Even though I lost her so long ago, God blessed me with an everyday reminder of her with Sergei. He's his mother's son — independent, strong-willed, and smart."

"And where is he now?"

"He was sent out to the front to prepare for the invasion. News is that it could happen as early as March or April."

Tanya's eyes shot up. "I'm still hoping that's just a rumor. Maybe the Germans will leave us alone. Feodora says that one of her friends in the Red Army says that Hitler wouldn't dare invade Russian soil. Nobody is that crazy."

"I sure hope you're right, but something in me tells me that Hitler will try."

Tanya looked Vera in the eyes. "What will we do if the Nazi's come to Leningrad?"

"Weren't you the one who was just telling me that we can't get nervous about tomorrow's trouble today? We'll figure it out, Tanya. For now, we just need to pray."

"Sure, yes." Tanya smiled hoping Vera

wouldn't be able to see through her hesitation. She could happily follow along with an old lady's misguided prayers, if it meant she had a safe place to live with her daughter.

Vera smiled softly, bowed her head and folded her hands.

Tanya followed obligingly.

"Heavenly Father, it seems as if Leningrad is on the brink of something terrible. The Nazis are pressing in from the west and the Finns from the north and we're trapped in the middle, unsure of where to go and what to do. Lord, protect us! Keep our city safe from this terrible persecution. We know You have a plan in this, and we trust You that Your will be done. Amen."

Tanya wiped an errant tear from her cheek, smiling bravely. Vera was so much like her own grandmother that she couldn't help but get a bit sentimental hearing her pray.

Even if she didn't believe in God.

# 26

*Ylivieska, Finland*

Anna could hardly believe they'd pulled it off. Not only had the Kalajoki Junior War Committee members been able to collect twenty boxes of foodstuffs, but they had gathered several steamer trunks full of wool blankets, winter coats, and crocheted mittens for the refugees. And they gathered it all just in time for Christmas.

Anna carefully stepped into the white wooden train station, steadying herself so she wouldn't slip on the wet wood-paneled floor. It had been snowing on and off for four days straight and the streets were covered with muddy ice, most of which had now been trampled into the train station by soaked travelers hoping to get inside.

Squinting against the rows of flickering lights inside the station, Anna turned toward Kaino and blinked to adjust her eyes. With the seemingly ever-present darkness in

December near the arctic, her eyes weren't accustomed to bright lights. She checked the clock on the wall. Thankfully they still had more than an hour before the train departed.

Her Papa and two of the Ranta boys had brought the boxes of supplies down to the station yesterday and loaded them into a cargo hold. They'd be loaded into the cargo area of the train by the porters before it left, which meant she had nothing to do but wait.

Anticipation made her want to break into a foxtrot. She was going to Helsinki. Of course, the purpose of the trip was to help the refugees, but she'd also get to see Matti . . .

As quickly as her excitement grew, so did her nervousness. She had no idea what to expect. With the way they had left things, she wasn't sure what he was even thinking. Although, his letters . . . well, they'd certainly hinted that he was thinking of her. A little at least.

"Let's go grab a cup of coffee from the café before we board." Kaino pulled her toward the tiny train station café.

With their too-heavy bags over their shoulders, they walked across the platform and slid into chairs at a corner table. Anna tugged off her damp wool gloves and rubbed

188

her hands together, leaning toward the fire that roared in the rock-hewn fireplace in the corner.

Flickering sconces on the walls illuminated other soaked travelers trying to warm up before what was sure to be a long ride.

When she looked at Kaino, she saw that her friend also wavered between excitement and nervousness about the trip.

"You all right, Kai?"

Kaino bit her lip. "Yeah. I think so. Just worried about seeing Johannes again. It's been so long."

"You and Johannes have so much history. I know things will pick up right where they left off."

"I hope so. Are you nervous about seeing Matti?"

"A bit. We've written every day, but I still wonder if the three weeks we spent together was enough to carry our relationship. What if it's all different this time?"

Kaino put a protective arm on Anna's shoulder and squeezed tightly. "It will be all right. You'll see."

The train whistle clanged in the station, and a voice on the loudspeaker screamed something about boarding.

Anna swigged the last few sips of her coffee and tugged her still-damp gloves over her hands. Tightening her scarf, she followed Kaino back into the waiting room and onto the platform.

"Do you have your ticket?" Kaino asked absentmindedly, fumbling around in the pockets of her red wool coat.

"Of course." Anna pulled hers out of her handbook — exactly where she had put it — and then pulled on a scrap of white from the side of Kaino's handbag. "Here. Looks as if we're in car ten, box four."

They approached the doorway leading to the platform and Anna paused, bracing herself for the sub-zero cold that came with Kalajoki winters. She had lived here her entire life, but the icy chill still took her breath away when she stepped outside. Steam and the scent of burning coal mixed with the freezing air, made Anna feel as if she were inhaling sooty icicles. Crinkling up her nose, she turned to Kaino. "Hurry. I'm freezing!"

They counted the cars and made their way down the platform, stopping in front of a car that had clearly once been red, but now boasted varying shades of grey, red and mud.

"Let's hope the inside is nicer than the outside." Anna sighed. Not the most luxurious travel accommodations. She quickly joined the crowd filing onto the train, pausing only to turn around and wave goodbye to no one in particular.

Kaino laughed and then tugged her onto the car, dragging her down the aisle through the dense cigarette smoke to Box four. "Knock knock!" Kaino knocked on an imaginary door, sliding into the car and scooted into one of the last two open seats in the box.

Anna glanced at her watch, making a mental calculation of the time. Quarter past seven. If all went well, they'd be in Helsinki in time for dinner. Of course, she had an entire day cooped up in this drafty box with screaming kids to deal with first. If only she could board one of those fancy fighter jets Matti had been writing about. He'd told her that a VL Pyry could fly from Helsinki to the Arctic Circle in less than two hours. Wouldn't that be magnificent?

Anna couldn't keep her thoughts from turning to their relationship. In his last letter, Matti had promised to meet her at the train station with a smile and a kiss. A giggle escaped Anna's lips as she reached down to straighten out her already-wrinkled dress, hoping that she looked somewhat presentable when she arrived. At the rate she was going, she would be a haggard mess by the time she stepped off that train.

Anna glanced over at Kaino, who was already leaning against the wall with an opened novel. She should probably settle in.

She pulled her well-worn copy of *The Maid Silja* along with a cloth-wrapped slice of limpua out of her bag and then scooted her sack underneath her feet. Doing her best to find a comfortable position, Anna opened her novel, hoping to get swept away into the story, the clacking of the train wheels echoing in the background of her mind, keeping rhythm with the too-slow ticking of the clock.

The train jerked, knocking Anna's book out of her hands.

"What was that?" Kaino wiped her eyes and rolled her shoulders before standing to peek out of the tiny circular window on the side of their car. "It seems like we're slowing down."

Anna looked at her watch. They were still more than four hours from Helsinki and the train wasn't scheduled to make any stops.

"We're definitely slowing down." Kaino pointed out the window and turned to Anna. "Should I go see what's going on?" She opened the sliding door that led into the main aisle in the center of the train and shook her head. "Everyone else has the same idea."

Kaino returned to her seat and sat.

Anna stifled the urge to fidget. The train continued to slow down until, with a slow jolt, it stopped.

Anna closed her eyes and swallowed the lump that crept into her throat. Maybe it was just a temporary slow-down. The conductor needed a break or something. Surely they'd be on their way soon.

Twenty minutes later, a concierge stepped inside their car. "We apologize for the delay. We've run into an unexpected blizzard, and the ice on the rails is making it impossible for us to move on. We're hoping to be moving in a few hours."

A few hours?

Anna looked at her watch again and realized that would put them into Helsinki well after midnight. Matti would have to head back to the barracks to sleep and her plans for a romantic evening would be ruined. She turned to Kaino, who wore a stricken expression.

"It's all right, Kai. We will still see them tomorrow." Anna said it as much to convince herself as she did to support Kaino. Weather could stop the train for days. Who knew how long they would be stuck out here?

Wide-eyed, Kaino stared out the window.

Anna stood and stretched her arms above her head, doing her best to shake off despairing thoughts. She should have expected something like this to happen. This trip had fallen together so seamlessly from the very moment they had planned it that Anna should have known. Because nothing ever turned out as expected. Especially in the winter in war-torn Finland.

She shivered, the cold air from outside making its way under the loose sliding door and straight to her heart. Maybe it was better this way anyway. Everything in her head warned her against getting too close to Matti, yet her heart seemed all too ready to shove those warnings aside.

But she knew better than to get involved with a man who was going off to war. He could die like Henrik. Or get wounded. Or change his mind about her as he fought in Russia.

Yes, maybe this was better. She slouched into her seat and forced herself to inhale. Maybe if she could turn this train around, she could forget all about Matti. Maybe she could move to America, go to the university, paint pictures, get on with her life.

It made rational sense. But the mere thought of leaving him made her stomach clench. Her rapidly beating heart told her what her brain couldn't seem to comprehend. Her heart already belonged to Matti whether she wanted it to or not.

# 27

*Helsinki, Finland*

Matti ran his fingers through his hair and paced back and forth in the long hallway of the Helsinki Central Railway Station. Butterflies pounded in his stomach, as if they had gotten tired of flitting and now were playing a loud concert, pounding, thumping and jumping around like crazy.

He laughed at himself. Seeing Anna had him more nervous than pretty much anything he had ever done.

Including fighting in the war.

Looking at his watch for the twentieth time, he made his way back down the long corridor. The train was already twenty minutes late and he was a nervous wreck, which wasn't good after having spent the afternoon trying to convince the guys — and himself — that he wasn't totally falling apart at the thought of seeing Anna again.

He wasn't nervous about Anna. He knew

without a doubt that she was the one. He had imagined his future with her a million times — the two of them building a beautiful cabin by the lake, raising berries and cattle, spending their days laughing and frolicking and doing all the things that married couples do.

That was exactly what he wanted.

Matti stepped up to the window and looked out onto the snowy Helsinki streets. *Lord, I know Anna is the right woman for me. And I pray that the next four days are a time where our relationship will blossom, so that we can eventually become man and wife.* He groaned. Had he just thought that? Prayed that?

Anna had changed him. For the better. Six months ago, he hadn't cared who he'd hurt with his anger. Now, he not only cared, but he felt compelled to fight hard for what he believed in because he knew that free Finland — for Anna and for their future — was worth it.

How could he convince her of the same thing?

A picture of her hopping on a ship to America flashed through his mind and his stomach clenched. No, that couldn't happen. He needed Anna as much as he needed fresh air to breathe or food to eat.

The big clock on the wall of the train station bonged five times and an announcer's voice boomed over the loudspeaker. "Train number one-five-four-three from Ylivieska has been delayed. We are unsure as to when it will arrive."

Gulping in a deep breath, Matti suppressed a groan before turning to get in line at the ticket counter. He didn't care how long he waited, he would see Anna tonight.

"Yes, sir. Do you have any information on Train one-five-four-three?"

"No. Only that the last train to come in from the north said that the tracks were freezing over, and a blizzard was passing through. We have no way of knowing when they will be able to get in."

Matti turned around and stared longingly out the window at the deserted platform.

He would wait.

As long as it took.

He wrapped his coat tightly around his shoulders and sank onto a hard, wooden chair. Closing his eyes, he tried to get comfortable enough to sleep, but his mind raced.

What if Anna didn't make it? What if her train was stuck out there for days and the ice storm trapped them and they all froze to death?

Matti shook his head. He was being silly. It was simply a weather-related delay. He would see Anna soon. He turned to see the bulletin board where people could write notes for arriving passengers. It was filled with slips of paper and names, and a slew of men and women crowded around the board to write their own notes.

No. He would never do that to Anna. He wanted to be here when she arrived.

Twenty minutes later, he stood alone in the cavernous building.

Alone to think. To pray. To worry.

He shivered, pulled his collar up high around his ears, and settled in. He would wait as long as it took.

The shrill of a train whistle jolted Matti from a troubled sleep at the same time the announcer came over the intercom. "Train one-five-four-three arriving from Ylivieska."

Matti bolted upright and blinked several times, trying to bring sense to his surroundings. Oh, yes. He was at the train station.

He glanced at his watch. It was well after midnight. He licked his lips and headed toward the water fountain to get a drink of water. He must look a mess!

Finding Platform three, he raced out onto the deserted walkway, the lone man willing to brave the sub-zero temperatures. Or the long wait for the delayed train.

He wrapped his scarf tightly around his nose, hoping to block out some of the fierce wind. Squinting, he stared down the tracks into the dark midnight air and spotted the bright light of the train as it moved toward him on the tracks.

Closing his eyes, he quickly prayed calm nerves and then swung his hands behind his back, clutching them there in order to keep from fidgeting.

The train slowed to a stop. The blast of the train whistle drowned out the clacking of the wheels down the tracks.

He adjusted the collar on his jacket and blew out a cold breath, steam wafting up into the air. A few moments later, bedraggled passengers filed off the train, stretching their legs before hurrying into the warmth of the station. He scanned the faces, looking for the woman he would recognize anywhere.

There. Toward the back.

He pushed his way through weary passengers, nearly sprinting now that he'd laid eyes on her. The wind whipped a wisp of hair across her face, and she reached up and tucked it behind her ear. Glancing up, she locked gazes with him. Her eyes smiled before her mouth did. "Matti," she mouthed.

"Anna!" He shouted and ran toward her, not caring who he had to push out of the way to get to her side. Finally arriving, he wrapped her up in his arms and spun her around. "It's great to see you!"

"You waited for me."

Matti lifted his hand to her hair and brushed a wayward strand out of her eyes. Then he looked into those green eyes. "Of course I waited."

Anna closed her eyes, her teeth chattering audibly above the sound of the howling wind. He wrapped his arm around her shoulders and pulled her inside. "You're freezing. Let's go inside." He put her gloved hand into his, and they hustled into the warmth of the train station.

"Oh, goodness! I forgot all about Kaino. Where is she?" Anna searched the station for her friend and spotted her sitting quietly on a chair in the waiting room, her head buried in her hands.

Anna walked over to Kaino, pulling Matti by the hand. She perched on the edge of the seat. "What's wrong, Kai?"

"He didn't wait." Her shoulders shook as she said the words. "Johannes didn't wait for me."

"Did you look at that board over there? Lots of people left notes for their loved ones there." The three of them made their way over to the train station's message board and frantically searched for a note bearing Kaino's name.

"There. See it up there?" Anna reached up to the top and pulled down a yellow note card.

Kaino read it and scowled. "He went home."

Matti's eyes widened as Anna wrapped her friend into a hug. "I'm sorry, Kai. It's so late that nearly everyone went home." She looked at Matti and smiled timidly.

He was glad he'd stayed.

Kaino sniffled. "I don't know what to do now."

Anna's cheeks puffed up as she looked from Kaino to Matti and back again to Kaino. All he wanted was a few minutes alone with Anna, to talk, to catch up. But he couldn't leave Kaino here alone.

"Maybe you can escort us both to our hotel, Matti?" Anna's voice sounded pinched.

There would be time to talk to Anna later. "Of course. What things are we bringing with us tonight?"

Anna glanced at the train and then back

at him. "The conductor said they would load our supplies onto the platform for us to get tomorrow. Tonight it's just too cold and icy. So for now, just my trunk. And Kaino's."

Matti grabbed Anna's trunk in one hand and Kaino's in the other and the women followed him out into the cold, as he did his best not to stare too hard at the woman he already loved.

If only he could find a way to tell her.

## 28

*Helsinki, Finland*

"So where are we going?" Since she'd been in Helsinki, she'd hardly had time to sit down, much less talk to him. And now, after two crazy days of delivering boxes to refugees, she was in the mood for a nice long conversation.

That and maybe a stolen kiss. She bit her lip. No kissing Matti. Not when so much was left unsaid between them.

"Suomi's. They have the best lingonberry cake that I've ever tried. And I want you to meet the guys in my company. That's where they like to hang out."

Anna furled her brows. She had wanted Matti to herself. But she had no claim to him, did she?

They walked up to a ten-story brick building with intricate white molding outlining the windows. The place was pitch-black, and Anna would've thought it was closed if loud music and boisterous laughter wasn't spilling onto the street.

"I think this used to be some sort of apartment building, but the new owners converted the upstairs into offices and the first floor into the now infamous Suomenlinna piano lounge. It's the place to come to in Helsinki for great music and the best hot cider in Europe." Matti's voice grew mock-serious, as if he were an official tour guide.

"I see. And why is it so dark?"

"The offices are probably closed, but with blackout orders, most of the buildings in Helsinki stay dark in the evenings. It's safer."

Anna shivered, partially from cold and partially from the thought that Russian planes could be scoping out their location at that very minute, waiting for one stupid person to turn on a light. She looked at Matti to distract herself. There was no use thinking thoughts like that.

He pulled her close. "Don't worry. This will be fun."

They walked up four steps and moved inside, stomping off their boots and removing layers of scarves, coats and hats. They handed their snow gear to the attendant and entered the main room, which boasted a large, wooden dance floor surrounded by small tables. In the back left, a bar made out of what looked like carved pine held a boisterous bartender who seemed to have four arms as he handed out steaming mugs to a crowd of soldiers around the bar.

"Over here, Ranta!" A loud, masculine voice called them to a table near the back.

"Hi, Käärme! Hey, Uotila!" Matti strode over to the men in his company, with Anna trailing behind him trying to keep her heart from beating out of her chest.

The men seemed nice enough. Blond-haired and strong, the six of them sat around a tiny round table, each holding a blue ceramic mug. They laughed and joked raucously.

"May I introduce Anna Ojala, my, uh . . . friend from Kalajoki? And Anna, these are . . . the men." Matti waved to his friends at the table as each shook her hand and offered a name.

"It's a pleasure to meet you. Matti has told me so much about you."

"And he has also told us plenty about you." A gap-toothed solider called Käärme winked.

"Don't even think about it, Käärme," Matti said. He put his arm around Anna's back and winked at her.

"Sit down, stay awhile." Uotila pulled out a chair for Anna before heading toward the bar. "Anyone want anything?"

"Get us a couple of coffees, please. With cream if they have it." Matti shouted above the din.

She sat on a plush purple bench and leaned forward. "So, please tell me what kind of trouble Matti has gotten himself into since he's been here."

Takala, the group leader, drew closer and placed his hand on Matti's back. "Last week, Ranta here got kitchen duty from our commanding officer because he was late to morning check-in."

Anna looked at Matti, her eyebrows raised.

He shrugged. "What? I got this letter from this girl back home, and I just couldn't help but give it one more read before reporting in."

She beamed.

"Anyway, it was oatmeal morning and Matti managed to burn it. The entire division spent breakfast picking tiny black flecks out of their mush. Let's just say that Matti will be getting outhouse duty next time he's late."

The guys erupted into laughter, and after seeing that Matti was also laughing, Anna chuckled as well.

Matti raised his hands in the air in mock surrender and looked at her. "It wasn't my fault. I was distracted. Remember what I said about a letter from Kalajoki?"

A round of laughter circulated the table. Soon the guys told more stories about their times at the fish packing plant and the barracks.

The pianist began a lively tune, prompting Takala to stand. "I think it's time for some dancing."

Anna looked to Matti, who quickly grabbed her hand and dragged her onto the dance floor. He spun her and foxtrotted around the room before pulling her close and swaying softly to the first slow song. As she inhaled the scent of him, she couldn't help but feel a sudden outpouring of desire. For him. For the life he represented. Maybe it wouldn't be so bad to be a Finnish soldier's wife.

Especially not if that soldier could dance his way into her heart as this one had.

She leaned her head against his shoulder and breathed deeply. The aroma of hot spiced cider filled her nostrils. His heart beat steadily and she pressed in closer to him, allowing his warmth to chase away the chill of the day.

And for the first time in months she felt safe and peaceful and . . . content? Yes, content. She closed her eyes and reveled in the feeling, allowing herself to get lost in the music and in his arms.

The sound of a siren jolted her.

"What was that?"

Matti's eyebrows dropped. He grabbed her by the wrist and guided her off of the dance floor toward his company mates. "They're bombing raid sirens. They installed them during the Winter War and we used to hear them almost every night, but I haven't heard them go off for months."

"What do they mean?"

"It means I have to get you out of here." Matti pulled her over to Takala, whose eyes were cloudy and dark. He dug in his pocket and handed Matti his keys without saying a word. Matti took them with a grim nod. He strode toward the coat check where he grabbed their coats from a pile, and they raced out the door just before a sea of people descended on the club's only exit.

"What's going on, Matti?" The sirens throbbed in her ears, making cadence with her rapidly beating heart.

"I need to get you out of Helsinki. I can't bear the thought of you getting caught in a raid."

"Out of Helsinki?" Anna yanked him to a halt in front of Takala's car. She grabbed his chin, forcing him to stop and look at her.

"Yes, you need to leave. I would never forgive myself if I let you get caught up in this war. I need you up in Kalajoki, where you are safe."

"But what about the refugees? Kaino and I were to deliver another load of items out to the camp at Vironniemi tomorrow." She couldn't keep the desperation from her voice.

"We'll get some of the men in my company to do it. I'm taking you to the train station." His lips narrowed and his eyes darkened. The seriousness in his voice took her breath away. "Now."

Anna turned from him and sank into the front seat of the car, her shoulders trembling as she realized she would be leaving Matti within the hour — before she had the chance to really talk to him. To tell him what she was feeling. And now she was going home, back to Kalajoki where the contentment that she had felt only minutes ago would surely be replaced with restlessness and bitterness.

She inhaled sharply as the car engine roared to life and squealed away from the club, all her hopes for these four days disappearing in a blur of darkened buildings. "Matti. I don't want to go," she whispered, hoping she would change his mind and convince him to take her somewhere else. Anywhere but the train station.

Surely there was somewhere safe in this city?

But he kept on driving, his jaw set and his eyes dark. He only stopped long enough to round up Kaino and fetch their belongings from the hotel before squealing next to a log mire of cars parked in front of the station.

An hour later as the train roared out of the station and into the snowy night, a troubling thought rolled through her head. In the desperation of buying tickets and finding her platform in the crowded station, she hadn't even had the chance to say goodbye.

# 29

*Leningrad, Russia*

The first pain struck at nine o'clock, right as Tanya settled into her bed. She clenched her abdomen. Her face contorted with pain. Was it her time? She gripped the edge of the bed, doing her best not to moan out loud. That would scare the living daylights out of Vera. Finally, after what seemed like hours, the searing contraction subsided. She slumped down into the pillows.

When would Feodora get home?

Probably not until midnight. If at all.

Did she have the strength to climb down the stairs to ask Vera for help? She must try. Tanya hoisted herself out of her bed, and gripped the wall as she maneuvered the rickety steps — hoping another contraction wouldn't start until she had made it downstairs.

It worked.

The next contraction hit right as she

stepped onto the first floor landing, causing her to cry out in pain. She gulped. Where was Vera? She cradled her lower abdomen and sank down to the floor to wait for the contraction to pass.

When it did, she stood and teetered down the hall to Vera's room. She hoped she wouldn't give the old woman a heart attack by barging in like this. "Knock, knock?" she whispered, willing her voice not to sound desperate. Was the door open?

"What is it, dear?"

"I think . . . it's my time."

"Oh, goodness!" Vera scrambled out of bed and slowly wrapped her robe around her shoulders. "You lie down in here, my dear. I'll go get water and towels."

"In your bed?" Tanya couldn't imagine taking her kind benefactor's bedroom, even at a time like this.

"Why, of course. Where else will you have this baby? Certainly not upstairs where it's cold and drafty."

Tanya started to protest, but her words were cut off by another sharp contraction. She moaned before reaching for something to support her weight. "Maybe . . . if I just . . . just walk . . . around . . ."

"Oh, no. You will do no such thing." Vera grabbed a stack of towels sitting on the chair next to the window and threw them onto the bed. Then she grabbed Tanya by the arm and led her to the bed, propping several pillows behind her head before gently laying a threadbare blue blanket across her trembling legs.

"Thank you, Vera." Tanya bit her lip and shuddered at the thought of what it would've been like to give birth in the Azoz Sanatoria. She didn't want to think about it.

A surge of pain tightened her abdomen once again and she screamed, her fingers twisting the bedsheets as she tried to ride out the wave.

Vera limped across the room and laid a calloused hand on Tanya's back, rubbing gently. "Heavenly Father, we thank You for choosing to give life to this precious baby. Protect her and Tanya right now. Ease her pain and help this baby to come into the world easy-like. Amen."

Tanya sighed as tears sprang to her eyes. She was strangely relieved by Vera's simple prayer. If only she could believe that Someone really was watching over her and this baby, maybe it would ease her pain. But that was all a fairy tale, wasn't it? The God she had once believed in would never have allowed her to be giving birth to Nicolai's baby without Nicolai there to see it.

Another contraction tore her from inside. She gasped for breath, pleading with her body to relax. When the pain finally subsided, she turned to Vera. "Please, pray more. Keep praying." She may not believe in God anymore, but she undoubtedly felt more peaceful when Vera was praying.

"I will, my dear. I will." And with that, Vera pulled out her own Bible and read scripture, praying the words over Tanya and her baby as minutes of agonizing contractions blurred into hours, each contraction steadily growing stronger. But through it all, Vera continued to whisper encouraging words and prayers into her ear, leading straight to her soul.

# 30

*Leningrad, Russia*

Feodora burst into Vera's room, jolting Tanya from her most recent contraction with a scream.

"Shh! She's right here." Vera rested in a chair next to Tanya's bed, gently stroking her sweat-soaked hair.

"Oh, dear. Is she all right?"

Feodora's voice was filled with worry, but Tanya couldn't focus on Fedora right now. She moaned louder than she'd intended to, the pain taking her to new levels.

Vera rushed to her side. "I think another contraction is coming on. Grab that hand!"

Feodora threw herself across the bed, grabbing Tanya's hand as she screamed, writhing back and forth as another contraction stole her breath.

"I . . . I can't . . . I can't do this . . ." she managed to gasp as the contraction subsided. She sank back into her pillows.

Another moan escaped her before she closed her eyes. Each ensuing contraction sapped every morsel of strength she had left in her body.

Feodora sank onto the bed next to her. "Will she be all right, Vera?"

Tanya opened her eyes to catch Vera's smile.

"Yes. I think we'll meet this little one within the hour."

Another scream. Tanya couldn't help herself.

Feodora clasped Tanya's hand into hers once again.

Vera rubbed her back, praying as Tanya rode out the contraction. "You're doing great, Tanya. It's almost time to push."

Tanya moaned as she relaxed once again, her body gasping for relief from the torture.

Vera pressed a cup to her lips and forced water down her throat, reminding Tanya that if she didn't drink, it would make the contractions stronger.

Tanya gulped, but most of the water dribbled down her chin as another contraction began. "Oooh . . ." She groaned, motioning toward a ceramic bowl that sat on the bedside table.

Vera seemed to read her mind and held out the dish.

Tanya vomited into it.

Vera tossed Feodora a wet rag. "Hold it to her forehead."

Tanya writhed and struggled to sit up straight, her legs arching toward her rock-hard abdomen. She grasped Vera's hand.

"I'll catch the baby. Can you stay up by her head and talk to her, Feodora?" Vera stood up and shuffled to the end of the bed. "I think it's just about time."

Feodora nodded frantically and moved to the top of the bed, stroking Tanya's hair gently as she did her best to assure her it would be fine.

"Nooo!" Tanya screamed before sinking back once again.

"You can do this, Tanya! Do it for Nicolai." Feodora's words sank in.

She grew more determined. She would have this baby — she must think of Nicolai. "For . . . for Nicolai . . ." The words stuck in her throat.

"Yes, that's right. Do it for Nicolai." Feodora looked her straight in the eyes and cheered her on.

Tanya clenched her fists and grimaced, letting loose an agonizing scream before bearing down and pushing with everything she had left in her.

"It's a girl!" Vera whooped. She whisked

the tiny baby into a towel and called out to Feodora to grab a knife from the butcher block in the kitchen.

"A knife?" Feodora looked at her, horrified.

"To cut the cord!"

Tanya moaned again, relief flowing through her veins. It was over. She must see the baby. She struggled to pull herself to her elbows and strained for a glimpse of her tiny daughter, who screamed wildly in Vera's arms. Tears glistened down her cheeks, and she was overcome with emotion as she saw her baby for the first time.

Vera hobbled over to Tanya and laid the bawling baby on her breast before gently toweling her off. "You've done well, my dear."

Feodora burst back into the room with a kitchen knife in her hand. "What do we do?"

"I'll take that. Ideally, we'd have scissors to do this, but I don't own a pair. A knife will have to do." Vera grabbed the knife from Feodora and gently sawed through the umbilical cord before moving back to her spot between Tanya's legs. "Now we catch the placenta."

"Pla . . . placenta?" Feodora looked queasy.

"You just stay up there with Tanya and

the baby and I'll handle that." Vera sank into her chair. "Back in '98, I helped my sweet sister deliver her baby boy, God rest her soul. Back in the day, we didn't have fancy hospitals or medical doctors. Women gave birth to babies at home." Vera's words came at a cadence that soothed Tanya's weary soul.

She shifted her attention to her sweet daughter, comfortably nuzzled next to her breast. Things had actually turned out all right. A wave of bittersweet nostalgia swept through her soul. If only Nicolai were here to see this. Oh, he would have fallen in love with this sweet baby girl! He would've made such a wonderful father.

Pain gripped her pelvis and she moaned softly, allowing the marvel of her baby daughter to carry her through the pain as she delivered the afterbirth. She stroked her daughter's downy soft curls and closed her eyes, wishing she could pray for this precious life. Ironic that the one thing her heart yearned to do was the one thing she wouldn't allow it.

No, she wouldn't pray for this baby, but she would love her. Tanya wiped away a tear and stared at her daughter, so infinitely beautiful, and let out a deep sigh. No, this baby girl would never know her father or his God, but she would know love. She would know how it felt to be cherished.

She would live her life never doubting that her mama would do anything for her.

# 31

*Leningrad, Russia*

Feodora stepped quietly toward the door. She was still wearing the red satin dress with a thigh-high slit she'd worn last night. "I'll go change," she said.

Tanya lifted her head from her pillow and frowned at her friend. What would Vera think of them now?

"All right, dear." Vera was always so kind, so sweet. Of course, if she had noticed Feodora's dress, that would all change.

The door slammed and Tanya could hear her footsteps as her friend raced up the stairs. She sank back onto the pillow, silently arguing with herself about whether Vera knew where Feodora had been. The old lady wasn't naïve enough to believe that she had been out visiting friends, was she?

She silently fumed at Feodora's brazenness. What could they do now? Leave it to Feodora to ruin the one good thing that had happened to her in a long time. Tanya chided herself for thinking like that. Without Feodora, she'd still be living at the sanatoria. Or worse.

Feodora reentered the room, wearing a more appropriate, cotton calico dress Her face was wet, clearly freshly washed, ruddy cheeks, and pale skin had replaced the thick gray eye shadow and bright red lipstick from the night before.

Vera left the room.

"Feodora! She must know!" Tanya whispered.

"I'm sorry, Tawnie. I was just so worried about you, and I didn't think to change."

"What will I do now? She'll kick us out for sure." Tanya let her gaze drift to the precious baby nestled close to her breast and her stomach contracted. She couldn't let anything happen to her. Ever.

Feodora stared at her wide-eyed.

Vera swung open the door, breaking the awkward silence. She carried a tray of tea — complete with blue flowered china. She set it onto the side table in the living room. The old woman turned to her with a smile. "Cream?"

"Yes, please." Feodora turned to Tanya, the corners of her mouth raised. Maybe Vera hadn't noticed her dress in the chaos of the birth?

"Here you go, my dear. You must be exhausted." Vera handed Tanya a delicate cup and signaled towards the sofa.

"Thank you."

Feodora took her cup from Vera. Her hands shook so violently that the cup and saucer clanked together. She sat down in a wooden chair next to the bed and looked from Vera to Tanya and back again to Vera. "Thank you for helping Tanya. Had I known, I never would have left last night."

"I was glad to do it." Vera reached out and took Tanya's hand. "She's become like a daughter to me in the last few weeks."

Tanya fidgeted with the handle of her cup, staring at the floor, the conversation gnawing at her nerves. What could they do? Say?

Vera broke the silence. "Feodora, Tanya, I know."

Tanya's gaze shot up.

"You know?" Feodora whispered.

"Yes, I know what you do — what you both do — for a living. I've known for weeks."

"Did Tanya tell you?" Feodora's gaze darted to Tanya.

"No, of course not! I didn't say a thing." Tanya pressed herself up onto her elbows, wincing at the pain that shot through her insides. "So why did you let us move in?" Shame spread over Tanya's cheeks.

"Because I believe that everyone deserves a chance at redemption," Vera said. "And while I wish you would leave that life, I also understand you feel trapped. I only pray that one day you will find a way to walk away and lead the life God has intended for you."

"God. If God were real, He would've never let this happen at all," Tanya whispered.

"I didn't have a choice, Vera. I couldn't pay for food." Feodora forced out the words, as if she struggled to believe them.

Vera gave Feodora a knowing look. "God provides."

"Well, it's been a long time since He's provided for me."

"He's never let me down," Vera responded, the softness in her voice contrasting with the steely determination of her words.

"I'm not sure I can believe that. I know what happened to your daughter. To your husband. How can you believe in a God that lets these things happen?" There. She had said it. At least everything was out in the open.

Vera continued to stare at her with kind

225

eyes. "I still trust Him, Feodora. And I pray you will learn to as well."

"Will you kick us out?" Tanya interrupted the conversation, desperate to know her fate.

"Heavens, no!" Vera's gaze shot up and she shook her head firmly. "As long as I have a house to call my own, you two have a bed and a home."

Relief swept through Tanya, warming her. She wished she could give the old woman what she wanted. If only things were different. "Thank you, Vera. I'm so grateful. And I wish there was another way for me to pay my way."

"I will pray that God will reveal a way. Until then, know that if you should decide to leave the life you lead, I will support you in any way I can. I haven't a penny to my name, but I trust God to provide a way for those who seek Him. I know He would do that for you. For us."

How could this woman be so kind and so forgiving? Tanya was certain she could never be like that. Sighing, she let the conversation drift off, sipping her tea slowly as she stared out of the dingy window onto the snow-clad street. If only she could find a real job with a real paycheck. She had tried that. And it hadn't worked even before she'd sullied her reputation. But now?

No one would hire her.

She let the truth seep into her soul like tea swirling into hot water. She had no choice but to keep serving the men in the officer's brigade. Her daughter's very existence depended on it.

# 32

*Helsinki, Finland*

The bright blue sky stood in stark contrast to the darkness that descended on Finland. The sun never really set these days in the land of the midnight sun, but even in the bright light, Matti still felt as though they hadn't emerged from one of darkest winters ever. The sunlight was simply a façade. If rumors were true, summer would be even colder and darker than winter had been.

A few weeks ago, Germany had marched into Denmark and Norway, destroying any hope Finland had of partnering with their Scandinavian allies. Now, the buzz around the base was Russia would march into the Baltics any day now. If they took control of Estonia, Latvia, and Lithuania, there would be nothing left standing between Russia and Germany. Except Finland.

The next few months would seal Finland's fate.

He pulled his latest letter from Anna out of his pocket and unfolded it, thanking God that at least his parents, brothers, and Anna were safe in Kalajoki — about as far as they could get from harm's way.

*Matti,*

*The newspapers up here don't paint a very pretty picture of what is happening in Helsinki. Is it really true that several of our Finnish officers have been traveling to Germany to meet with the Nazis? How can we possibly align ourselves with them when they've caused so much terror?*

*I'm so scared! For you, for Finland, for everyone! Every day now I brace myself for the news that we're moving off into another war — and I'm not sure whether I should pray for it or against it.*

Matti agreed with Anna about the war. He'd always felt that fighting for Karelia was worth every effort, but now that it looked almost certain the Nazis would be involved, he wasn't so sure. Could he go off and fight — possibly die — to facilitate the evil schemes of an evil regime? He wasn't so sure.

*Regardless, I'm praying. I pray every day that God will fill you with peace and hope that defies all odds. I pray that you'll find the*

*strength to do what is right even when the world seems wrong.*
  *Anna*

He gritted his teeth as he contemplated Anna's words. Did he really have the courage to do what was right even when everything seemed wrong?

The heat of the sun, now shining bright in the middle of the sky, broke Matti's reverie. He had to get over to check-in fast, or he would get kitchen duty again. He'd day dreamed his way through breakfast. He would grab a cup of coffee and call it good.

Matti strode into the mess hall. He grabbed a slice of hardtack and a cup of coffee before trying find a place to sit. Even if he didn't have time for a full breakfast, he needed a few minutes to unwind. The last few days had been . . . strange. The air seemed ripe with news, as if any minute, the dam would burst and they would hear that war had begun.

He scanned the room. Markos sat alone at a corner table. Matti caught his friend's eye and hurried to sit down, stopping short when he noticed the terror etched on Markos's face. "What's going on, Markos?" He glanced around the room and realized the same expression on Markos's face was mirrored on most of the men in the room.

"Haven't you heard?"

"Heard what?"

"It seems as if we'll be marching into Karelia."

"When?"

"This week, most likely."

Matti's pulse sped up. He was shocked to hear the news he'd waited on for so long. This was a good thing, right?

"Why are you smiling, Matti?"

"We've been waiting for this, Markos. We have to fight for Karelia."

Markos frowned. "There's more, Matti."

"More?"

"The Germans are marching in from the East as we speak. It sounds as if we're to assault Russia on all sides. I don't know for sure, but it seems the plan is for us to march straight through Karelia and into Leningrad."

Matti's mouth dropped open. "Leningrad? Why would Finland march into Leningrad?"

Markos shrugged, looked around as if there were German spies hiding under the tables.

Matti blew out a deep breath. "This is all speculation, right? We don't know this for sure?"

"No, nothing is for sure. But that's the

rumor I'm hearing."

Matti bit his tongue. This was what he had wanted, right? To take back Karelia? To push the Russians out of his homeland? Matti took a swig of coffee, grimaced at the bitter taste in his mouth, and wished for the hundredth time they still had sugar and milk. They were lucky to even have coffee, so he should be grateful. He stood and hurried outside to join the crowds at roll call, praying that instead of hearing another assignment at the fish packing plant, he would hear an assignment to pack up and head out.

*Lord, give me another day here. I have to write Anna before we leave.* After all, his line of communication with Anna may soon be cut off. He'd have to warn her.

Once they marched into Karelia, there was no saying how long they'd fight before he had the chance to write her again.

# 33

*Leningrad, Russia*
*June, 1941*

"Yes, ma'am, we're organizing citizen response teams to help fortify the city in hopes of protecting the citizen populations."

Tanya tried to focus on what was being said.

"This is just precautionary, is that correct?" Vera's voice was tense.

"No, ma'am, as we heard when Molotov spoke on the radio yesterday, German forces bombed our bases in the Baltics early yesterday morning. They're marching into Russia as we speak. The 4th Panzer German tank division is headed straight toward Leningrad. Up to the north, the Finns have congregated on our border and we think they will also attack soon."

Tanya kissed Verushka's downy head and pulled her closer. How could she keep this precious little one safe in the midst of a

233

crazy war that seemed intent on sweeping them all into the bloody fray?

"But just last week the papers said the war was simply a provocation. That nothing would actually happen." Feodora chimed in, terror shining in her eyes.

"I know. They took us by surprise, but we do know they are headed this way. We have troops surrounding the city, reinforcing defense lines and getting ready to protect us. But, as a precautionary measure, we're putting together a citizen coalition to help with fortifications."

"What about the Nazi-Soviet pact?" Tanya remembered an article she read about the pact that claimed to be the peaceful resolution to the whole situation.

"It doesn't look as if they're honoring it, does it now?" The man turned and looked down the street, obviously agitated and unsure how to answer their probing questions.

"What can we do?" Vera pushed aside their questions, her voice steely. She put her hands on her hips and looked at the man.

"Thank you, ma'am. We're mobilizing the entire civilian community to help build fortifications." He pulled a folded map from his pocket and pointed to clusters of red lines drawn in at various points on the outskirts of the city. "Meet at one of these locations and a civilian task force will tell you what to do."

"We're women. We can hardly help." Tanya pointed at the baby and then looked at Vera, who suddenly looked very old and frail.

"This seems to be our only shot, ma'am. If every citizen comes — young, old, weak and strong — then maybe we'll be able to get our defenses built before the Germans and the Finns arrive."

All three women promised the soldier they would do whatever they could to help. He saluted them and turned toward the next house to start his spiel over again.

Tanya's mind raced. The Nazis were coming to Leningrad.

News that they had been anticipating for months now, yet when it finally came, it seemed surreal. Impossible, even.

Tanya sank down into the sofa cushions, positioning little Verushka onto her breast so she could eat.

Feodora sat next to her tickling the baby's tiny toes and kissing the balls of her feet.

"Shall I make tea?" Vera asked, already heading toward the kitchen.

"What will we do, Fe?" Tanya broke the silence.

Feodora looked out the window as more

soldiers marched by, clearly on their way to mobilize more of the population. "All we can do. Wait. Hope. And help where we can."

"But I'm so scared. What will happen to Verushka? To us?" Tanya brought the baby's tiny hand up to her lips and kissed it.

Feodora's eyes grew wide. She reached out and stroked the baby's face, a look of weary terror on her face. Then she glanced at the kitchen, leaned closer to Tanya, and whispered, "What about money?"

"What do you mean?" Tanya looked at her, confused, before realization dawned. Their source of income was drying up.

After she'd recovered from childbirth, Tanya knew that as soon as she recovered, she wouldn't have a choice but to return to the work she had been doing. Verushka had to eat, and Tanya had to pay rent. She swallowed hard as she thought about evenings in shady hotel rooms doing . . .

Well, she had no choice.

On the first night, Vera hadn't seemed to notice when Tanya left a sleeping Verushka upstairs in her crib while she went out.

But after a few nights, Vera met her at the door with a teary sob. "You don't have to do this, Tanya!" she had nearly shouted at her.

"But I do. How would we eat otherwise?" Tanya set her jaw and kept her words calm.

"God will provide a way."

"I don't believe in God." Tanya let the words slip out before she truly contemplated what they would do to Vera, the woman who had given her everything.

Vera stood for several moments, just staring at her before she turned away. As she had walked down the hallway, Tanya heard her praying out loud. "Lord, please help this stubborn girl to turn from her sinful ways and back to You."

Now it seemed that Vera's prayers had been answered. Not about turning back to God, but about her sinful ways. They wouldn't make money with the soldiers if the soldiers were all off fighting.

A tight ball rose in her chest. She stared at her friend. How would they survive the month, much less the war?

Vera had no income.

And now, neither did they.

Feodora turned her head toward the kitchen door before sneaking her ever-present flask out of the pocket of her house-coat. She took a swig and tucked the flask back into her dress pocket.

Tanya leaned forward and shaded Verushka's eyes, as if covering her eyes would shield her from the pain.

Vera plodded into the living room, a teapot steaming on a tray in her hands.

Feodora popped up to help her pour.

Tanya switched Verushka to the other breast.

"Vera, we . . . we're scared." Feodora said.

This would most definitely be a difficult conversation.

Vera straightened her spine and squared her shoulders before turning to Tanya. She clasped her hands in front of her chest. "You two look at me right now."

Tanya looked up guiltily, like a child who'd just been caught stealing penny candy.

"This is a hard time for Leningrad, for us, but we will not start wallowing." She wagged her fingers at the two of them, her face resolute. "The four of us, we will stick together. We'll do whatever we can to keep this little girl safe."

"But we hardly have any money." Tanya couldn't help but whine a little.

"I will trust God to provide. And I pray that one day you two will learn to do the same."

"So, what now?" Tanya choked out.

Vera held up her hand again. "First, we'll go to the store and stock up on flour, rice, and beans. Starting today, we will be vigilant about every bite we put into our mouths."

Tanya felt a surge of gratitude that Vera was taking charge.

"And second, we'll go out there and help build those fortifications tomorrow."

"Build fortifications?" Tanya hoped her voice didn't sound as terrified as she felt.

"Yes, we're building fortifications. We'll do whatever it takes to make sure those Germans don't come into our city. I'll not see the place destroyed that I've loved since I was a little girl." Vera sat down and smiled. Then, with her most dainty voice she asked, "May I refill your tea?"

# 34

## The Karelian Border, Finland

Matti had been right about one thing — it would be a long, cold summer. Six nights of sleeping on the icy metal bed of the company's truck had left him sore, stiff and craving a warm bed and a hot cup of coffee, two luxuries he wouldn't find out here on the front.

Matti took a deep breath and stretched his arms above his head. He surveyed the horizon. Home sweet home was just over the tree line, a dozen or so kilometers away. Or a million when one considered the line of Russian tanks and guns that stood between him and the dusty dirt road where he'd grown up.

At least he was here, and though there wasn't any coffee, he was happy to be unassigned from rapid resettlement duty and assigned to the infantry again.

Several loud thumps echoed in the distance. Had the war begun somewhere along the front or were the Russians practicing? Either way, it was only a matter of time.

Sixteen Finnish infantry divisions plus several cavalry divisions had lined up along the Karelian side and were awaiting orders to storm across the border. With the Nazis rapidly moving in from the East, war was imminent.

Takala rose from his sleeping bag and stepped over the other sleeping soldiers with a scowl. He hopped out of the bed truck and made his way to the makeshift mess. He joined Matti, who stood next to their company fire, stirring a pot of mush in an iron pot. "Don't burn the rations, Ranta."

"Who, me?"

Takala patted him on the back before propping himself onto a log next to the fire. "How are you holding up?"

Matti clenched his jaw.

"What is it?"

"You are my commanding officer. Can I speak without fear of reprisal?"

"Are we talking treason here?"

Matti looked at him, horrified. "No, of course not!"

"Then speak freely."

"All right, I guess I'm almost more con-cerned about this so-called alliance with the

Germans than I was about the Russians living in Karelia in our houses and hosting military retreats at our resorts."

Did the dark clouds in Takala's eyes mean that he had thought the same thing? Not that he could ever say it, being a commander and all.

"I've heard rumors that we're not stopping in Karelia. That there are plans to march into Leningrad."

"Officially, the line is that we're preparing to march into Karelia. That's it. Which is something I thought you'd be happy about."

"I am. But something doesn't feel right about it."

"Beyond that, it's all speculation. And why worry about tomorrow when today is so darn miserable we have to eat burned mush for breakfast."

Matti looked down, quickly stirring his pot and noticing black flecks seeping into his oatmeal. Great. "Serves you right for putting me on kitchen duty again. We all know I'm better with a gun than a spoon."

With a grin, he banged his spoon against the pot and called out to the guys that breakfast was served. And considering the fact that it could be their last warm meal for weeks, they'd better enjoy. Black flecks and all.

■ ■ ■ ■

The whining rumble that echoed across the camp brought Matti back to his time in the trenches during the Winter War. He knew that sound. He threw on his boots and grabbed his already-loaded rifle before most of the men in his company had even managed to lift their heads. "Air raid!" He shouted above the roar that drowned out the terrified shouts of confused men coming out of a deep sleep. He sprinted to the safe position. About four hundred meters to the southeast, he turned.

His fellow soldiers were still frozen in place.

"Get moving! Now!" he shouted above the thunder. He raced back and grabbed a couple of the fresh recruits' arms. "You have to move!"

The shadow of Russian bombers came into view over the horizon — so many of them, in formation, heading straight toward their camp.

Leaping into the trench his company had dug earlier in the week, Matti dove to the floor and covered his head with his arms as dozens of other soldiers leapt in behind him. Matti braced himself for the first tremors of bomb blasts.

They never came.

The drone of plane engines still rumbled above at a fever pitch, yet no bombs fell from their undersides. Was this some crazy surveillance mission?

Matti dared a quick glance into the sky.

Dozens of bombers flew in formation heading in a northwesterly direction. Straight toward . . . No!

"They're heading toward Helsinki!" The realization dawned as the final planes flew over their trenches. Matti stood, gesturing desperately toward the camp where radios could warn Helsinki of the coming on-slaught.

Takala leapt out of the trench and sprinted toward the radio mounted in their com-munications tent.

Matti was fast on his heels, desperate to give Helsinki a few minutes warning.

Not that it would do much good. All of Finland's troops were congregated at the border.

Why would the Russians attack Helsinki unprovoked? Especially when the city was full of innocent women and children?

He couldn't think about that right now. He had to help.

He raced into the tent behind Takela. His

commanding officer was screaming, "Russian bombers spotted heading north-northwest at 0-five-hundred hours. I repeat, Russian bombers are heading straight toward Helsinki."

It was all they could do. But it wouldn't be enough.

The adrenaline from the attack drained out of his body, replaced by a hopeless desperation from knowing Helsinki was probably being bombed.

Right then.

He looked around him, assessing the state of the other men in his company. They were scared, but no one was injured. A bit tired from the desperate race to the trenches, but no one was hurt.

Matti propped himself up in the back of the flatbed truck and leaned back against his pack. Nothing to do but wait for Takala to brief them.

Wait and pray.

*Lord, protect Helsinki right now. Blind those Russian fighters so they drop bombs on unoccupied land. Or not at all. Keep the civilians and children in Helsinki safe. Save Finland.*

Right now, with enemies on all sides, God was his only hope for a good resolution.

"Attention!" Takala's voice startled Matti.

His eyes shot open

"They took us by surprise, soldiers. We had no clue it was coming. We're marching along following all of the orders of their crazy Peace Treaty and then . . . Bam! They bomb Helsinki anyway." Takala's glare made Matti glad he'd stayed on his good side.

"We have received word that while most of our airfields and bases remain intact the Russians have managed to hit several civilian targets, including some shops in Porvoo and a school in Lahti."

Gasps erupted around the room.

"Fortunately, it was early in the morning and no children were at school, but the building was destroyed."

Matti straightened, his clenched fists digging into his thighs in an effort to keep from hitting something.

Takala continued. "We are still assessing damages and trying to figure out what sparked this attack, but in the interim, our division has been put on alert. I'm not sure what that means, but be prepared for orders to come down the chain shortly."

Matti glanced at Takala, instinctively raising his hand to his chin. He sank back down onto the hard bed of the truck, hoping they would be able to launch a counter attack before more innocent civilians were hurt.

Slamming his fist down, Matti reminded himself to breath.

Inhale. Exhale.

It took all that was in him not to grab his rifle and run for the border to confront the Russians who clearly didn't know a thing about honor.

But he was fighting for a just cause. They were fighting against an enemy willing to hurt innocent people to get what they wanted.

An enemy that connived evil instead of good and clearly didn't understand what it meant to be loyal, honest, or true.

They were fighting this battle against pure evil.

How could they lose?

# 35

Tanya folded Vera's light blue cotton sheet in half long-ways, and then again. Propping baby Verushka on her hip, she wrapped the folded sheet around her midsection, over her shoulders and then back behind.

Just then, Vera came out of her room, wearing trousers for the first time since they'd met. She had her hair wrapped in a kerchief, wisps of gray falling out from the front. Vera secured a tan wool sweater around her waist and tied it tightly before looking at Tanya with solemn eyes. "Are you ready?"

She pulled on her make-do baby sling to make sure it was tight and called up the stairs. "Feorora! We're leaving."

Feodora raced down the stairs. A whiff of vodka gave Tanya insight to the dark circles under her friend's eyes.

Tanya patted her on the back. "Oh, Fe . . .

248

you didn't."

Feodora scrunched up her nose. "I had to."

They stepped out the door.

"Good morning, Leningrad!" Feodora slurred, allowing the vodka to lighten up the somber mood that seemed to hover over the entire city. "These three women are here to help win the war!"

"Shut up," an older woman shouted at her.

"No one is in the mood, Fe." Tanya zipped her fingers across her lips, warning her friend against her exuberant chatter. Everyone just wanted to get the job done.

When they arrived at the end of the block, Tanya and Feodora joined a crowd of others — mothers, teenagers, children, and grandparents — as they marched in military fashion due east toward the Moscow Gates, the closest sector of the city marked on the Civilian Response Team's map.

It would be a long walk, but Tanya didn't mind the exercise or the time to think.

They plodded on in silence, their footsteps echoing off gray-tinged buildings, lit only by the bright light of the morning sun. Overhead, tiny, dark clouds floated in an otherwise blue sky, setting a somber mood for the city that was seeing its first few days of nice weather all year. Regardless of the sunshine, the typical hustle and bustle of Leningrad was gone, replaced instead by a silent parade of travelers, all trudging east toward a common goal.

Tanya patted a sleeping Verushka on her back and glared at the Moscow station they trudged past.

"This street was my first glimpse of Leningrad." Tanya waved a hand over the square.

"Oh, I didn't realize you got here through the Moscow line."

"I came from Moscow, silly."

"It looks so beautiful from here," Vera chimed in. "No wonder you stayed."

The tall, ornately carved cream and yellow buildings stood in stark contrast to the hastily built tenements just blocks away, showing off the beauty of the city that had captured the hearts of so many. Tiny buds were just starting to peek through on flowering limes, and jasmine vines brought a fragrant life to the city. On summer days like today, Tanya could see why Vera and Feodora loved Leningrad so much.

It really could be a magical place. It also could be a place of devastation, as Tanya well knew.

Just blocks away from the splendor of central Leningrad, they'd find unimaginable poverty. Prostitution. Drug use. All the things Tanya had grown to detest when she was living at the Azoz Sanatoria. All the things she had experienced all too intimately.

She reached her hand up to Verushka's downy head and stroked her soft skin. Shuddering, she felt a wave of protectiveness rise up. She had to protect her daughter from such things.

Coming to a street corner, Tanya glanced over to see a lamppost covered with sheets of paper, hastily tacked one on top of the other. A picture of a stern-looking Russian soldier holding a gun aimed at a swastika-clad monster was juxtaposed next to a poster advertising the Prokofyev Ballet's upcoming performance of *Romeo and Juliet.*

Hope, fear, and death tacked next to despair, trust, and life.

Block after block, a city of oxymorons revealed itself to the parade of resolute travelers, each caught up in their own efforts to memorize a city that could well be destroyed in just a few weeks.

The foursome headed toward the Moscow Sector where a command station had been set up by a rag-tag group of older men who called themselves the Citizen Army of Leningrad. These men — too old to enlist in the Red Army themselves — were already working to dig a line of trenches along the edge of the city. Later, they explained, they would fill the trenches with twisted wire, wooden fortifications and anything else they could think of to protect the city's borders.

"How can we help?" Vera seemed to have more enthusiasm than she had capacity.

"How about you women start wrapping this wire around the wooden frames over there?"

Feodora headed for a spool of barbed wire and pointed to Tanya to grab the other end. Tanya reached over a sleeping Verushka and did her best to help Feodora lift the wire without jostling the baby. Slowly they wrapped the wire around the plywood frame, meter after meter of wire. One hastily constructed frame of plywood and sticks.

Minute after minute, hour after hour.

And while they may not have been the strongest or the most energetic workers, the three women had wrapped hundreds of meters of barricades by the end of the day.

Tanya was exhausted. But also relieved. Because for the first time in a long time, she felt as if she had taken control of her own situation.

And right now, control was one thing that seemed to be in short supply.

# 36

*Leningrad, Russia*
*June 26, 1941*
*MORE THAN ONE MILLION LENINGRAD-*
*ERS HELP BUILD DEFENSE LINES!*

Vera walked in the door, pointing to the headline on the front page of the latest issue of the Leningradskaya Pravda. "One million people! Can you believe it?"

Tanya looked up from feeding Verushka. "I can believe it, Vera. You saw how many citizens were out there working yesterday."

Feodora looked up from the tiny pink blanket she'd been knitting for Verushka and scrunched up her nose.

Vera's eyes grew dreamy. She had lived in Leningrad long enough to love the city.

Tanya, on the other hand, had only seen the ugly side of the city — the derelict Vyborg Quarter full of clapboard houses and slummy apartments, full of hungry beggars, starving children, and women forced into prostitution to pay for bread.

Tanya's love for Leningrad wasn't quite on par with Vera's.

But what she lacked in love, she made up for in pure desire to save her precious daughter. And that meant she would fight alongside Leningrad to the very end.

"Should we head down to the grocery store and try to stock up on supplies today? There wasn't much to be had last time I was there." Vera seemed to read Tanya's mind.

"No use." Feodora's words were slurred, revealing she'd had another flask of vodka for breakfast. "The man helping me build fortifications yesterday told me nearly every gastronom in town is completely out of food."

Tanya's gaze shot up. "Completely out?"

"Yep, I guess the rich Leningrad house-wives made a run at the stores the morning the Germans marched into Russia. They bought up everything in stock. He told me one woman bought up twenty pounds of caviar!"

"Caviar?" Vera clucked her tongue. "Won't exactly keep them full for long."

"Exactly. But as of yesterday, there was nothing left in the stores."

"What do we do now?" Tanya hated to be

negative, but they would need more than a few days' supply of food.

"The first thing we should do is go down to Kirov's and see if the rumors are true." Vera's common sense shone through in their moment of panic.

"I'll go with you!" Tanya said, anxious to get out of the stifling house.

They walked together down the street toward Kirov's. As they rounded the corner near the familiar store, the crowd gathered underneath the blue and white awning.

A quick glance in the window revealed the stark truth. Every shelf was completely empty.

A sign on the door explained that they would reopen once they were able to re-stock.

Tanya and Vera exchanged a wary look. Tanya looked away toward the horizon, the despair of the moment overcoming her soul.

Vera may feel confident trusting a higher power, but she wasn't so sure. Not that she had a better option.

## 37

*Kalajoki, Finland*

"And now, Citizens of Finland, on this, the twenty-sixth of June, 1941, we interrupt our regularly scheduled programming for an emergency address by President Risto Ryti." The scratchy voice boomed from the radio in the living room.

Hearing the words, Anna's heart thudded to a stop. Her paint-soaked brush clattered to the floor, leaving a green trail of watercolor paint across the wood's surface. Dashing to the kitchen to grab a wet towel, she raced back into the parlor. She crouched on the floor mopping up the paint without looking. Instead, she stared straight ahead at the dark mahogany wood radio that sat on the table next to the window.

President Ryti cleared his throat, the muffled coughing sound echoing across the airwaves. "Our peace-loving people, which for more than a year have strained to rebuild their country to flourish in the aftermath of the previous war, has once again been made the target of vicious attack. It is the same enemy, which, during an excess of half a century, has ravaged, shattered, murdered, and waged wars against our small nation. They have violated our territory, slain peaceful citizens — mainly the aged, women, and children, and destroyed the property of peaceful citizens . . ."

Anna sank down onto the floor next to her father's legs.

Mr. Ranta whispered "amen!" before grabbing his wife's hand and holding tight.

"From the instant of commencement of hostilities between Germany and Soviet Union, numerous instances of border violations have been committed by the Soviet Union, for which we have expressed our most vigorous protests, all to no avail."

"What's he talking about?" Anna's gaze shot up, imploring her father to explain. "The Russians attacked Finland yesterday?"

"Shhh." Her father reached out to her with a finger in the air.

The solemn voice on the radio continued. "In this manner has commenced our second battle for defense only some nineteen months since the previous attack. This new attack toward Finland is a culmination point for that mode of politics, which the Soviet Union has pursued ever since the Moscow Peace Settlement toward Finland, and the purpose of which has been the destruction of our independence and the enslavement of our people."

Everyone in the room sat straighter in their chairs, leaning so as not to miss a word.

The president continued, explaining the incredible loss Finland had faced during the Winter War and the massive relocation that followed, resulting in hundreds of thousands of refugees. He also explained that the loss of Karelia had resulted in diminished defense capabilities for all of Finland.

The radio crackled, dipping and fading as the entire room sat in silence, desperate to hear.

President Ryti continued, explaining the many ways Russia had broken the terms of their agreement over the year. They had lied about almost everything, constantly pushing for more concessions from peace-loving Finland.

It was now Anna's turn to say amen, an errant tear of joy slipping down her face.

"Being accustomed to keeping the given word, people of Finland wanted to keep the agreement which we had been forced to make in Moscow. Our starting point was that, as we live in this corner of the earth from generation to the next in close proximity as neighbors of Russia, relations with them must be accomplished. Once again, we wanted, regardless of what happened; commence building of permanent peace with the Soviet Union.

"This wish of peace was tested time and time again, as can be concluded from the previously mentioned constant demands."

If anyone understood a wish for peace, it was Anna. She desperately wanted peace — and still, at times, clung to her belief that perhaps Finland would be better just settling down and rebuilding homes for the refugees from Karelia. But now it looked as though that quest for peace had a high cost: innocent lives in Helsinki. How could the Russians have done such a thing?

Matti had been right — they should've marched back into Karelia months ago instead of clinging to hope in a treaty that Russia had never intended to honor.

The chilly room suddenly felt stifling. Anna pulled out her handkerchief and dabbed her forehead. The last time Finland had declared war, she had been scared and upset, but it had all seemed so far away. This time it hit her hard. Matti was down there, probably already in harm's way. The thought of it made her throat close in fear.

She gasped for a breath and forced herself to pay attention once again, even though she wanted to close her ears, to pretend the words hadn't been said.

"Our possibilities of successfully coping with this, our second defensive battle on this occasion, is quite different than previously, when we, by ourselves, were squeezed by this eastern giant. The military forces of the great and powerful Germany, under command of the ingenious leader, Chancellor of State Hitler, will successfully stand side by side with us to do battle against the Soviet Union's military forces . . ."

"What did he just say?" Mr. Ranta spit the words out first.

"Did he just say that we are in an alliance with Nazi Germany?" Anna shook her head, panic setting in. Not only was Matti fighting in an official war, but he would potentially have to fight alongside Nazi soldiers.

"This has to be a mistake." Her father looked stricken.

"Maybe this isn't what it seems," Mr. Ranta started again. The desperation in his voice turned Anna's stomach.

Rising, Anna sought out the comfort of her mother's arms.

Her mother's sobs drowned out the final words of the president's address.

They were at war. Aligned with Germany.

And Matti — her Matti — was out there somewhere. Probably fighting right now.

# 38

*On the Karelian Border, Finland*

The men in the company huddled around the lone transistor radio in the officer's tent to hear the president's official address. Most listened only half-heartedly. They already knew what was to be said. They had witnessed the horror of yesterday first-hand.

Takala leaned over and whispered into Matti's ear, "I hear the Russians lost twenty-five planes over Helsinki yesterday. We lost none."

"We just lost schools and office buildings," Matti was not in the mood to look on the bright side.

"Stinking Russians." Takala scowled.

"When will we go in and take back Karelia?"

"Soon, Matti. Very soon."

Matti's thoughts drifted to Anna and his parents up in Kalajoki, who were almost certainly listening to the presidential address and worrying about him. If only he could call them, reassure them that he was all right.

*Lord, be with them as they hear this message. Help them to see that only through war will we regain what is rightfully ours. Give them peace even as they hear this terrible news.*

Matti shut his eyes and imagined Anna. Knowing her, she had escaped into her art. He pictured her sitting in her living room with a sketchbook in her lap, her hands racing over the rough-textured paper with precision and ease. He pictured a beautiful sketch of some exotic beach or distant city — always something new and different, never the familiar. Yes, she was sketching right now. Sketching to escape a home she didn't love.

The home that he was fighting to save.

*Lord, fill Anna's heart with peace and joy even in the midst of this trouble. Because trouble is in this world we now have, but You, Lord, You have overcome the world!*

Opening his eyes, Matti surveyed the men in his company — men who would soon be fighting — maybe even dying — with him. Each one listened intently to the president's address, their jaws clenched shut in weary apprehension.

Everyone was terrified. Not just about the war, but also that they would soon be thrust into it.

*Lord, give me the words to say to help my friends have peace. Help them to feel Your presence so they can fight with courage. And Lord, help us to take back Karelia soon.*

Matti stood and paced, his head not willing to settle on the truth that made his heart ache. Today changed everything for Finland.

His life would never again be the same.

## 39

Leningrad, Russia

"You won't believe this." Feodora slammed into the house waving a white leaflet.

Tanya set Verushka down on the floor to play with some of Vera's spoons.

Feadora held it out showing her.

**COMRADES! STAND AS ONE IN DEFENSE OF OUR FREEDOM!**

"Keep reading!" Feodora huffed, waving the pamphlet in front of Tanya's face.

"Give it to me. I can't read with you moving it like that."

"I'll just tell you. They've drafted the entire civilian population into mandatory military service to dig trenches and construct shelters. If you are between the ages of fifteen and sixty-five and are caught not working on the war effort, you could be shot. On the spot."

"Let me see that."

Tanya read the military order slowly,

confirming what Feodora said. All men, women, and children were ordered to report to the nearest military checkpoint at eight o'clock on Monday morning. Those in defiance of the order were subject to military discipline, which could mean execution.

"But what will I do with Veruskha?"

"I'll watch her." Vera swung into the room carrying a tray of tea and a newspaper. "You have to go."

Tanya swallowed hard. She couldn't leave Verushka, could she? But she had to. She had no choice.

"Plus . . ." Vera held up the latest copy of the Leningradskaya Pravda. "The paper says that within a few days, our boys will turn the Germans back and drive them all the way back to Berlin."

"It does?"

"Yep! Right here, it says a sergeant . . ." Vera opened the paper, put her glasses on her nose and squinted at the paper before continuing. ". . . Sergeant Hirsch was shot down by our boys over Tallinn a few days ago. He's now in custody and singing like a sparrow. He says the Germans are sick of fighting and none of them want to be part of this war. Apparently, they're running as quickly as they can to our ranks the second they see the size of our Red Army divisions."

"Well, that's a relief," Feodora said. "Maybe this war will be over before any of these fortifications we're building have to be used."

"That's my hope. But in the meantime, you two had better get down there on Monday morning and register."

"The paper also says the bakery on the corner of Gostiny Dvor has upped his production and is making mass quantities of white bread," Feodora added.

"Bread?" Finally. Tanya couldn't help but lick her lips.

"Verushka and I will go down there while you work tomorrow." Vera reached out and chucked the baby's chin. "Won't we, my love? Won't we?"

Both Vera and Feodora had smiles on their faces, but Tanya couldn't help but let a tear escape. How could this be happening? How could this be her life now?

"Verushka will be fine, Tanya." Vera rubbed Tanya's back, probably trying to erase the worried look from her face.

"I hope so."

"I know so, my dear." Vera touched her cheek. "I know so."

"No. It can't be." Tanya moaned and covered her face with her hand as they walked up to the military checkpoint.

"It can't be what?" Feodora seemed distracted this morning. She was awfully cheery today, but Tanya had to wonder how long it would last. Her supply of vodka had to be running low.

"That's Lieutenant Pudovkin. Right up there, next to that gray truck."

"Lieutenant who?"

"Lieutenant Pudovkin. The guy I attended that first officer's ball with."

"Oh. Lieutenant Pudovkin. That's great!"

"How is it great?" Tanya's mortification grew worse by the second. How could she work alongside a man she had kissed . . . for money?

"We'll have an inside scoop on what's going on. Maybe even get plum assignments. If we have to do this, it will help to know someone higher up."

"Or, he'll call us out in front of all of these people. Tell everyone what we . . . what I did."

"He won't." Feodora grabbed Tanya's hand from her face and dragged her toward Lieutenant Pudovkin. "Trust me. He doesn't want anyone to know about what happened either."

Feodora strode up to the Lieutenant and gave an uncoordinated salute. "Feodora

Yezhof and Tanya Egerov reporting for duty."

"Hello Miss Yezhof, Miss Egerov." Lieutenant Pudovkin looked straight at her.

Tanya knew her cheeks flamed in shame. Would he call her out? Embarrass her in front of all of these people?

"You may go stand over to the left with the women's corps. I'll be over to give you instructions in a few minutes."

His tone seemed benign enough. For now.

Ten minutes later, when Lieutenant Pudovkin came to brief them on their assignments, Feodora had already introduced them to all of the other women waiting under the shade of a huge fir tree. She was in the process of planning a celebratory party for their little corps after the war.

Why not plan a party? They had known each other for a whole ten minutes after all.

Tanya forced herself to smile. Feodora's boisterous and fun-loving personality was a wonderful asset, even if it was a bit grating at times.

Lieutenant Pudovkin interrupted her thoughts with instructions. "This corps has been assigned to help dig a service trench in the southwest sector of the city by Avteve. The trench will be used to get supplies to the front as well as to shelter civilians and military officers in the event of an invasion.

"Please break into groups of three and then head back to the supply truck and grab two shovels and a pickaxe. You will work together to excavate the ground."

"And how will we get to Avteve?" A woman with blonde hair and a perfectly pressed lavender dress called out.

"Unfortunately, we'll have to walk, madam. Fuel supplies are low right now."

"But that's more than five miles," the woman moaned, looking at her high-heeled black boots in dismay.

Tanya rolled her eyes at the woman, giving Feodora a secret look that told her what she thought of Miss High Heels. She was in for some surprises now that she had been enlisted to work alongside the riffraff of society. She was probably the type who had excluded Tanya all those months when she was starving and desperate.

Feodora scowled at Tanya and shook her head firmly. Then, she turned and held her dirty hand out to the woman and grinned. "I'm Feodora. Want to be in our group?"

Tanya mouthed the word "no" to Feodora, but she was already walking toward the truck arm-in-arm with the woman.

"Oh. OK, sure. I'm Agripina. Agripina Borowski."

"Beautiful name. Now, do you have any other shoes at home that you can grab on the way so you'll be a bit more comfortable?"

"I do have more shoes but . . . well, they have even higher heels." The woman burst into tears.

"Well, then these will have to do. We'll walk slowly." Feodora linked one of her elbows into Agripina's and patted her gently on the shoulder. "Let's go get our supplies."

The three of them walked over to the flatbed pickup that was parked on the side of the road, where an older man wearing a red armband gave them two shovels and a pickaxe as well as a map to their rally point at the trench.

"Shall we go?"

"Do we have a choice?" Agripina whined.

The three headed off in the direction of Avteva, slowing to allow for Agripina's delicate steps on the cobblestone streets.

"Wait!" Lieutenant Pudovkin ran up behind them, catching up quickly. "I'll walk with you."

Feodora said "Fantastic" at the exact second Tanya said "We're fine on our own." But Feodora's voice was louder, and Lieutenant Pudovkin didn't seem to care that he was associating himself with women like them.

"Thank you, Lieutenant Pudovkin. I would love to hear what's going on with the war. The papers say we're giving the Germans a good whipping."

"I wish that were true, Miss Yezhof." The dark look on his face revealed that the papers weren't giving them the whole story. "News from the front is dismal. And this morning at our briefing we learned that the Germans have already broken through our two best defense lines protecting the city."

"What does that mean?"

"It means we'd better pray the Luga Line down on the Velikaya River holds."

"The Luga Line? Where is that?" Tanya asked.

"The Velikaya River is only a hundred kilometers from here. At most." Feodora's boisterous tone betrayed her fear. "I thought the Germans were already being driven back to the border."

"I thought so too. But, they broke through our lines at Pskov yesterday and are marching straight toward Luga." A glimmer of fear flashed on the Lieutenant's grim face. "You know, I could get in a lot of trouble for telling you this."

Feodora ran her fingers over her mouth,

symbolizing that her lips were sealed. Then she looked at the back of Agripina's head and grimaced, signaling to Lieutenant Pudovkin that she wasn't so sure about Agripina's loyalties. Maybe they should be careful.

"Anyway," he continued cautiously. "We're recruiting a volunteer corps to head down to Luga and reinforce the line. We've already signed up 20,000 citizens and are looking for more if any of you are interested."

"No, thank you!" Agripina shook her head adamantly.

"You may change your mind after you see the working conditions today, madam."

Shaking her head again, Agripina seemed to disagree.

A lump of bile rose in Tanya's throat, and she quickly pushed it down. There was no way she could go to Luga. Not with Verushka here in Leningrad.

Or could she?

Trying to calm her heart, which now seemed to be fluttering into her throat, Tanya turned to Lieutenant Pudovkin. "What exactly would it mean if we joined the Volunteer Corps?"

"It would mean that instead of working here every day, you'd take the train out to Luga for a week or two and help construct

273

the defense line. The Red Army would supply your meals and transportation and when
you were finished, and we'd ship you back
here safe and sound."

Free food. Tanya's interest was piqued.

"Is the work there difficult for someone
like . . . me?" Agripina asked. Tanya doubted
Agripina had ever worked a day in her life.
So, yes, the work would be hard for her.

"Yes, it's hard. But you'd be doing something meaningful. Luga is the last line of
defense for our city, and you could literally
help save Leningrad. Think about it, and if
you're still interested after we work today,
find me and I can get you signed up. I will
be leading the next train load down to Luga,
so at least you'll know someone there."

Feodora and Tanya looked at each other.

Could this be the answer to Vera's prayers?
Tanya shoved the thought aside, remember-
ing that she was making her own way. But
still, this was an opportunity. It wasn't ideal
— she would miss Verushka dreadfully —
but it meant three full weeks of provisions,
when before, they'd had none.

"We're here." The Lieutenant's voice
pulled her out of her thoughts, and she
turned to him as he pointed at a place in
the line where only a few groups were digging. "Why don't you three start digging

over there? Just dig the trench and haul the soil up in one of those carts and over to those mounds."

"What will we do with those mounds?" Tanya asked, curious about what they were building.

"Tank barriers."

"Those are huge!" Feodora whispered.

The three women made their way over and leapt into the trench, digging their shovels into the hard clay soil. Shovelful after shovelful, wheelbarrow load after wheelbarrow load, they worked their way back and forth as the trench grew slowly but surely.

It was tedious, boring work, but at least they had each other for company. Some of the other groups worked in silence, but Feodora would never let that happen with them.

"So, my dear, tell us about yourself." Feodora turned toward Agripina, reaching out the olive branch of friendship again.

"Well, I'm an only child. My dad is . . . was . . . a professor at the university. He taught literature before the Bolsheviks removed him from his position. And my mother is a poet. We live down in the university sector."

"Oh, it's absolutely beautiful down there!" Feodora gushed, going on and on about the intricately painted white-trimmed buildings that made up the famous university grounds.

Agripina agreed with a nod. "It is beautiful. Although not as beautiful as it was a few weeks ago. Did you know that they hid Peter I's bronze horseman in a sandbox? Just took him off of his pedestal and buried him."

"And they just up and took every painting out of the Hermitage and shipped it to Siberia," a voice across the trench chimed in.

"They did? The papers say everything is going so well." Tanya frowned. "Why would they go to such great lengths if the Nazis are just turning around and running for the border?"

"Because the Nazis aren't turning around and running for the border." Agripina grimaced, as if her words smelled as bad as the bags of rotting garbage that lined the road.

Tanya blew out a deep breath as tears gathered in the corners of her eyes. Could the papers be wrong?

"I'm sorry, Tanya." Agripina offered a faint smile. "I didn't mean to upset you. I sometimes let my emotions run away from me.

"It's OK."

"Tanya's just sensitive because she has a baby girl at home."

"Oh, I love babies." Agripina's eyes brightened. "Tell me about her."

"Well, she's six months old and has sandy-blonde hair and blue eyes just like her daddy."

"Your husband?" Agripina interrupted.

"My late husband. He died last summer."

"Oh, I'm so sorry."

Choking down a sob, Tanya continued. "Her name is Vera, but we call her Verushka. She has tiny dimples that make her eyes sparkle every time she smiles. And one crooked tooth right up top and center."

"She's about the cutest thing ever," Feodora added. "You should come meet her sometime."

"I'd love that. I've always loved babies, and I rarely spend time with them. My parents were both only children, so I don't have any siblings or cousins."

Tanya swallowed a lump in her throat, feeling bad that she had so quickly judged Agripina as spoiled and selfish. She seemed nice enough. "Well you can come play with Verushka any time."

Agripina smiled as her gaze floated off into the distance.

Tanya suppressed an urge to run straight

home, grab her daughter, and escape this city. This place where nothing made sense and everything seemed on the verge of death.

# 40

*On a train toward Luga, Soviet Union*
Now they had really done it. And Tanya blamed Feodora entirely.

OK, so it wasn't all her fault, but at this moment in time, she needed someone to be angry with. And she couldn't let the blame fall on her shoulders, not when she had been the one to hesitate this whole trip. She knew it was good for them — they desperately needed the food — but she couldn't bear to be apart from Verushka.

But Feodora had prevailed on her. They needed this. They needed to help. For cause and country. For Leningrad.

Oh, and for the free food.

It was all over once Vera had gotten wind of their dilemma. And in true Vera form, she had convinced Tanya that maybe the Women's Volunteer Corps was an answer to prayer. It gave them financial relief and provided them with an opportunity to help in a tangible way. Plus, she would take impeccable care of the baby while they went, which meant all of them would be contributing to the war effort.

How could she say no to that?

Tanya had relented and they had signed up.

As soon as they'd signed up, Feodora had started on Agripina.

She had walked three miles into the university quarter and straight into Agripina's fancy house and told her that it was an adventure that they all needed to be a part of. A few more lines about sisterhood, and suddenly Agripina was on board too. High-heeled boots and all.

And now here they were, the three of them, stuck on a speeding train to hell, or so it seemed.

Tanya shuddered as she dared to peek out of the tiny train windows. Bombs exploded in open fields, dropped by Nazi bombers that dotted the sky like millions of geese flying south for winter. Tanya tucked her head down and scrunched closer to the floor, shivering at the destruction that was inflicted outside.

From the sound of it, the bombing was bad and getting worse.

Tanya willed her heart to stop beating into

her throat and wished once again that she still believed in God. If there was a time to pray, this was it.

Feodora was crouched next to her on the train car's floor, a flask of vodka in her shaking hand.

"What do we do now?" Tanya whispered.

"We take a swig for our nerves and hope for the best!"

"No. We pray." Agripina glared at them from underneath her seat and reached across the aisle to grip Tanya's hands. "I don't know about you ladies, but I feel as if we need some divine intervention right now."

Feodora tucked her flask in her pocket and bowed her head, looking to Agripina for instructions. "Can't hurt."

Tanya was fighting a losing battle. "You two go ahead. I'll just lie here."

Agripina ignored Tanya and began to pray.

Tanya lifted her head to whisper to another woman crouched under the seat in front of her. "How much farther to Luga?"

"It's a two-hour trip. We left Leningrad more than an hour ago. I'd say we are at least halfway there."

"So, another full hour to hope we don't get hit by a stray bomb."

"This is nothing," a voice from across the

aisle whispered to them. "I heard that last week, the Nazis were strafing the train that carried one of the other Volunteer Corps out to Luga."

"What's strafing?" Feodora popped her head above the seat.

"It's when their planes fly low to the ground and drop bombs from about ten meters away."

Stifling an involuntary moan, Tanya closed her eyes, trying to block out the entire situation. Was she really here? On a train headed to the front while Nazi bombers did everything they could to stop it from reaching its destination?

She pinched her arm, praying she'd wake up from the nightmare. But no relief came. So she hunkered down, covered her head with her hands, and allowed the rumble of the train to lull her into a state of numbness, her heart yearning to plead with the God of her childhood that she would live to see her daughter again.

All while her head reminded her again and again that she didn't believe anymore.

# 41

*Luga, Russia*

Luga smelled like a farm. Like chickens and cows and goats — a scent that would forever remind Tanya of the pure sense of relief she felt stepping off of that train and onto solid ground again. If she never stepped on a train again for the rest of her life, it would be too soon.

Feodora, Agripina, and Tanya searched for Lieutenant Pudovkin from the corner of the train station. Had he requested the position to lead their corps or had his request something to do with her? At this point, she didn't care. After the train ride, it was comforting just knowing him.

"Good afternoon, ladies. That was quite a ride." The lieutenant sighed heavily in a clear attempt to lighten the mood. "Let's hope things quiet down now that we're here." He pointed down the road and to the north. "You're now a part of the People's

Volunteers. We're building a one-hundred-mile defense line along the Velikaya River. Your job is to lend a hand with the digging and hauling."

"Hey, at least we have experience with that," Feodora whispered in Tanya's ear.

Did the girl have nerves of steel? How could she be calm at a moment like this?

Tanya swallowed hard, turned toward the supply cart, and hefted out shovels and pickaxes. She had no choice but to start working.

She took two steps before the sound of another incoming train drowned out her thoughts. Turning, she watched as the train screeched to a halt. Dozens of Red Army soldiers leapt off and hurried into formation.

"Who are they?" Tanya managed to say.

"Not sure." Feodora looked at the soldiers and seemed confused. They had heard that most of the Red Army soldiers were fighting at the front and would fall back to the Luga line only when necessary.

"Hey! Lieutenant Pudovkin?" Feodora pointed at the soldiers. "Why are they here?"

"Those are fresh reinforcements from the Finn border in Karelia. The Generals think that the Finns won't invade, so all of our manpower up there is being moved down to reinforce Luga."

Tanya took some comfort in the fact the Red Army was reassigning troops from Karelia to protect them.

She turned back to the dirt road in front of her and trudged on, trying to ignore the sound of soldiers as they readied themselves for war. Five minutes later, they reached their work point and the three women began to dig, removing piles of soil from the trench and moving them to the large piles that stood on the banks of the river to keep tanks from driving up the banks. Within a few hours, their lines towered ten feet above the ground.

Tanya couldn't imagine any army ever breaking through this. The line was just too strong — the piles too high.

The thousands of civilians working to build this line had to outnumber the enemy twelve to one.

Which was a relief because the Luga line was the only barrier standing between her sweet baby daughter and the Nazi 4th Panzers.

Suddenly feeling quite confident, Tanya began to hum a tune as she worked, smiling tentatively at Feodora, who joined in. Around them, more and more ladies joined the music, and before long hundreds of women proudly sang Russian folk songs as they dug the defense lines centimeter after centimeter, meter after meter, kilometer after kilometer.

Maybe Feodora's idea to join the Volunteer Corps wasn't such a bad one after all.

Air raid sirens pierced the air.

Tanya looked around in confusion, trying to make sense of the noise.

"Take cover!" Agripina raced toward them and grabbed Tanya's arms as she spun toward the trench they were in the middle of building.

Stunned into action, Tanya leapt into the trench and ducked her head, just as they had practiced while working in Leningrad. At the time, she'd hoped the air raid drill was only precautionary and the Nazis wouldn't dare bomb an unarmed civilian corps.

But the train.

No, the Nazis would stop at nothing to reach their objectives. Even killing innocent civilians. Women. Mothers.

Tanya flinched as the sputter of anti-aircraft fire echoed through the trench, signaling that the air raid sirens weren't just a drill. Nazi bombers were coming. She crouched down tighter and stole a glance at

Feodora and Agripina, their faces stricken and mud-streaked.

She reached out and took one of each of their hands in hers. Gripping them tightly, she pulled them close to her body. If she died, she wanted to do it clinging to someone she loved. Agripina peered above her folded arms, gave her a hesitant smile, and then curled in, shoving her trembling body as close to the still-unreinforced walls of the trench as she could. Three loud booms shook dirt clods loose above them, raining down a waterfall of dirt and pebbles.

But no one dared move. Not when the growl of Nazi bombers were so close.

Two minutes later, the air raid sirens stopped.

It took them several minutes before they crept from their prone positions, brushing themselves off and looking around the trench to make sure everyone was accounted for.

They were.

Then the tears came. Tears of relief flooded down Tanya's cheeks as her heart rate skittered to normal.

"Help! Someone help! I've been hit!"

Tanya's heart rate hammered back into her throat as screams came from above them and to the west.

Feodora scaled the trench, not stopping to assess her own safety, and ran toward the cries.

Tanya stood frozen in place. She looked at Agripina who seemed to be facing a similar internal battle to her own. It was so dangerous to leave the safety of the trench right now. But did they have a choice but to go help?

Their hesitation swept them into a cloud of others who also weren't sure what to do. By the time they scaled the trench walls, hundreds of soldiers and volunteers ran around in chaos, trying to assess the damage. To the south, a bomb had fallen, exploding one of the gun emplacements that a team of university students had been building. Shrapnel had flown into a half-finished trench where a women's corps hunkered down, spraying the poor women with a needle-sharp shower of burning metal and fragmented wood.

"Tanya! Agripina! Come help me!" Feodora screamed and waved her hands over her head.

They ran to her, where she kneeled by a woman on the ground. "Are you all right?"

Feodora leaned close to the injured woman and stroked her face before pulling up her shirt. Several pieces of shrapnel were embedded in her left hip and lower back.

A wave of dizziness caused Tanya's entire body to sway. "We have to get her medical help. Fast!"

"Medic! Over here," Feodora shouted.

No one came.

"Here, let's load her onto this piece of tarp." Feodora grabbed a folded piece of gray canvas that sat next to the construction supplies. "We'll carry her over to the medical tent ourselves."

Agripina and Tanya stood staring. Shocked.

"Girls! We need to help her. Come help me," Feodora snapped at them. She grabbed the tarp and leaned close to the woman's glazed eyes. "Now, you just relax. We'll have you fixed up in no time."

Tanya took a deep breath and resolved to stay strong. She grabbed the woman's left arm and lifted her onto the tarp, careful to keep her on her right side so that they wouldn't bump her injured flank.

With a moan, the woman settled into their makeshift stretcher.

"You're doing great. Just great," Tanya whispered into her ear, hoping to keep her calm.

Hoisting the tarp, Tanya and Agripina took the ends, while Feodora held the injured woman's hand, stroking it as the three of them made their way to help. When they arrived at the tent, Feodora shouted, "We have someone."

"Set her down there," the nurse pointed to a cot near the entry. "I'll get to her in a second."

"But she needs your help."

"So do all of these. I'll get to her."

Tanya grasped Feodora's shoulders and pulled her outside. They had taken her to the hospital tent. It would have to be enough.

"Come on. Let's go see who else needs our help." Feodora grabbed them by the hands and led them past the tent flap.

"I'm not sure I can," Tanya whispered, the events of the last hour filling her with a sense of dread she couldn't shake.

"We have no choice."

"She's right, Tanya. We have no choice. Without us they have no hope."

Tanya straightened her spine and marched forward, resolute to bring hope to those who needed it most. Because if anyone knew what it was like to be hopeless, it was her. For the first time since Nic's death, she had a thread of a future that just might blossom into the hope that had eluded her for so long.

And it felt strange that hope was blossoming right when she was at risk to lose everything.

# 42

*On the Karelian border, Finland*
The pounding of boot steps reverberated through the night. Matti closed his eyes, trying to calm his pounding heart. Taking one hand off of his rifle, he flexed and then relaxed each of his fingers, doing whatever he could to keep his body and his mind relaxed.

He paused for a second, calculating his bearings to make sure he stayed in his assigned position behind Käärme and to the left of Takala as they jogged two-by-two toward the Russian border. Matti squinted and surveyed the path in the dim light of a Karelian white night.

Towering birch trees surrounded them, the whites of the trunks glowing in the midnight sun, casting dark shadows across their path. In front and behind their company, dozens of other companies ran in similar formation, creating a giant snake of camouflaged men weaving their way through the eerily quiet forest.

After halting at their pre-determined stopping point, Takala gathered the men into a tight huddle for a quick pep talk a if they were getting ready to compete in a high school skiing tournament not going to war.

"How are we doing?" Matti whispered.

"Fine." Even if they weren't ready, they hardly had a choice.

"This is our day, our time to take back what's ours. Let's stick together and run for our objective. I'll see you on the other side of the border!"

Two minutes later, the men headed out again, this time crawling on their bellies through heavily vegetated birch forest, rifles slung across their backs, supplies strapped to their stomachs.

As he inched his way forward, Matti prayed silently, willing his breath to come in short, even bursts that wouldn't be detected by a hidden enemy. *Lord, protect me. Protect my men. Help us to take back Karelia easily and without major casualties. Protect us, Lord. Only you can protect us.* He kept a careful eye on the moving boots in front of him, his heart keeping careful rhythm with the thumping of knees and elbows on the hard ground as they crossed the border.

A crack of rifle fire boomed in the distance.

Matti froze and ducked his head for half a second before continuing forward.

Several more cracks reverberated through the air, several hundred feet to their left, but around them, all remained quiet.

Ten minutes later, Takala leapt into a remaining trench from the winter war.

The rest of the company followed.

"We're here," he whispered.

"We're in Karelia?"

"Yes. We'll rest here for a bit before heading on to our target."

Matti set up his rifle on the lip of the trench and hunkered down, using his sight to survey the countryside for any enemy combatants. The countryside was silent. Had they really just invaded Karelia? The Winter War had been brutal . . . but this? This was a walk in the park.

The rumble of airplanes overhead reminded him their invasion wasn't over. Looking to the southwest, Matti spotted a tiny, insect-like formation of Russian bombers heading toward the border. "Bombers overhead!" Ducking as close as he could to the muddy trench, he took cover while the crackle of anti-aircraft guns reverberated through the air.

Whew. At least the good guys had seen them coming.

Matti couldn't help but think back to the Winter War when they had been dismally outnumbered and short on supplies. Oftentimes, their anti-aircraft guns sat silent as Russian planes flew overhead and bombed at leisure, the exhausted and shell-shocked Finnish troops without ammo to respond.

But not anymore.

Suddenly, the Finns seemed to have endless supplies. And firepower.

An explosion in the sky made Matti tremble and he didn't have to look to know that a Russian bomber was going down. He'd heard that sound before. A few seconds later, a second ear-splitting boom told him that at least one of the Finns had good aim today. He swallowed the bile that crept into his throat and clenched his shaking hands at his side. Even if the Russians had started it, Matti hated the thought that lives were being lost today.

And for what? So that the Russians could keep a tiny tract of land that wasn't theirs to begin with? What a shame.

But the explosions sounding around the trench told Matti that shameful or not, it was happening. Anti-aircraft fire opened up again, this time to the southeast of them.

Takala stole a glance at his men. "Stay put. This isn't our battle," he reminded them.

As infantrymen, they had their own assignments and targets, and getting caught in the middle of an air-to-ground battle wasn't part of the plan. Instead, they hunkered down and waited for the planes to head back to Soviet soil so they could move toward Viipuri.

Scanning the trench as more flack bursts echoed, Matti looked at each of his company members, hoping a calm look would bring reassurance. The men sat with varying states of panic, fear, and resoluteness showing on their faces. Could he be a calming influence on some of the new guys who had never been in battle before? But he didn't have to.

As quickly as the air raid started, it stopped, and an eerie silence fell over the trench.

"All right, men. It's time." Takala's voice sounded calm and steely. "Grab your weapons, keep low, and head straight south-southwest. Viipuri is just two clicks away. Intel says we will find pockets of resistance holed up in houses, so check every corner before proceeding. Rally point behind the town square at eleven hundred hours. Questions?"

"No, sir!" They all seemed to know the drill, fresh faced as they were.

Matti gripped his gun tightly and double-checked to make sure he had all of his ammo still strapped to his hip. Then, with a quick prayer, he crept out of the hollow and ran across the open meadow alongside hundreds of other Finnish soldiers who were also heading straight toward Viipuri. As he sprinted forward, Matti braced himself for the sound of rifle fire, flinching in anticipation of having to hit the ground at the explosion of a Molotov cocktail, but nothing happened.

They made the two-kilometer trek in complete silence.

Had they managed to invade Karelia without a lick of resistance? It seemed that they had.

Marching along the familiar roads, Matti ran his hand along the rough-hewn planks on the wooden fences that lined the way, allowing the sights and sounds of home to take him back to his childhood — to happier times, when this city was his parents' favorite vacation spot. As he sneaked along, he thought of the weeks they had spent vacationing at Viipuri resorts along the Gulf of Finland. And the afternoons wading in the cool waters, to seafood dinners, to winter days cross-country skiing through these forests.

Maybe he'd bring Anna here after this war was over. Maybe they'd honeymoon on the shores of the Gulf . . . Matti stopped himself. He needed to focus. He was marching into Viipuri . . . into Russian occupied Viipuri . . . and he was so distracted by nostalgia he could get himself shot.

He backed against a rock wall and peered around the corner into the square where they were set to rally in ten minutes. Carefully checking each of his touch points, he looked at College and shook his head.

Viipuri was theirs.

# 43

*Kalajoki, Finland*

Anna's father ran into the farmhouse kitchen waving a copy of the newspaper. "We recaptured Viipuri!" He spread the newspaper on the table so they could see, and then ran into the living room to turn on the radio.

Anna's heart thudded to a stop. Matti was in Karelia. Fighting. What if he had been injured or . . . worse?

She followed her father into the living room and turned up the volume on the radio as loud as it would go. She dropped onto the sofa beside her father, rested her head in her hands, and prayed silently. *Please, Lord, help him to be all right.*

Finnish troops entered Karelia on the tenth of July with four divisions marching straight into the capitol city.

Anna drew a deep sigh. That didn't tell her anything at all. How would she tolerate the wait?

Her father rubbed her back and whispered, "They'll not exactly tell you the fate of a specific soldier on the radio, Anna."

She glared at him.

"But the papers said that the resistance was weak."

"It did?"

"Russian resistance was nearly nonexistent as our boys marched back into the Isthmus, recapturing major cities and villages alike."

"The Russians have one of the strongest armies in the world. Why would they let us just march into Karelia without a fight?" Anna looked at her father in confusion.

"Because they're too busy fighting the Nazis to the south." Mr. Ranta tramped into the living room holding the newspaper, and found a seat in an armchair. "It says right here that the Russians sent three Karelian divisions south last week, assumedly to protect Leningrad from the Nazis."

That was the best news she'd heard in a long time.

Maybe the Nazis weren't so bad after all. Just as long as they didn't think they could help them reoccupy or govern Karelia. The Finns could do that just fine, thank you very much.

Mr. Ranta grabbed his wife and swung her up in a spin. "We're going home, my love."

"We're going home!" Mrs. Ranta raced toward the fields where the boys were planting to tell them the good news, stopping to hug Anna along the way. "Matti will be home soon, my dear."

And everything in Anna's heart prayed she was right.

Anna grabbed her pencils and a sketchbook, needing to get outside before she started dancing through her parent's living room. It would definitely dampen her mood if she crashed into her mother's china cabinet or something of the sort.

They had Karelia. The Finns had Karelia.

And Matti was coming home soon.

He had to be. They had recaptured Karelia, what else did they have to do? Now that Karelia was in Finnish hands, the soldiers could come home and do normal non-war things like, for example, get married.

Anna sashayed out of the front door and skipped out to the orchard like a giddy five-year-old. Once in the orchard, she pulled out her sketchbook and began to draw a sky covered in fireworks. Celebratory fireworks. Below, she drew hundreds of people stood with eyes raised to the sky, cheering and laughing and smiling. She scrawled the words "victory" in curvy cursive across the top and then stepped back to look at the page. It needed a bit more color in the sky and the fireworks could use some flecks of white paint, but overall it was pretty great. She smiled, laughing at her new reality.

She'd have Arvo make a wooden frame for the sketch and give it to Matti on the day he came home.

Leaning back against a knotted log, Anna allowed herself to daydream for the first time in months. It was July. It would take a couple of months to stabilize Karelia, but surely that would be done by September. October, at the latest. Maybe they could plan a fall wedding.?

Something simple, maybe even when the weather was still warm so they could get married outside? She could string leaves together to make brightly colored garlands and they could dance in the moonlight . . .

"Anna?" Anna jumped at the sound of Kaino's voice, coming from behind the barn. "I've been looking all over for you. Did you hear the news?"

"Over here, Kai!"

Kaino raced over to her friend and plopped down. "Did you hear?"

"That we retook Karelia without even a fight?"

"Well, yes! That's news. But there's more. I just heard that the United States has reopened applications for visas. Any Finnish citizen with a familial sponsor in the United States is welcome to apply."

Anna swallowed hard. That was news she would have jumped at a year ago, but now, with things between her and Matti so uncertain?

He wanted to settle down on the banks of Lake Lagoda and raise babies. But would she ever be happy knowing she had missed the chance for what she'd dreamed of for so long?

# 44

*Kalajoki, Finland*

It wouldn't hurt for her to apply, would it?

Anna rolled over and pulled her pillow up under her elbows, propping up her head so she'd be able to stare out at the rolling hills of the Kalajoki countryside. It was beautiful. And serene. And most likely the last place on earth where there was peace to be had with the entire world wrapped up in this terrible war.

Yes, it was a great place to be.

So why couldn't she squelch the feelings of restlessness that always seemed to creep up when she thought of living her entire life in Kalajoki? She considered her options as she ran her finger along the visa application she had picked up yesterday at the immigration office in town.

Was it a betrayal to consider applying without talking to him? It wasn't as if he was her boyfriend.

She used her finger to scrawl *Anna Ojala* on the page, imagining what it would look like to see her name written on the official document.

"No, wait." She bit her lip and smiled, rubbing her finger over the imaginary letters she'd just written. "Anna Ranta." She pretended to rewrite her name, this time with a series of imaginary hearts down the side of the page.

Much better.

Matti wouldn't be upset if she applied, would he? He would understand that she was planning for her future. No, their future.

"Even if I apply, I don't have to go," she whispered, as if saying the words out loud would take away some of the sting. Frowning at the blank paper in front of her, she considered her options.

Maybe he'd be glad she had the foresight to apply. He'd understand that he was gone and she'd had no choice but to see what happened. It wasn't as if she was leaving without talking to him. Most likely, she wouldn't get a visa anyway.

This was a rare opportunity. With hundreds of thousands of people trying to get out of Europe, the fact that there was even an immigration quota for Finland was a miracle.

She may never have this chance again.

Grabbing a pen before she changed her mind, Anna quickly scrawled her name and birthday onto the application, filling in the rest of the blanks covering her general information.

After she finished, she hid the pages in her sock drawer away from prying eyes. Her parents would be appalled if they knew she was applying for a visa when Matti was off fighting. In their old-fashioned loyalty, they would think the whole idea reeked of dishonor.

Her mother would cry and her father would rant about a woman's place. Or something like that.

No, they could never find out about this. They simply wouldn't understand.

## 45

*Luga, Russia*

They may have been hailed in the papers and on the radio as the brave resistance fighters of Russia, doing whatever it took to save Leningrad from destruction and doom, but for Tanya, the resistance fighting felt a lot like digging. From sun up to sun down.

For two weeks now, they'd spent every day camped out in the northeast section of the Luga line, digging sticky clay soil out of trenches and moving it to fortified tank defense mounds.

Shovelful after shovelful. Wagonload after wagonload.

It really wasn't so bad, not when she had Feodora and Agripina to talk to, but the days did drag on. She missed Verushka fiercely.

Pushing her shovel into the ground once again, Tanya wiped sweat off of her brow and turned toward Feodora. "Another day as a proud resistance fighter for the motherland."

Feodora pointed a shaky hand toward one of the tin box rations that they had been surviving on since they had arrived. "But at least we get a delicious, well-rounded meal three times a day. That is, if you consider a tin of canned ham a well-rounded meal."

"I know too well that food is food."

Feodora looked at her intently. "I just wish they had some . . ."

Tanya patted her friend's back in understanding.

Feodora's flask had been empty for about a week now and her friend had worked through flashes of anxiety, nausea, and trembling for the last seven days. The trembling was slowly subsiding, but Feodora was miserable.

"Have the headaches stopped?"

"Somewhat. It still pounds behind my eyes."

"And the nightmares?" There had been many nights that Feodora had awakened their entire tent with her screaming.

"They just keep coming back."

Tanya gritted her teeth and blinked back tears. Feodora had such a kind heart and amazing tenacity. How could God have allowed her to suffer so greatly?

Because God didn't exist, that's why.

"Is there anything I can do to help, Feodora?"

"You could . . . pray."

"Pray?" Tanya's mouth dropped open. Feodora had always felt like Tanya did about God. She had once believed, but after everything that had happened to her, she was a bit more realistic about religion.

"Actually, I'm glad you asked because I've wanted to talk to you about that."

"About praying?" Tanya whispered. What had happened to her friend?

"Well, in the last few weeks, Agripina has been talking to me about God."

"And?"

"Well, she's led this incredibly sheltered life. Her parents are rich and she's never wanted for a thing. She's gone to mass every Wednesday and Sunday every week for her entire life. And yet, she always felt as if something was missing. Until . . ."

"Until?"

"Until she met us. She said she had prayed the morning she went out to work the lines in Leningrad that God would reveal Himself to her in a powerful way. And she believes He did."

"She thinks God revealed Himself by letting her meet a ragtag single mother and her alcoholic best friend?"

Feodora drew a sharp breath. She clenched her lips together. "That's not fair, Tanya."

"I know. I'm sorry. I just can't believe that God is up there in the sky worrying about us." Tanya waved her hand over the line they were building, the scent of gunpowder from last night's air raid still heavy in the air. "How could He care about a woman's prayer to find friends when there is so much else going on?"

"I don't know all the answers, Tanya, but I do know that when I finally prayed God would forgive me, things got a whole lot easier. It was like a weight was lifted."

"So just like that, you believe in God again?"

"I don't think I ever stopped, Tanya. For a few years there, I let my own worries and struggles push God aside. But He was always there. And somewhere deep inside, I think I always knew that."

"So what now? Will you, you know, change?"

"I hope not!" Feodora stood up and spun around, her arms flailing above her head. "What's there to change about this?"

Tanya laughed for the first time in days.

"Actually, I hope I do change. I've spent

too long not trusting anyone and allowing my fear to guide me. Right now, I'm trusting God to get me through these headaches and while they still hurt awfully bad, I'm also glad I'm getting there. Who knows? Maybe this is what it takes to break this addiction."

"And when we get back?"

"I'm trying to trust God to provide for us when we have no income." Feodora's eyes clouded as she must have realized the uphill battle they faced when they returned. "I don't want to go back to . . ."

"All right, you trust. I, however, cannot blindly trust some God when my baby's life is at risk."

"I understand how you feel, Tanya, I really do." Feodora's eyes glistened. "I'll pray that your heart will be softened."

A tiny part of Tanya ached, wishing she could believe again. How she yearned for the comfort of having someone she could trust. But she was also realistic. She knew what trusting in God had gotten her before.

"Oh, and Tanya?" Feodora's eyes were pleading. "I'm so sorry."

"For what?"

"For getting you into . . . you know."

Tanya glanced away from her friend and dug her toe into the ground. "It's okay, Fe.

You saved my life. And Veruskha's. Neither of us had a choice."

# 46

*Luga, Russia*
The whining of air raid sirens awoke them with a start.

Tanya sat up quickly and looked at Feodora, the confused look on her friend's face mirroring what she felt.

Glancing out the tent flap, she tried to gauge the time based on the position of the sun, but it was difficult to tell. The midnight sun sure wasn't making it easy to work under cover.

She struggled to her feet and grabbed her helmet and gas mask before helping Feodora who was still groggy from being awakened so quickly.

One of the unit commanders screamed into their tent. "We have orders for an immediate evacuation of all women from the Luga area. The entire line is crumbling. Grab your things and run for the train depot. Now!"

Tanya snatched her tiny knapsack and grabbed Feodora's hand. They ran out of the tent, searching the cloudless skies.

To the west, a perfectly formed triangle of tiny, black planes headed straight toward them.

Tanya froze. The planes grew larger as they got closer until she was clearly able to see the red, black, and white Nazi swastikas painted on the sides of each plane.

"Run!" She dropped her knapsack and sprinted down the dusty road that led to the train station, refusing to look backward as the roar of the engines grew so loud she could no longer hear her own heartbeat.

A plane sank low on the horizon just in front of Tanya, dipping its nose and pouring bullets onto a group of unsuspecting women in the middle of their mad dash to the station. Two women dropped to the ground amidst a chorus of screams, silenced by Nazi bullets that did not discriminate.

Tanya wanted to stop to help, to see if the bullet-ridden women were still alive, but another low-flying plane dove from the sky and headed straight toward her. She raced for the relative safety of the station. Could sub-machine gun bullets penetrate walls? She would soon find out.

Ducking into the front doors of the station, Tanya bent forward and gulped deep breaths of air. She had made it.

"Fe, that was close . . ." Feodora wasn't beside her. "Fe? Feodora!"

Her gaze skittered around the station, her wide-eyed comrades emitting a chorus of groans and screams. One woman in the corner had a bullet wound on her arm. Another lay in her friend's arms.

"Feodora! Fe!"

Where could she have gone?

Tanya forced herself to search the panicked faces in the station one-by-one, hoping, fearing at the same time. Where was her friend's familiar golden hair and boisterous smile? Where was she?

The reverberation of more machine gun fire echoed through the building and, Tanya dove to the floor. Surely Feodora wasn't still out there, was she?

She raced toward the glass doors at the front of the building and as she reached the bare windows, another plane dove down on the nearly empty street, it's nose aiming straight toward a hodge-podge group of stragglers — the last of the volunteers who were rushing for cover inside the station.

"Nooo!" she screamed, waving her arms for the women to get inside to safety.

But no human could run that fast. The

patter of bullets began and death poured out of the nose of the plane, pummeling the shell-shocked victims. One after another, women fell, hitting the ground with a cacophony of screams.

Feodora stood in the middle of the group, her arm around a frail-looking woman whose face twisted into a grimace as she struggled to take each step. A dark stain of blood ran down the woman's leg. Feodora had stopped to help another victim.

Tanya caught Feodora's eye and screamed, "Come on, Feodora. Come on."

Thirty meters to go. Then twenty.

Then fifteen.

The Nazi fighter took one last dip toward the stragglers, pumping the trigger on the nose-mounted machine guns. The first few shots hit the ground, erupting in tiny geysers of clay-colored mud, each tiny eruption filling Tanya with relief that another Nazi bullet had fallen without harming someone.

"Run!" Tanya screamed again, reaching out to her friend as if she could pull her more quickly.

In one horrific moment, one of the bullets found its mark. Feodora jerked forward, a stunned expression of both fear and confusion on her face before she hit the ground in a cloud of dust.

"Feodora!" Tanya raced out into the street without caring about the danger. She reached Feodora and wrapped her hands around her friend's shoulders, dragging her limp body into the station.

"Help! Someone help me!" Her cries were lost amongst the hundreds of other women who were also desperately seeking help. "Please! Help!"

Agripina shoved her way through the crowd and crouched next to Feodora. "Oh, no."

"The plane . . . it . . . it . . ."

Agripina fell down at Feodora's other side, brushing Feodora's blood-soaked hair off of her dirt-stained face.

Tanya listened for sounds of breathing. "She isn't breathing."

Agripina leapt to her feet. "Someone! Please! Help. My friend has been shot!"

A woman raced toward them, blood covering the front of her white shirt. She sank to the ground next to Feodora. "I'm a nurse. Get back."

"She was shot in the back."

"All right." The nurse gently rolled Feodora onto her side. A pool of blood had puddled under her body. Sticking two fingers against her neck, the nurse sat quietly for several minutes, moving her fingers to different positions before turning sad eyes toward Tanya and Agripina. "I'm sorry. She's gone."

"Gone?" Tanya screamed. "Can't we get her to the hospital tent for surgery or something?"

"No." The nurse gripped Tanya to steady her. "It looks as if she was killed instantly."

Killed instantly?

Tanya collapsed into Agripina's trembling arms, closing her eyes in an effort to block out the pain. How could this have happened?

Agripina gripped her shoulders, sobbing audibly.

How could Feodora . . . be gone? A moaning wail escaped her lips as she melted onto the floor, her head pressed against her friend's still form. Lying there, she screamed in anger, ranting against a God whom she didn't even believe existed. "How could You have let this happen? How? How?"

Her screams were interrupted by Agripina, who pulled her up and looked her straight in the eye. "Tanya. They're telling us we have to get on a train now. I know you're sad. I know you don't want to leave, but they think another air raid is imminent. We have to get out of here now."

"But . . . what about Feodora?" Tanya

searched Agripina's face for answers, for hope, for anything that would help her friend.

"We have to go. Now."

"I can't leave her!" Tanya screamed back. "I can't."

"We have to."

Agripina's arms pulled her one way, but her heart brought her back to the platform. To Feodora. She writhed against Agripina's tugging, desperate for one last glimpse of her friend.

"Feodora!" Tanya reached out the door and screamed in despair. She had to go back for her, she had to bring her onto the train.

Agripina pulled her back, forcing her towards the train. How could she be leaving Fe there alone on the cold, hard floor?

The doors slammed shut and without so much as a whistle to signal their departure, the train sped out of the station, racing through the open fields toward Leningrad.

Racing away from death and destruction and failed hopes.

Racing away from the defense line that Feodora had given her life to build.

Racing away from the failures and losses of a Russian army that couldn't seem to hold off their enemy.

And toward Leningrad.
The city that had just lost its last hope.

# 47

*Leningrad, Russia*

The streets of Leningrad seemed normal.

Tanya and Agripina trudged down boulevards lit by both the sun and the moon in its early evening light, all but ignoring the stately buildings glowing in the warm air and the birds that flitted back and forth between the trees that lined the nearly empty Leningrad streets. A couple passed by, hand-in-hand, talking in whispers to each other as if they didn't have a care in the world.

"It's as if they don't know what's coming," Agripina said bitterly.

"Or what has already come to pass." Tanya's voice was weak. Strained. Another wave of pain flooded her body and she choked on a messy sob before giving in and allowing the tears to flow. Hiccupping, Tanya studied Agripina, wondering if she looked as haggard and battle worn as her friend did. Agripina's dress — probably once sold on the racks of an expensive boutique — was torn at the collar and the hem. Bloodstains soaked the front and mud streaked down the sleeves. Mud-stained tracks of tears stained her pale face as well.

Glancing down at her own torn and blood-stained clothes, Tanya reached up and did her best to comb her fingers through her hair. "I . . . I need to straighten up. I can't let Verushka see me like this."

Agripina carefully removed a light yellow shawl from her knapsack — she hadn't lost hers in the rush — and wrapped it around Tanya's shoulders. "Here. Take this. It'll at least cover the blood stains on your dress."

"But what about you?"

"They won't even notice me when they see you."

Tanya wrapped the shawl around her shoulders and took a tentative step up the crooked stairs to Vera's front door.

"Vera?" She opened the door without knocking. "We're . . . I'm home."

Vera hobbled in from the kitchen, the baby on her hip, her grin replaced by a look of dread when she saw Tanya and Agripina standing in the shadows of her doorway. "Oh, dear. What has happened?"

"She's . . . she's gone." Tanya collapsed

into Vera's embrace.

"What happened?" Vera's voice was tight, barely audible.

"There was an air raid and the Nazi planes were shooting at us." Agripina answered for Tanya, her eyes slick and wet.

Vera pulled Agripina into their hug.

A moan escaped Tanya's lips as she clung to what felt like her last lifeline. "Where's Verushka? Where's my baby?"

"She's napping. Go have a seat over there and I'll wake her up." Vera laid a gentle hand on her back and led her to the couch, gently sitting right beside her and wrapping her into another warm hug.

Agripina perched on the edge of the couch next to Tanya and looked at her. "We'll get through this, Tanya. We will."

The sound of a baby crying echoed from down the hall.

Tanya's chest ached. Her baby. She was finally home for Verushka.

Vera entered the room with the baby on her hip. "Mama's here, Rushkie. Your mama is here." Verushka's head lay on Vera's shoulders, her eyes half-closed in sleep.

Tanya stood up on wobbly legs and pulled her baby onto her chest. "Oh, baby, I have missed you."

Verushka leaned her head back and stared

at Tanya, blinking several times in confusion before leaning down and nestling into the hollow of Tanya's neck.

"I'll make tea." Vera scurried off to the kitchen and Tanya sank down onto the couch cushions. If only this moment was happy. It should have been happy. She reached up and stroked Verushka's hair and felt the baby's shoulder's relax. Within a few minutes, Verushka's breathing grew rhythmic. She was back asleep.

"Feodora was . . . she was the first friend I've ever had. The first real friend, at least." Agripina's squeaky voice broke Tanya's reverie.

"Mine, too. She was the only person who ever was there for me." Tanya gazed at the spot on the couch where Feodora usually sat and allowed another moan to escape her lips. How could she survive now that Feodora — her best friend — was gone?

Vera came into the room and set the tea tray on the coffee table. She joined them on the couch, gently stroking their backs as the three of them grieved for their lost friend, for their lost hope.

Tanya was tired of being strong, tired of suffering while life seemed to trample her.

"At least . . . she knew Jesus." Agripina said softly.

Vera's gaze shot up. "What do you mean?"

"I mean, we talked. Feodora and I. And she realized that she had been running away from God for a long time. She prayed and asked for His forgiveness and, well . . . she was different at the end. Just different."

"Praise God." Vera clapped, tears shimmering in her eyes as if her grief was mixed with joy.

Tanya stared at her foot, not wanting to listen to the hopeful words that her friends spoke. There was nothing to praise anyone about right now. Not when Feodora was dead.

Vera put a kind hand on her leg and squeezed hard. "I know you loved her, Tanya. And you were a great friend to her. And while there is nothing I can say to ease the pain of your loss right now, I will be praying."

Tanya shook her head slowly. Prayer wouldn't help. Nothing would now.

"I'd better . . . get home." Agripina stood, the pained smile on her face doing little to mask her grief.

"Oh, no, my dear. You can't go out by yourself right now, not on a night like tonight." Vera crossed her arms over her chest.

"She's right, Agripina. It's not safe out

there. You have to stay here tonight and we'll walk you home in the morning."

Vera rubbed her hand over her shoulder as she wiped her cheek.

"Ga goo ba!" Verushka woke up and leaned back, cooing in her lap.

"Oh, Vera! Listen to her!"

"I know. Isn't it adorable? She's been babbling like that for a few weeks now. Oh, you should've heard her when we were at the grocers last week, she was putting on quite a show." Vera's mouth thinned into a straight line. "I'm sorry Tanya . . . I don't mean to go on and on about all you've missed."

"No, it's all right. I want to hear it. Every detail."

Verushka cooed some more and then pointed a pudgy fist towards the kitchen. "I think she's hungry."

"Let me get her a bottle, Tanya, so you can get cleaned up."

"No, I want to feed her." For the first time since she'd arrived home, Tanya felt sure of something. She hugged Verushka closely and showered her with another round of kisses. "I don't want to miss another minute with this little one."

"All right, there's a bit more powdered milk in the walk-in. Only a few days' worth but you can take the rest."

A few days' worth?

"While you're in there, I'll go heat up some water so you and Agripina can get cleaned up." Vera's brave face was pale and drawn, as if trying to distract herself from her own pain.

Tanya understood the feeling. "I'll be out in a bit." Tanya bit back a sob, hoping she could make it until Veruskha's bedtime without another quivering meltdown. She walked into the kitchen, inhaling the familiar scent of her baby. "I've missed you so much, little one. I wish I still had milk so I could nurse you."

Luga had not only stolen her best friend and her time, but also her ability to nurse her child.

Verushka didn't seem to care, though. She seemed perfectly happy to drink powdered milk from a tin cup. Tanya sat the baby on her lap and closed her eyes, allowing her tiny daughter to comfort her in a way no one else could.

If anyone could soften the blow of losing her best friend, it wasn't the God Who had abandoned her right when she needed Him most.

No. It was Verushka, the tiny baby who seemed to be her one and only bright spot in a dark world.

# 48

*Leningrad, Russia*

"Tanya, I know you don't want to think about this, but, well, here." Vera shoved the Leningradskaya Pravda in front of her.

She squinted, trying to focus on the tiny print. "What is it, Vera?"

"They're asking parents to voluntarily send all children under ten on trains to the Urals where they'll be met by local families who will take care of them until the city is safe again."

"To the Urals?"

"Yes, I guess they figure if the Nazis make it to Siberia, then we're really in trouble."

"Who would want Siberia anyway?" Tanya laughed, the smile feeling strange on her face.

"So, what do you think about sending Verushka?" Vera's voice was tentative.

"There's no way I could. Never!" Tanya looked up, trying to read Vera's thoughts.

"I don't know, Tanya. I want to keep Verushka safe, but I also can't imagine she'd be safer away from her mama than she would way out in Siberia."

"I don't think I can do it. Be without her again."

"I'm not sure I could . . . say goodbye to her either," Vera said. "Plus, we should be fairly safe here. Smolny is miles away and that's the Nazis primary target. Why would they bomb a tiny street in the Vyborg Quarter?"

"My thoughts exactly," Tanya said, snuggling her baby close and kissing her head. "I just couldn't bear to be away from you again, baby girl!" Tanya settled back onto the couch, the newspaper still on her lap. Rubbing the baby's back, she quickly scanned the headlines, trying to distract herself from thoughts of Feodora.

It didn't work. Stories of air raids and strafing attacks and Nazi victories filled the pages, making Tanya ache with dread and fear.

"Last week the papers were espousing the strength of the Red Army. Now it looks as if they're trying to scare us."

"I have a feeling they are trying to be realistic. Make sure that everyone knows that action now is our only hope. Plus,

329

everyone has heard stories from Luga."

At the mention of Luga, Tanya bit her lip. Would she ever hear that word again without crying?

"Tanya . . ." Vera sat next to her, taking the baby and kissing her nose. "Why don't you head over to Agripina's this afternoon and talk? She was there and is probably feeling much like you are right now."

"Do you think it's safe?"

"Yes, just stay away from Smolny and you should be fine." Vera's eyes were distant too, as though she was doing her best to be strong, knowing if she broke down, they'd both break.

"I'd love to see Agripina." Tanya stood and took a deep breath. She slipped on her shawl. "I'll be home later. Thank you."

Stepping out into the bright sunshine, she blinked to get her bearings before heading toward the University quarter. Nothing looked the same. It was as if the city had been transformed overnight from a state of quiet trepidation to a war zone.

Sandbags lined the streets, piled up under shop windows that were crisscrossed with paper strips and newspapers in an effort to keep them from shattering in the event of an air raid. Parks contained huge guns, manned by men wearing red Volunteer

Corps armbands. Every street light and wall in the city seemed to be plastered with posters calling on the citizens of Leningrad to volunteer.

"I've already done that," Tanya mumbled. "A lot of good it did too." Lumbering forward, one step in front of the other, Tanya did her best to ignore the guns and the signs and the terrified looking men who hauled furniture and scraps of metal to various anti-tank embankments around the city. "One, two, three . . ." Tanya counted her steps, knowing if she stopped to look, she'd dissolve into a mess of tears and grief. "Just keep walking."

The rumble of planes broke her concentration and instinctively, Tanya covered her head and ducked behind a pile of sandbags. Were they bombing Leningrad today? She scanned the street and considered making a run to an alleyway about one hundred yards ahead. But that would put her in the wide open street for several seconds.

Right where Feodora had . . .

No. She couldn't think of Feodora right now.

She closed her eyes and covered her head with her arms, bracing as the roar of the plane's engines grew louder. But the familiar thud of bombs never came. Instead, she felt the pitter-patter of paper falling on her back as thousands of tiny leaflets rained down on the streets around her.

Snatching one up, she read the roughly printed words carefully.

*If you think you can defend Leningrad, you are mistaken! Surrender now to German troops and you will survive, but oppose the great German army and you will be destroyed in a hurricane of German bombs and shells.*

A wave of nausea swept through her as she looked down the street. Thousands of leaflets flittered in the summer air, eventually settling on the ground, making it look as though it had snowed in August. Tossing her leaflet into the trash can on the corner, Tanya scooped up a huge load of the vile leaflets and shoved them in as well before kicking the garbage can.

Just wait until Agripina heard about this.

Her emotions shifted from sad to angry. The Nazis couldn't rob her daughter of her homeland. Not after they'd already robbed them of Fe.

Tanya looked both directions to make sure no one was watching before scooping one more off the ground and stuffing it into the pocket of her dress. Ten minutes later, she was on a tree-lined street with stately, gated houses. She checked her address to be sure she had the right one, ambled up the walk, and knocked gently.

A woman in a black dress and white apron answered. "May I help you?" She barked gruffly.

"Yes ma'am, Tanya Egerov here for Agripina."

"Is she expecting you?" The woman's scowl matched her cold demeanor.

"No, she isn't. But I think she'll want to see me. I was with her in Luga."

The maid cringed at the word Luga, and Tanya realized that Agripina's family may not have supported her venture in the Volunteer Corps. "I'll ask her. You may wait out here."

Tanya blinked in surprise as the door slammed in her face. Sinking down onto the step, she remembered the many slammed doors when she'd first moved to Leningrad. Apparently, there was still something about her that made people cringe.

Two seconds later, the door banged open and Agripina rushed out. "Oh, Tanya! Come in! I'm so sorry about your welcome. I will definitely be talking to Magda about that."

"It's all right." Tanya choked back tears. Seeing Agripina reminded her of Feodora.

"Come in! Let's go to the parlor and I'll have Magda bring us tea."

Tanya stepped inside the ornate entry room, a giant crystal chandelier hung above antique furniture. She had never seen anything like it, and had to resist the temptation not to stop and gawk at the gorgeous paintings and golden vases that lined the stately hall.

"Sit down." Agripina pointed to a peach-colored sofa that looked as if it had never been used. "How are you, Tanya?"

"I'm all right. It is so wonderful to see Verushka. When she is around, I am able to distract myself with her for a time. But then when the house is quiet and I'm all alone, I remember the truth. She's not coming back."

"I know. Every morning I wake up and expect to find her lying on a cot beside me. Without her it's so quiet."

Tanya quickly wiped tears from her face, trying to find the right words to say. "She was the person who gave me hope when things seemed impossible. I don't know how I'll survive without her."

Agripina laid a hand on her leg and squeezed. "I will pray that you . . . that we both . . . find the strength."

"I don't . . . want to talk about God right now."

"I respect that. But I do want to tell you

Feodora's biggest worry was you would . . . go back to your old lifestyle if things got desperate."

"She told you that?"

Shock flashed on Agripina's face as Tanya spit out the angry words.

"I didn't mean any harm. I don't judge you, Tanya. I just want to help."

"Well, you can help by keeping your mouth shut." Tanya drew her face into a frown, shame heating her cheeks. She couldn't believe Feodora had told Agripina her secret . . . as if she'd found God and suddenly she was all high and mighty. "I think it's time for me to head home."

"Oh, Tanya. I didn't mean to upset you. I just wanted you to know that I'm praying for you, and I will be here for you no matter what you need. We are in this together."

"I wouldn't want you to have to lower yourself to associate with a woman like me, so I'll stay away." Tanya regretted the words as soon as she said them.

Agripina sniffled. "I loved Feodora too. Her past and all. I would never judge you for making choices that I never had to make."

"Good day, Agripina."

Her friend stood wide-eyed as Tanya stormed out the door, racing down the street to get out of view before she crumbled onto a park bench. Why had she gotten so angry with Agripina?

It wasn't her fault that Feodora had revealed her secret.

And Agripina hadn't been cruel about it.

But still, how could Tanya ever be friends with someone who knew what she had done? Agripina lived in a beautiful house with a maid and a housekeeper. She couldn't understand the desperation Tanya felt every day.

Agripina would always look down on her, no matter what she said.

It was probably better to stay away and let Agripina worry about her own life and troubles while Tanya worried about hers. She hardly knew the woman anyway, so there was no need to invest in someone who would never understand her. Yes, it was better to just walk away and forget about Agripina. But why did it feel as if she was ripping a scab off of her heart with every step she took?

# 49

*Somewhere in Karelia*

"Our orders are to hold the pre-winter war border right about here." Takala pointed to a line on the map he'd drawn about fifteen kilos north of the Leningrad suburbs, and then passed the map around the group so the men could look closer.

"What do you mean, hold the border?" Matti stood with a frown, hands on his hips.

Takala gave him a look that would've scared Hitler. "It means when we get our orders we march to Kirjasalo, set up camp, and then hold our line. We've been told that nothing comes in or out of the city while the Germans prepare to attack."

"We're not invading Leningrad?" College ducked his head, seemingly to avoid one of Takala's looks as well.

"No, doesn't appear so. We're just supposed to hold the border — to make sure no supplies or weapons or artillery make it in to military groups inside the city."

"Like a siege?" College said the words that Matti was already thinking.

"Yes, I guess it's like a siege. Hopefully, a very short siege while the Germans march through Leningrad toward Moscow."

"But what about women and children in the city?" Matti's head pounded. "They'll starve without supplies."

"Assuming they've been preparing for the invasion and will have stocked up, they'll probably hole up for a few weeks eating canned goods and be fine until the border is opened." Takala had clearly been fed this line by his higher-ups.

Matti hoped his friend was right.

Käärme was studying the map closely.

Takala grabbed the map and pointed to an arrow at the pre-winter war border. "We may hit resistance right here. Intelligence says that there is still one Russian division stationed there to hold the border. Which is why we'll be marching at zero-two-hundred hours so that we can do it under the cover of darkness."

"Will we have air support?"

"Yes, the flyboys from Tiedustelulenta-laivue 12 will support our push."

Takala continued to give them instructions, pointing out specific rally points and targets. Then, he tossed the map into the fire and used a stick to make sure it was completely burned. "Don't want anyone in that Russian division getting hold of that."

The men stared at him in solemn silence. They were going into Russia.

Käärme pulled out a flask and began passing it around the group, encouraging the men to get their liquid courage.

Matti frowned. He had hoped the war would bring some maturity to this group, but they were still the same wild party boys they had been before. Of course, they hadn't faced any real resistance either.

"Put that away, guys. We have a job to do tonight." Takala said sternly.

Matti's gaze shot up. Maybe Takala had changed?

Käärme blinked in surprise and then tucked his flask into his coat pocket. "Sorry. I thought we could celebrate our progress."

"We'll celebrate when we get there, Käärme. Until then, let's stay focused."

Rain filtered through the branches of the birches, giving music to their slow and methodical march toward Kirjasalo.

"Come on, men, just a little further," Takala whispered from the front of their queue.

Matti burrowed his head and took another hunched step forward, praying they would reach Kirjasalo without any resistance. As much as he wanted to fight, he wasn't sure he was ready to face Russian soldiers this morning. He trudged on in the dim light of a northern summer night, the squish of clay-like mud on his boots telling every step. Anxious to see the edge of the forest, he raised his head above the line of soldiers in front of him. An unexpected bullet whizzed by his ear. He slammed his body into the muddy ground.

Rookie mistake.

"Enemy fighters at right!" Matti hissed as the men in his company sank into the muddy terrain and aimed their rifles in the direction where the bullets had come.

He flattened himself onto the ground behind a stump and squinted, trying to get a read on who was shooting at them. Scanning the horizon, he spotted a small Russian troop hunched behind a ledge to their southwest.

"There. Do you see them?" he whispered to Takala, who crouched behind him with rifle ready.

"Yes."

The muscles in Matti's shoulders tightened as his fingers trembled over the trigger. He dreaded what the next few minutes would bring. They had faced so little resistance in the last weeks that Matti had almost forgotten what it felt like to have the adrenaline of battle pumping through his body and the fear of death in his heart — a feeling he'd hoped he'd never feel again.

A burst of rifle fire opened up.

Matti squinted to see as shells whistled around his ears. He straightened, making himself as thin as possible before slowly moving his rifle over the stump and taking aim at one of the black barrels that peeked over the ledge. Swallowing a sick feeling, he hesitated as explosions caused the woods to tremble.

A shell burst about fifty meters to his left, raining down dirt and leaves on his helmet. He reached up to brush the dirt out of his eyes and a bullet whizzed by, his arm hairs rising with its seemingly magnetic pull. Jerking his arm back behind the tree, Matti closed his eyes. *Whew. A close one.*

"Cover them!" Takala shouted as he pointed toward Käärme and College, who eased out from behind their hiding spot in a grove of trees and rushed the Russian unit's flank.

Matti took a deep breath and gripped his rifle tightly before peeking out behind the tree and opening fire at the Russians who shot at his friends. "Oh, no, you don't!" Matti shouted at a Red Army soldier who seemed to have a clear shot at College.

A bullet hit the Russian soldier right in the rifle scope, knocking the weapon out of his hand.

Two seconds later, another Russian soldier popped up, shooting wildly as Takala and Matti desperately tried to get a scope on him. One . . . two . . . there!

The Red Army soldier went down.

The forest fell silent.

# 50

*Kirjasalo, Karelia*

"I recognize that guy over there." Matti pushed his canteen to the side and pointed across the mess tent toward a soldier who made his way toward the chow line.

"I've never seen him." Käärme looked up from the letter he was writing and squinted at the man walking toward one of the other Finnish encampments on the ridge.

"I've seen him before," Matti said, squinting. Matti's skin prickled. "Johannes!"

Johannes stopped and narrowed his eyes. Recognition lit his face. "Oh, hi. Matti, is it?"

"Yes! Matti Ranta. I'm Anna Ojala's boy . . . I mean, friend."

"Oh, yes." Johannes's eyes narrowed, as if he were confused. "How are you?"

"Hit a bit of resistance yesterday as we marched down, but we made it all right. Glad to be here."

"This camp sure beats sleeping in bags in the woods, doesn't it?"

"I hear you. Three warm meals a day and coffee to boot."

"And don't forget mail service!" Johannes said.

"Speaking of, have you heard from Kaino?"

"She's good. She keeps talking about a fall wedding." The side of Johannes's mouth wrinkled as if the idea of a wedding made him queasy.

"You don't want to marry her?"

"I mean, she's great and all, but we're still so young."

Matti frowned. "Anna's last letter was stained with tears. I think she was hoping for a fall wedding too." Matti didn't add that he would be happy to give her one if he could just get home. He had no desire to sow his wild oats.

A cloud of confusion crossed Johannes's face. "Oh, she still writes you?"

Now it was Matti's turn to be confused. "Why wouldn't she?"

"I thought with her planning to go to America, you two maybe had called things off." Johannes rambled.

Matti's heart pounded in his chest so hard he wondered if Johannes could hear it. "Go

344

to America? What does that mean?"

"Oh. You didn't know?" Johannes stuttered. "Anna applied for a visa to the United States a few weeks ago. It could come through at any time. Kaino was fretting about how much she would miss her."

Matti closed his eyes. Anna. Had she been lying to him this entire time?

"I'm . . . I'm sorry. I feel as if I just inadvertently delivered a Dear John letter."

"No, it's fine. I'm glad I know." Matti said, realizing what a fool he'd been. Here he had been pining away, working so hard to get home and marry Anna and all the while she'd been scheming to leave him. And she didn't even tell him about her intentions.

"Well, it was good seeing you. We're stationed just down the road so I'll see you around."

"Yes, good to see you." Matti turned around and raced toward the woods, desperate to get away and find some solace. But no peace came. Not when the woman he loved had just betrayed him.

How could Anna have done this to him? All this time he had assumed she was waiting for him, working on her war committee meetings and on the farm. Her letters had come almost daily, filled with news of life on the farm, of her plans for their future.

Never once had she mentioned a visa or America.

Was this her strange way of breaking up with him? Or did she plan on stringing him along until he finished with the war?

Oh, yeah. She said she wouldn't send him a Dear John letter on the front as she had done for Henrick. She must be waiting until he got home to tell him. That, or she was just leaving and would never say a word.

Either way, she clearly wasn't the woman he thought she was.

*Lord, what do I do?* He didn't stop to wait for an answer. Instead, he raced back to camp and grabbed a piece of paper and an envelope. He wasn't letting a woman make a fool of him.

*Anna,*

*I have been dreaming of building a future with you for months, but it turns out you are not the woman I thought you were. I'm glad I figured it out before it was too late. I wish you the best in your life and pray you find happiness wherever you go.*

*Matti*

There. Short, sweet and honest.

Matti quickly folded the letter, doing his best to ignore the ache in his heart as he thought about what had just happened. He sealed the envelope and ran to toss it into the mailbag before the last transport of the day headed north. No need to drag this farce on any longer.

Matti bit down hard on his lip. He was a soldier. He wouldn't cry over a girl, even if he'd thought he loved her. No, he wouldn't let this destroy him.

Because no girl was worth that.

## 51

*Leningrad, Russia*
*September 8, 1941*

Tanya covered her ears with her hands, doing her best to block out the sound of the air raid sirens. "Up and out of there, Verushka." She scooped the baby out of her bassinet and put her in Vera's bed next to her.

The baby cooed and then fell back asleep, leaving Tanya alone with her thoughts. The sirens had been blaring since six that evening, bringing with them a constant supply of nightmares and flashbacks to her time in Luga. She hadn't slept a wink.

And now the sirens blared again, signaling another attack on the city somewhere. At the rate the Germans had been bombing tonight, this was probably the start of the invasion. Which was maybe a good thing. Leningrad was about as prepared as it could be and the sooner they got started, the sooner it would be over.

A soft knock sounded on the door.

"Tanya? Are you OK in there?"

Tanya opened the door. "Verushka's fine. I'm . . . shaken up."

"I thought you might be, dear. Do you want tea?"

Tanya sank into the soft green velvet of her chair, wishing that maybe she could pray. It would be nice to talk to Someone Who could actually do something to help.

Fifteen minutes later, Vera came back, holding the Leningradskaya Pravda.

"It looks as though it's begun." Vera set the paper on the table in front of her. "But we already knew that. The bombing last night left little doubt."

"I'm surprised the Pravda still printed last night." Tanya yawned.

"You know what they say — rain or shine — and now we know, bombs won't stop them either." Vera pursed her lips and handed Tanya the wet paper.

"I guess we just hole up here for a few weeks and wait for it to blow over?"

"We have a little food and lots of firewood and good company. We can't ask for much more."

"No, we can't. The street looks exactly the same as it did yesterday. You wouldn't know that half the city was on fire if the sky wasn't glowing orange."

Vera pointed to a dark cloud of smoke to the north. "I think that's the Badayev warehouses. It says here that they were bombed last night and the entire complex is on fire."

"What are the Badayev warehouses?"

"The city's biggest storehouses for food. According to this, more than one thousand tons of flour were burned. If they don't get the fires out, we could lose equal amounts of sugar, meat, and butter."

Tanya's heart sank.

The city was already rationing food. If they lost their biggest supply, they'd all be in trouble.

"Let's just pray they get those fires out." Vera's words drifted off and the two women fell into a comfortable silence, as Tanya contemplated the fate of their city.

They had known the Germans were marching toward them for weeks now, but Tanya still carried a glimmer of hope that maybe the men on the front would be able to hold off the invasion.

"I wonder if we'll see them. The Germans. Will they just march down our street with Nazi flags and rifles?" Tanya broke the silence first.

"I hope not! I've been praying they'll just march on through on their way to Moscow and leave us alone."

"Well, keep praying. We don't want them to camp out here in Leningrad."

"Keep praying? Are you changing your mind about God?" Vera gazed at her, as if trying to read her heart.

Maybe she did.

"Tanya. Have you changed your mind about God?" Vera's dark eyes seemed to bore holes into her consciousness.

Tanya opened her mouth to respond but no words came out.

# 52

## Kalajoki, Finland

Anna stared across the table as Mr. Ranta scooped a spoonful of salmon and potato soup into his mouth.

"What are you saying?" her father asked him.

"I'm saying that I saw Mr. Korkonen at the store and he told me that he is concerned that Kalajoki doesn't have enough food stored up for winter."

Last winter had been very sparse for all of them — Finland had lost more than half of her fish packing capacity with the loss of Karelia. Coupled with the flood of refugees, many in Northern Finland had gone hungry. In fact, in the last few weeks of spring last year, their family had survived on bread and milk alone.

"Isn't this winter supposed to be different?" Anna interrupted. "We have Karelia back. Why can't we just go in and start packing fish again?"

"I wish we could." The wistful look in Mr. Ranta's eyes told Anna that he missed his home and his livelihood. "I'd love to go back. But right now, they're saying no civilians in or out of Karelia."

"But surely that will change before long?"

"I hope so, but regardless, I think we should plan for food shortages again this winter. Better safe than regret it later."

Mr. Ranta and Anna's father had developed a trusting friendship during the year and a half they'd shared a home.

Now her father looked worried. "What can we do?" he asked.

"I think we need to start limiting food intake in our household. Try to stretch food as far as we can. Mr. Korkonen said that we should stock up on simple things like canned fish and flour. Then, at least, we have the supplies to survive."

Anna sighed. This was exactly why she wanted to go to America. So she didn't have to worry about things like war and food shortages. Surely Matti would understand that when he got home. She'd just tell him how hard it had been for them to get by for the last two winters and explain that they could build a wonderful life together in the land of promise. She was certain he would agree. "Hey, have you heard from Matti lately?" She looked toward Mr. Ranta.

After more than a month of silence, she had gotten several backlogged letters after he had reached his camp on the border.

"Oh, yes, I almost forgot. You got a letter from him today." Mr. Ranta took the letter out of his pocket and handed it to Anna.

She fingered the letter and frowned. It seemed thinner than his usual letters. She quickly spooned soup into her mouth, anxious to find a private place to read his words. Oh, how she missed him. "May I please be excused?" She looked hopefully at her father.

"Sure. Just come back and help your mother with the dishes when everyone else is finished."

Anna raced out of the room before he changed his mind. Tearing open the envelope as she slammed the door shut, she anxiously read Matti's words. She sank onto the couch, the words seeming to punch her in the chest. She scanned again, hoping she had read them wrong.

*It turns out you are not the woman I thought you were.*

What could that mean? She racked her brain, trying to think of what she had written in her last letter. Was it that she had told him she was hoping for a fall wedding? Did he think she was pushing him too quickly?

*I'm glad I figured it out before it was too late.*

A wave of nausea swept up from her chest. She crinkled the letter in her hands.

She had scared away Matti — the only man she had ever loved. Sobs bubbled up from her heart and she wept. All of her dreams and hopes for her future had been destroyed in one short letter. She had given up everything for him, waited for him, put her entire hope for the future in him. And he had thrown it all back at her because he'd been scared away when she actually wanted him to settle down. Anna clutched her stomach, trying to push back the pain that seemed to penetrate her entire body. "Matti," she cried out, sniffling.

Even though he wasn't the man she thought he was, he was still the man she loved deeply. It would take her a long time to get over him.

Maybe forever.

The irony was that exactly one day after Matti broke up with her she got the letter saying her visa had been approved. At least she didn't have to make a tough decision.

Anna moaned. She should be thrilled to

be in possession of that letter, but her heart couldn't seem to let go of Matti. And her head couldn't seem to accept that he didn't want to be with her anymore. Anna pulled out the letter from the embassy and read it again.

*Anna Ojala, your visa to the United States under the sponsorship of Mrs. Mary Simo in Astoria in the State of Oregon has been approved. Please submit your travel paperwork to our offices at your convenience.*

So it was settled. She was going to Oregon.

She would have to tell her parents soon. She had money set aside from her time working at the market to buy her passage.

She was finally going to America. Her dreams were finally coming true. So why did she feel as though she'd just lost everything she'd ever wanted?

# 53

Verushka let out one last wail and sank into Tanya's shoulder, finally giving in to sleep. "I think she's asleep."

"Praise the Lord." Vera sighed softly from the chair next to the fireplace where she'd been sitting hunkered under a blanket all day.

Tanya gently stroked the baby's soft head and rubbed her hands over her icy feet. She set the sleeping child on Vera's lap and tightly wrapped another quilt around both of them. Maybe Vera's body heat would keep the baby warm.

She turned to Vera's old dining table, lying top-down next to the hearth. The legs had already been burned, and half of the antiqued Russian pine top was chopped ready to go into the fire. Tanya looked out the window, glaring at the snow and ice accumulated on the streets. Even if they only had one fire a day, there was only enough wood left for three or four more days.

A moan from Verushka pulled her out of her thoughts. A fresh wave of grief burrowed up into her throat. Her baby was so hungry, so cold. "Oh, Vera, what will we do?"

Vera's eyes closed and her mouth began to move in what Tanya knew was silent prayer. The old woman had grown more quiet over the last few weeks, often retreating into her chair for hours at a time.

Sighing deeply, Tanya closed her eyes as well, allowing herself a moment's respite.

What would they do? Vera's carefully planned out food stores had run out five days ago, leaving them with nothing left to feed themselves or the baby. A trip to the gastronom yesterday had revealed that there wasn't any food left in the city. Grocery store shelves were empty. Restaurants were closed. And thousands of starving people braved the icy cold streets in hopes of finding something to eat.

"Maybe you could visit Agripina?" Vera's question startled Tanya out of her pensive worry. "Maybe her family has some stores."

"I can't go to Agripina."

"Why not? The streets are no colder than the house is." Vera frowned at the dwindling pile of furniture that was now their only source of heat.

"No, it's not the cold, Vera. Agripina and I had a falling out," Tanya said.

"And?" Vera waited.

"It's just that every time I see her, I can't help but think of Feodora."

Vera's shoulders trembled. "I miss her too."

"I just wish the Germans would invade!" Tanya couldn't help but giggle through her tears at the irony of that statement. A month ago, she would've been called crazy for saying it, but now nearly every Leningrader felt the same way. It wasn't that they welcomed the violence of an invasion, but anything seemed better than the waiting. And freezing. And starving.

Vera once again closed her eyes. She looked so tired and weak that Tanya had to wonder how much of her own food she was secretly passing to Verushka.

Tanya was doing the same thing . . . as much as she could. But it wasn't fair to Vera, especially considering how much it seemed to be affecting her.

"Vera, are you giving your food to Verushka?" The words slipped out of her mouth before she could hold them in.

"Oh, honey . . ." Vera's voice trailed off, her eyes drifting to the tiny sleeping form in her lap. "We need to get help soon, don't we?"

"Yes, we do."

"Would you like me to go see Agripina?"

Tanya studied the old woman. Vera couldn't go, not when she hardly had the energy to get out of her chair. No, Tanya would have to face her old friend. Face the memories. And maybe even the talk of God.

Why was Agripina's name like salt in an open wound? Was it because she reminded her of Feodora? Or was it the fact that Agripina knew her terrible secret?

"I will go to Agripina tomorrow." Tanya promised Vera before she could change her mind.

Tanya wrapped her scarf tightly around her neck and headed out into the freezing cold air. The wind beat against her cheeks, stabbing icicles beating into her skin. She pulled her scarf up to cover her nose.

"Here we go," she whispered.

She hadn't been outside in weeks. When the first air raid started, they had hunkered down and spent their days inside, hoping to avoid the next bombing raid. It had been fun for a while — they'd read books and played games and listened to the radio. Then the temperature had dropped and the

360

first snow had come early.

Then they ran out of food. And fuel.

Vera's once cozy house had quickly become an icy, dark prison. Tanya shivered in the nearly empty streets, wondering if she was risking too much to go out right now.

Searching for signs of German soldiers, Tanya saw only cold and weary pedestrians, most likely out in search of food. Every person she passed had cloudy eyes and a reserved face, as if realization of their situation had finally dawned.

Tanya turned onto Agripina's street. She ducked her head and stepped quickly, not allowing herself to think about the way she had left things with Agripina.

What if Agripina turned her away at the door?

"It's time to find out." The steam of her breath floated in front of her as she tapped the brass knocker.

The maid peeked her head out of a crack in the door, looking pale and gaunt.

"Hello. Is Agripina here?"

The maid stood grim faced and gestured for her to come inside. Stepping out of the cold, Tanya fidgeted in the front entryway while the maid hurried to find Agripina in the darkened house.

Five minutes later, Agripina whirled into

the room wearing a fur-lined parka and high leather boots. Even in the cold, her smile sparkled below her dark, cloudy eyes. "Tanya! You're all right."

"I'm sorry Agripina. I shouldn't have left as I did last time." Agripina's smile softened her heart in a way that no words could.

"It's all right. We are all under so much stress! It's a wonder we don't all scream and yell at each other more often."

"How are you?" Tanya blinked back tears at her friend's kind words of forgiveness.

"I've been better, Tanya," Agripina's voice trembled. Tanya noticed the dark circles that showed under her eyes over what was once porcelain skin.

"It's horrible. . . . what these Germans are doing."

"I know. This is worse than an invasion, if you ask me."

"I agree. We don't have any food left." Tanya looked at her friend hopefully.

"We're down to our last stores." Agripina looked toward the kitchen. "But let me go see if we have anything. If anyone should eat, it should be a mama with a baby."

"Oh, no, I couldn't ask you to give up your last provisions."

Agripina grabbed her gloved hand and led her into a huge kitchen. Opening a door on the side, she stared at empty shelves. "We have two cans of sausages and a tiny bit of powdered milk. Would Verushka want those?"

"I can't take those. That's all you have." She shuddered at the thought of her friend starving while they ate her last provisions.

Agripina pressed the cans into Tanya's hand and smiled. "No, really, it's all right, Tanya. We'll be fine. I heard that the city is now selling bread to citizens. It's part of the new rationing program."

"A rationing program?" Tanya's eyes pleaded with Agripina for any news that would save her baby.

"Yes. Every citizen is entitled to 250 grams of bread a day."

"How much is that?"

"No idea, but it's something. Here, let me find you the details of where you can go to register."

Agripina came back a few minutes later with a small piece of paper, reading from it as she talked. "It looks as though you go to one of the kiosks that they've set up all around town and you register. Then you show up and trade stamps for bread once a week."

Tanya was glad there was something for them. "I can't help but wonder if this is what the Germans want. You know, just kill off the entire city and fill it with good Germans."

Agripina's face darkened. "No one is that cruel, Tanya. No one."

"I'm not so sure." Tanya hesitated. Did she really want to reveal her thoughts to Agripina?

"What's going on? You can tell me, you know." Agripina read her mind, giving her no choice.

"I guess I just can't sit here and let my baby starve. I have to do something to save her."

"Isn't that why you came to me?"

"Well, yes, but . . ." Tanya waved at the empty pantry. "You can't exactly help much. And I wouldn't expect you to."

"So, what are you thinking of doing?"

"Maybe if I . . . maybe I can find someone, somehow to get us some food."

Agripina's mouth dropped open. "No, Tanya. No."

"Do I have a choice?"

"We always have a choice. I know you don't like me to talk about God, but I do believe that God has a plan in all this. We have to trust Him. We have no other option."

"But I do have other options. I can . . .

364

well, I can use what I have to get food for my baby." Tanya put on her bravest face. She would do whatever it took for Verushka.

"Let's think about this. Let's say you head out to the lines. The Red Army soldiers are taking quite the beating, so that leaves the Germans. Do you think they want anything to do with a Russian prostitute?" Agripina's face contorted as she said the words.

"They're far from home. Maybe they want a night of comfort?" Tanya hated her words.

"But they hate us. Look how they've treated us. They'd kill you on the spot."

Tanya's eyes brimmed with tears as she considered her options. "Well, then, what about the Finns? They're camped out on the north end of the city."

Agripina looked out the window, her brow furrowing into a frown. "Tanya, please. Just go home and wait this out. And . . ."

"And what?"

"This may sound crazy, but I feel as if God has told me that Verushka will survive this. She'll be all right."

"But she needs me to help her survive. I'm her only hope."

"God is her only hope, Tawnie. Can't you see that?"

"I . . . I wish I believed." Tanya let the words that had filled her heart over the last few weeks slip out. It would be so comforting if she could turn to God and trust Him like Vera and Agripina and even Feodora did.

Agripina wrapped her in a hug, warmth emanating from her and causing Tanya to sink into her friend's embrace. But she pulled back. "You know He loves you, even though you've walked away from Him. He is up in heaven now, intervening at His Father's feet, that your heart will be softened to Him, that you'll turn to Him in your hour of need."

"Come to me, beloved." The words were almost audible, and for a flurry of a moment, Tanya's heart considered it. Had she ever really stopped believing at all? Not really, she had always felt His presence even through these months without Him. Oh, what it would be like to throw herself into the arms of her loving Savior. Should she? Could she?

No. She had drifted too far.

"I can't." Tanya's voice trembled as she looked at her friend's teary eyes. "He would never take me after what I've done."

"There is no sin that can separate you from His love, my dear."

"Says the girl who has lived a perfect life."

Agripina sighed. "Hardly. Trust me, I've

had my share of sins, one being living in this house of luxury and allowing potential sisters in Christ to struggle on the streets without ever noticing their need."

Tanya swallowed hard, blinking back icy tears. "I wish I could turn to God, Agripina, but I just can't. Not when I've learned the hard way that the only one I can truly trust is myself."

# 54

"I will be leaving on November eighteenth for Hango." Anna finished her dissertation, not daring to look into her parent's eyes.

"You already bought your tickets?" Her mother looked up, panic showing in her eyes.

"Yes, I went down to the station yesterday and bought everything I need. I'll even have some money left over to give to Aunt Mary once I arrive." Anna smiled, hoping her trembling voice wouldn't betray the fact that she was as torn up about this trip as her parents were.

"But what about Matti?" Mrs. Ranta's chin trembled as she joined the conversation for the first time.

"He doesn't want to be with me." The words tasted bitter on her tongue.

"That doesn't sound like Matti." Mrs. Ranta said firmly, not even looking up at

Anna. "It must be a mistake."

"No!" Anna pulled the folded letter out of her pocket as proof. "Read for yourself. He says I'm not the woman he thought I was."

Mrs. Ranta took the letter and read carefully. "Did you two fight?" Mrs. Ranta set her jaw firmly, clearly both angry and confused.

"No! I did nothing other than ask if he wanted to get married this fall."

"That wouldn't have scared him off. All he talks about in our letters is coming home to marry you."

Anna let out a small moan. This wasn't going well at all.

"No, this can't be. We need to write him and ask him what's happening before you leave. He wouldn't ever break it off with you like that." Mrs. Ranta set her jaw with determination.

"It's too late." Anna clenched her teeth.

"So you're leaving with no consideration for how it would make him feel? Of the danger this could put him in?" Mrs. Ranta had tears in her eyes.

Her throat tightened. Henrick had died after reading her letter and now Mrs. Ranta acted as though she was doing the same thing to Matti. But this was different. Matti had broken up with her.

"My mind is made up." She tried her best to keep her face neutral.

All four adults in the room paled.

"Now that things have settled into a routine, you'll be fine without me," Anna continued, desperately trying to fill the silence. "I'll write, of course."

Her father looked at her intently. "Is there anything we can say to change your mind, Anna?"

Anna shook her head firmly.

She was being honest. There was only one person who could change her mind, and he had already told her he didn't want anything to do with her.

# 55

"Here, eat." Tanya handed a piece of stale bread to Verushka. The baby reached out toward the bread, fumbling to grasp it in her mittened hand. She clutched and devoured it rapidly, not pausing to chew. "Slow down, baby girl. Here, have some water to wash it down."

Verushka ignored the cup of icy water Tanya offered and instead grabbed another chunk of bread from her hand and stuffed it into her mouth.

"Poor baby, you're so hungry." Tanya wished she had more bread to give her daughter. Their daily ration of 250 grams wasn't enough for anyone to survive on, especially since the bread was made with more sawdust than flour. At least it tasted like it was.

Even with Tanya and Vera both giving Veruskha half of their own daily rations, the baby was still starving.

A moan rose from the other room. Tanya looked over her shoulder toward Vera. The poor woman had grown weaker and weaker as the weeks of the siege passed, and now, she could hardly get out of her chair in the living room.

Tanya stood up and grabbed the wall for balance. She made her way over to her friend. "Vera? Are you all right? Can I bring you some water?"

Vera opened her blue eyes and blinked in confusion. This wasn't good. She didn't recognize her.

"Here Vera, have some water." Tanya held a tin cup to her lips and tried to force liquid through them. Vera moaned, the water dribbling down her chin. "That's it. I'm going for help."

Vera moaned again, not seeming to comprehend Tanya's words.

She had to do something. Or else they would all die. Tucking another wool afghan around the old woman's body, Tanya stood quickly and waited for a wave of dizziness to pass. She went back into the kitchen and grabbed Verushka. "Come on, love, let's go see Miss Agripina." Tanya wrapped the baby tightly against her in an effort to block out the cold and steadied herself against the wall, hoping she had the strength to walk the two kilometers to Agripina's house.

She stepped outside and sucked in a deep breath, the cold stinging her insides. It was hardly any colder out here than inside, really. The walls only served to block out the wind.

Tanya set off down the street, doing her best to avoid staring at the gaunt faces of the people passing her. The townspeople trudged along, their looks of desperation mirroring her own. Up ahead, a man lay face down in the street. Tanya wasn't sure if he was dead or just resting, but she didn't have the energy to check. What could she do about it anyway?

Snuggling Verushka close, she focused on the road ahead, willing herself to take another step forward. She stumbled and almost dropped Verushka as her knees buckled beneath her.

She made her way to a wrought iron park bench to rest. Closing her eyes, she pulled Verushka close and tried to catch her breath.

After twenty minutes of rest, she felt strong enough to make the trek. Pulling the baby into the crook of her arm, she walked slowly, hoping to make it without another stop.

It took her more than half an hour, but

she finally arrived on Agripina's stoop, cold and weak . . . but alive.

She raised her fist to the door and tapped with as much strength as she could muster.

Agripina answered. "Oh, Tanya!" She pulled her inside.

"Where's your maid?"

"She . . . passed away last week." A whimper escaped her lips as she said the words.

"Oh, Agripina, I'm so sorry."

Tears welled in her friend's eyes. "Tanya, that's not all. Both of my parents died yesterday. There just wasn't enough food."

Tanya's stomach tightened in guilt and she moaned audibly. She had taken their last can of sausages for her daughter. She had killed Agripina's parents. "Oh, Agripina, I'm so sorry. I should have never taken your food."

"No," Agripina shook her head firmly. "It's not that. There isn't food in the city. No one in Leningrad will survive this if it lasts much longer."

"Do you have any food for yourself?" Tanya studied Agripina's emaciated form.

"I'm doing better than most. I am young and strong and I'm doing all right on my daily rations."

"Oh, Agripina, no one can survive on those."

"Maybe I can. If the Germans invade soon, I can hold out."

"Can you come home with me? We can work together to try to find something to eat?"

Agripina hesitated as though considering Tanya's offer. "I can't leave my parents' house. It was my grandparents' house, and my father has always worked hard to keep it in my family. Even after he lost his job at the university, he worked hard to keep the house up. I can't bear the thought of someone assuming it's abandoned when the Germans invade."

Tanya pulled her friend into a tight hug, realizing desperation was felt around the city.

"So you're sure you can't leave?"

"I'll wait and pray. I just have a feeling God is telling me to stay for now."

Tanya nodded. She had to get back. "Promise to come see us as soon as this siege is over?" Tanya started toward the door.

"Tanya?" Agripina's eyes betrayed her anguish. "You walked all the way over here. Do you have the energy to make it back with the baby in your arms?"

"I have to try."

"Here, take my ration for today. Eat it so I know you'll be all right." Agripina walked to the kitchen and returned holding a small square of bread.

"Oh, no, I can't do that, Agripina."

"How about half? If you don't make it back, Verushka won't either."

Her friend was tossing her a lifeline.

If only God would do the same.

# 56

Tanya nearly fell into the house.

She set a wailing Verushka on the floor and walked over to Vera. "I'm back."

Vera didn't move.

"Vera?" Tanya shook her shoulder gently. "Vera!"

Verushka wailed louder.

"Vera! I'll get you some water." Tanya rushed to the kitchen, ignoring the baby's cries. Racing back into the room, Tanya shoved the glass of water to her friend's lips and poured it into her mouth. But it only dribbled off of her chin. "Vera, please wake up."

Tanya shook her shoulder again, felt Vera's neck for a pulse, and willed herself not to sink into a puddle of despair.

Vera was gone.

She had been much smarter this time and

brought the pram. At least she didn't have to worry about dropping the baby.

They had set off hours before dawn on a journey strangely reminiscent of the early morning walk Tanya took that fateful morning over a year ago after Nicolai died. Empty streets. An empty heart. And an unwavering desire to complete her mission regardless of what made sense. Or what seemed right.

Tanya had finally reached her end.

Yesterday, after Vera died, she briefly considered trying to borrow her ration card to get more bread. But then she remembered what had happened last week when a woman showed up at the kiosk to collect her dead husband's ration, only to be arrested by the Leningrad police. There was a food shortage and they took cheating seriously.

Instead, Tanya combed Vera's hair and dressed her in her best dress. With a kiss, she set her out on their front stoop in a pile of snow, wishing she could honor the dear woman with a decent burial or a service. But there was nothing she could do.

So she cried for everything lost and everything still to lose. Hours later, the tears hadn't stopped. This, right here, might be her end. And she was all right with that —

she didn't want to live in this world anymore anyway.

But Verushka . . . Verushka deserved a chance.

It was then, in the wee hours of a forlorn night, that Tanya devised her desperate plan.

She layered every article of clothing she owned onto Verushka's trembling form before piling her into her bassinet and layering on blankets. Not that it would help. The entire city was an ice-covered graveyard.

She set off after midnight, heading due north on quiet streets. A few hours later, she trekked onward, navigating her way more by sound than by sight. Weak with hunger and exhaustion, she willed herself to keep walking, knowing that any misstep or hesitation could mean death for both her and Verushka.

Did she have the strength to walk all twenty kilometers?

Did she have a choice?

Verushka woke and started to cry, her cold and hungry wails breaking the early morning silence.

"Shh, shhh. It's all right, little one! I'll get you some food." Tanya tightened the blanket around Verushka, tucking her snug with a hand-knitted quilt, hoping that maybe she would fall back asleep. She stuck her finger into Verushka's mouth and the baby suckled hungrily before realizing Tanya had nothing to offer.

They trudged on, mama and babe, step after step, until she reached the outskirts of the city. Continuing northward, she stopped at an intersection and looked both ways, trying to figure out which way to go. She risked standing under a streetlight for long enough to pull out Vera's compass. She calculated due north. Then she tightened the scarf around her head and hoped it would keep her hair in place before plodding on.

She needed to look presentable when she arrived. Trudging forward, she reminded herself that if she didn't make it up to the Finnish lines before daylight, she'd have to stop and rest for the day. She'd heard German soldiers were shooting anyone outside of the city limits on sight, so she couldn't risk being spotted by a patrol.

A wave of determination passed through her and she quickened her pace. Today she would have bread. Either that or she would be dead.

"Just keep walking," she whispered, her breath coming out in a puff of fog in the cold early morning air.

As the kilometers passed, Tanya allowed

her mind to go numb. With each step, her mind repeated a constant track of "keep walking, keep walking, keep walking." Her steps only slowed every half hour or so when she reached down and felt Verushka's pulse. Still breathing.

"Thank goodness," Tanya said out loud. "Come on, baby girl. Hang in there."

Three hours later, the sun rose over the edge of the horizon and Tanya had stumbled her way almost twenty kilometers to the edge of the massive birch forest that sat on the edge of the border town of Kirjasalo. There, she hoped she'd find a desperate Finn soldier who was willing to trade . . . well, whatever it took.

She ducked behind a tree and sank to the ground in exhaustion. Looking around, she saw no signs of life. Her back was still exposed to the south. She forced herself to stand one more time.

With a weak breath, she checked on Verushka. She was still sleeping, probably too weak to even cry about the hunger pains. "Hang on, baby. I'm getting you help."

Making her way deeper into the forest, Tanya pushed the pram over rocky ledges and tangled vines until her legs trembled with exhaustion. Finally, she spotted a cluster of boulders and edged the carriage into a corner where she hoped it was adequately hidden.

She could no longer stay awake.

# 57

*Kirjasalo, Karelia*

"Wait up!" Takala jogged up to Matti and Käärme as they strapped their rifles onto their backs for their early morning patrol. "I'll go with you this morning, Ranta. Käärme, you just earned yourself the morning off. I can't sleep and I need to get out of that tent."

"As you wish, boss." Käärme clapped his hand across Takala's back. "Thanks."

"You owe me."

"Yes, sir." Käärme headed back to his tent and the two men set off due south, carefully making their way down a worn path through towering white birch trees as the sun started to rise.

"*Brrrr!* It's cold." Takala wrapped his parka tightly around his shoulders and shivered.

"Usually we have snow by this time of year," Matti explained. "Maybe soon we'll be able to do ski patrols."

They walked on in silence, each carefully observing the edges of the road to look for something out of the ordinary. But everything was calm. Peaceful, even.

Takala waved his hand toward a huge stack of moss covered rocks that were clustered on a hillside. "Just look over there . . . the green of the moss covering the towering trees. It's like a picture from a Christmas card."

Matti looked up at the evergreen trees that formed an emerald green canopy over their head and smiled slightly. "Home sweet Karelian home."

Takala put his hand over his eyes and looked out into the forest, pointing out a white speck from behind the boulders. "What is that?"

"I don't see anything." Matti squinted.

"Right over there." Takala pointed again toward the cluster of rocks, already reaching for his rifle.

Matti looked closely. There was something white behind those rocks — maybe an old shirt someone had left out there or something. He put his finger to his lips and gazed toward the rocks. "I'll check."

"I'll come too."

The two men crept off the path, silently making their way through the thick underbrush, doing their best not to make a sound. Creeping around the biggest boulder, Matti peered around the rocks. Was that a wheel?

"It's a baby carriage," he whispered to Takala, gripping his rifle to his chest as he crept closer.

Takala reached the carriage first and peered inside, his eyes immediately growing wide. "There's a baby in it!"

Matti threw his rifle down and ran toward the carriage, reaching down to grab the tiny child wrapped tightly in pink blankets. She was warm. He fumbled through her blankets to find her pulse. "She's alive."

Turning to search the area, Matti scoured the rocks for any sign of the baby's mother . . . there! Matti spotted her next to a cluster of three boulders. He ran over to her. "Ma'am! Ma'am?"

"откуда Вы приехали" The woman looked up at them with wild eyes, frantically scrambling to her feet.

"Russian. She's speaking Russian!" Matti's face twisted into a frown. There shouldn't be any Russians out here in the military zone.

"I know a little Russian." Takala leaned in closer.

"I do too," Matti whispered as he leaned in and did his best to prop up the woman.

"I grew up near the border so I learned it in school."

Takala bent down eye level with the woman, gently reaching out to put his hand on her shoulder before asking her name.

"Tanya," came the whispered reply.

"What are you doing up here?" Matti asked softly, trying his best not to scare her.

She scooted into an upright position, her eyes showing clarity that they hadn't a few minutes earlier. "I-I'm from Leningrad. I'll do anything you want if you give me bread for my baby."

Matti's heart wrenched, compassion filling him as he saw the desperation in the woman's blue eyes. No one — not even a Russian prostitute — should have to watch her baby starve.

Takala looked frantically from Matti to the woman and back again, obviously torn as to what to do. "Our orders say that all Russians should be taken prisoner on sight."

"But she's starving. She needs our help. Who knows what they would do with a woman and a child in prison camps." Matti shook his head at his commander, praying that he would have some empathy.

"Go get our packs. Let's give her something to eat while I try to figure out what to do," Takala barked, his face taking on a hardness.

Matti ran off, returning a few moments later with two heavy packs.

"Ranta, we could get into a lot of trouble for this, you know," Takala said as he grabbed the pack.

"If we let an innocent child starve because we have orders . . . I couldn't forgive myself."

Takala frowned.

"Let's start by getting these two something to eat." Matti pulled out a ration pack and tore it open, removing a small rye cracker and handing it to the woman.

She turned her head and clamped her mouth shut.

"Why is she doing that?" Takala asked.

"The baby," Tanya whispered.

"Go get the baby. We have to feed her first."

Matti ran to the pram and gently scooped up the tiny baby, who remained asleep, even through all the yelling. "Do we have any milk? Something a baby could eat?"

Matti dug frantically in his bag. "No. No milk. Tanya, is your baby able to eat some hard tack?"

Tanya shifted, trying to pull her body further into a sitting position, her eyes cloudy.

"Try to wake her up." Takala gently took the baby from Matti, cradling her in his arms and stroking her face.

The baby's soft cry echoed through the rocks. Takala held the cracker and put it in the baby's mouth. She devoured it and instantly reached for another.

"Now will you eat?" Matti said to Tanya in Russian. "We have enough for you too."

But the woman just shook her head.

"What's the baby's name?" Matti asked.

"Vera," Tanya whimpered weakly. "We . . . call her Verushka."

"And how old is she?"

"She's . . . ten months old. Born . . . January twenty first." Tanya's words came in wisps, barely audible in the early morning silence.

"OK, well, you and little Vera will be fine." Matti tried to reassure her, wiping away the tears that streamed down her cheeks.

"Bring . . . her to me."

Takala gently placed the baby in Tanya's trembling lap, making sure she had a cracker in both of her hands before he let her go.

Silence fell over the forest as Tanya closed her eyes and nuzzled her baby's head. After what seemed like an hour, Tanya looked up to Matti. "Water?"

He ran back to his pack and grabbed his

canteen, squatting down to give the baby a swig before turning to look Tanya in the eye. "Tanya, we have enough for both of you. I promise."

She hesitated before grabbing a cracker and eating it slowly, closing her eyes after each bite.

"So, tell me what you're doing up here?" Compassion flooded his soul.

"I . . . I had no bread, no way to feed . . . her. I thought that maybe I could find a soldier who would trade . . . you know . . ."

"Have you done that before?"

"Before the war, I . . . I uh, I lost my husband and so I dated the officers in the army for money." Tanya confessed readily, as if purging her soul.

Matti's heart flooded with compassion. The poor woman had been desperate for so long.

"God forgives you," Matti whispered softly.

"God . . . I don't believe in Him anymore." Tanya's words were barely a whisper.

"Why not?"

"He took everything . . . everyone . . . from me."

"And you wonder how a loving God could allow all this suffering?"

Tanya opened her mouth and then shut it again.

Matti lowered himself onto the hard ground next to Tanya and looked her straight in the eye. "I can't explain why things happen when they do. I don't know your story or what has happened, but I do know that God is here. He is everywhere. And He loves you."

"He could . . . never love me."

"He led you here, to us, didn't He? I have a feeling we're amongst the only soldiers in this entire encirclement who wouldn't have taken you prisoner or worse."

Tanya smiled weakly. "He did . . . do that."

"Did you pray for a miracle?"

Tears welled up in Tanya's eyes. "I didn't, but my friends did. My friends Vera and Feodora and Agripina all prayed fervently that somehow, some way, little Verushka would survive this siege. Every one of them believed she would survive. Even when things looked impossible."

"Do you believe now?"

"No," Tanya whimpered.

"Even after God brought you here?"

Realization dawned in her crystal-blue eyes. "I can't."

"You must."

"But what if He won't take me?"

Matti turned back to Takala who leaned against a tree, listening to their conversation.

They were talking about much more than the baby's survival. "He will. God takes anyone — saint or sinner — they just have to trust Him and be willing to give their whole life — heart and soul — to Him."

A wave of understanding showed on her face. "I do want that. I want Him."

"Will you pray with me?"

She nodded slowly, her blue eyes sparkling with tears.

"Father God, thank You for bring Tanya and Verushka to us. Thank You for leading them here so that we can help them. Lord, we know that You are real and You are working in our lives and I pray that You fill Tanya with a sense of peace right now that goes beyond human understanding. Help her to feel Your presence and to know without a doubt that You are real. And that You love her . . ."

Tanya interrupted, her voice gaining strength as the words poured forth. "God . . . please . . . forgive me. I want to come back to You."

Her words came out weak and feathery but Matti understood them perfectly. He leaned closer and rubbed Tanya's arm, helping her take another bite of her cracker.

Did that really just happen? Had he just led a desperate Russian prostitute to Jesus?

Praise God.

Matti looked up at Takala, who stared at him wide-eyed.

Maybe next he'd start working on Takala's relationship with the Lord.

He smiled and turned his attention back to Tanya, slouched down against the rock. Baby Verushka lay on her lap, fiddling with a string on her dress.

"Are you feeling better?" Matti hunched forward.

Tanya managed a weak smile. "Much better. My heart feels . . . so light."

"I meant physically, but I'm glad you're spiritually better too."

"I'm better than I . . . have been in years." Tanya's smile radiated with a strength that seemed superhuman.

"I'm glad. Now let's try to figure out what we're going to do to get you out of here to someplace safe."

"No," Tanya's voice was getting weaker. "I . . . can't . . . I'm so tired."

Matti gripped her shoulders and turned her toward him, desperate for her eyes to focus on his. "Stay awake, Tanya." He shook her gently.

But her head flopped forward.

Matti cried out, "She's dying, Takala. Help me! Do something."

Takala leaned over and put his fingers in front of her lips. "She's breathing, but so weak." He grabbed his canteen and dripped water into her mouth.

Matti's throat tightened as emotion filled his chest. He had only known Tanya for a few minutes, but he already felt an eternal connection. He would save this woman and her baby even if it meant losing everything.

# 58

*Kirjasalo, Kalajoki*

As if sensing something was wrong with her mama, Verushka started to wail loudly.

Matti scooped her out of Tanya's arms and wrapped her tightly in the blanket from her pram. He patted her back and burrowed her close to his chest. "It's all right, little one. Shh Shh."

Takala craned his neck around the trees. "Do you think anyone can hear her?"

Matti searched the area behind them. "I doubt it. But we need to do something fast. Another patrol is bound to come by any moment."

"Let's just waltz into camp with an unconscious woman hoisted over our shoulders while pushing a baby in a baby carriage." Takala cracked half a smile.

"All right, we have to think. What can we do?" Matti pulled another rations kit out of his pack and handed Verushka a cracker.

Hopefully she would calm down.

Takala kneeled next to Tanya, dribbling water into her mouth. "Wake up!" His eyes grew wide. "Please, wake up."

Tanya moaned and looked up at them, seemingly confused.

Takala bent down and broke off a piece of the cracker and put it on her tongue.

She chewed slowly. After a moment, she whispered, "H–hh–help . . ."

Matti bent down and put his hand on her shoulder. "Tanya, please do not worry. We will take care of you."

Takala glanced back at him and whispered. "How?"

Matti shrugged. Squinting into the woods, he prayed he wouldn't see a patrol.

Tanya moaned again. "Ve-rrruuuu . . ."

Matti gently set Verushka on Tanya's lap and made sure she was wrapped tightly. The baby cooed.

"Tanya, please eat more. Slowly." Takala held the cracker and helped her take another bite.

Tanya ate, her eyes closing and her mouth seeming to move in silent prayer.

Takala pulled Matti aside. "Maybe we could try to bring them back into Leningrad — see if someone there could take care of them?"

"They're starving in there . . . she just risked her life to escape. If she goes back, she'll die. We have to get her into Finland."

"Finland? How would we ever get her to the border? And even if we got there, where could we bring them? Everyone is starving everywhere."

"If I could get them to Anna . . ." Matti caught himself. Anna was leaving. He swallowed a lump of pain and focused on the baby. "If I could get them to my mom up in Kalajoki, I know she'd take her in. She would find a way."

Takala looked toward the north, scowling. "Kalajoki. . . ."

Matti took a deep breath. "Yes, Kalajoki. We just have to get them up there."

Matti kicked a rock at his feet and sighed. This was impossible. There was no physical way to get Tanya and Vera out of Russia.

Unless. . . . could he? "I could take them."

"How could you take them? You have to report back into base in an hour."

"But what if I don't? You could tell them something happened on this patrol . . ." Matti's voice quickened, the idea churning in his head. He could make it over the border.

"You'll just hike through Karelia with a woman tagging along and a baby in your arms and hope for the best?"

"Why not?" Matti shrugged. Tanya had done it. Why couldn't he?

"And what am I supposed to do? Just pretend you're not around camp? People will ask."

Matti frowned, the beginnings of a plan whirring through his mind. "What if you say I wandered off the path in my patrol to investigate something suspicious in a clearing?" That part was true at least.

"And then?" Takala looked at him, his expression softening as he heard the rest of the desperate plan.

"And that I never came back. Let them search for me for a few days."

"Then as soon as I get them up to Finland, I'll find a way back down here. I'll make up a story about getting lost in the woods and hiding from Russian soldiers for a few days or something." Bit by bit, the plan fell into place in Matti's head. It could work.

Takala stood and stared at him for several minutes.

"Do you think they'll buy it?" Takala finally asked.

"We have to at least try."

Matti ran a gloved hand over his glistening forehead, walked around the clearing

397

and began to collected pine boughs. "Come help me. I'll make a sled of some sort."

Takala stepped toward Matti, resignation showing on his face. "Do you promise you'll come back? I'm . . . I'm not ready to have to face the loss of my best friend. Soldiers get shot for things like this."

"I'll make it." Matti grabbed a six-inch bough and set it on the snowy ground. "I will get her up there and get back down here as quickly as I can."

"It'll take a miracle from this God of yours, I think." Takala sighed.

"Well, I think it's clear that He's in the business of miracles right now." Matti pointed at Tanya and the baby.

"If you make it back, I just might believe it."

"When I make it back, we'll talk." Matti looked at his friend.

"Do you have any supplies?" Takala motioned to his pack.

Matti shook his head. "No."

It was Takala's turn to scowl. "I'll try to sneak into camp to get you some food and stuff. Otherwise, you'll end up in the same situation that Tanya is in."

"What if someone sees you in camp?"

"I'll figure that out when it happens." Takala blew out a big breath. "As I said, this will take a miracle for it to work. I'll be back as quickly as I can."

Matti reached up with his knife, cut a low-hanging branch, and laid it on the ground next to the others. He collected more until he had twenty boughs lying across the snow. Then he pulled a length of rope from his sack and began to weave them together to form a rough sled. As he worked, he prayed. *Lord, please help this to work. Tanya and Verushka must survive.* Twenty minutes later, Matti spotted Takala's green-clad form sprinting toward the clearing.

The baby let out a tired wail from her mama's lap.

Matti twisted rope around another bough and looked toward his friend.

"Here's food, a parka, a warm blanket and an extra canteen." Takala took his hand and inhaled. "Oh, and I grabbed some extra T-shirts . . . I thought you could use them for, for . . . you know."

"For what?"

"For diapers."

Matti's heart raced. "I forgot about that."

"Well, you must be used to the smell. She stinks!"

"So, are you volunteering to change her?"

"No, thank you." Takala laughed, but then his face grew sober. "So, do you . . . still think you should do this?"

"I do." Matti did his best to force a smile. "It's our only choice."

Together the men walked to Tanya and crouched down. "Tanya, we will leave in a couple of hours to try to get into Finland. It'll be a long night, so try to get some sleep right now."

Tanya nodded, her eyes glistening. She patted her now-sleeping daughter on the back and whispered, "Thanks."

With the baby finally quiet, Matti and Takala went back to the pine branches to finish the construction on their rudimentary sled. As he tied a rope around a small branch to make a handle, Matti thought of another kink in his plans. "Takala, what will I do once I reach Helsinki? I can't exactly take the train up to Kalajoki if they think I'm AWOL."

Takala scowled again. They crouched in silence for a few minutes before Takala spoke again. "My sister lives in Helsinki. Her husband Aabraham has a truck . . ."

He bent over to pull a piece of paper out of his pack and began scribbling. *Aabraham, as a favor to me, please give my friend Matti Ranta anything he asks for. I will pay you back double as soon as I'm home. Pauli.* He finished by scribbling down an address in the suburbs of Helsinki. "There. Just give that to him." He whispered.

"What if someone stops me and asks for ID?"

"I guess we just pray that no one does." Takala grabbed his shoulder and looked him in the eye. "Matti, I can't help but feel as though everything that has happened today has been an act of God." Takala clenched his jaw and shook his head.

Matti stared at his friend for several minutes, blinked, and then put his hand on Takala's shoulder. "My friend, I couldn't agree more. When I get back to camp, we'll have coffee and talk this through."

"I think that's the best we can do." Takala pursed his lips into a frown. "Let's hope it's enough."

"No, let's trust it's enough." Matti patted his friend on his back. "Thank you, my friend." Matti sat down next to Tanya and leaned against the log. He saluted his friend and then whispered, "I think I need to get some sleep."

"And I should be heading back to camp?"

"Yes. You should. Goodbye, friend." Matti gave a weak smile.

"Not goodbye. Just see you soon. You'd better come back here next week, or I'll really start to worry."

"Just pray, Takala. Just pray."

"I will. The entire time." Takala turned and strode off into the woods, leaving Matti alone with his thoughts.

A starving, sick and desperate woman and her tiny baby were in his care. Now what?

# 59

Matti squinted at his watch and frowned. How long had he been hiking through the woods? He couldn't see the hour in the pitch-black, but he guessed it was well after midnight.

In an attempt to avoid being spotted by patrols, he had taken a long and circuitous route around Kirjasalo, pulling the sled with a sleeping Tanya and Verushka for ten kilometers west before slowly edging his way north. Now, hours later, he figured he'd gone at least fifteen kilometers. Maybe even twenty.

He stopped and lifted the wool blanket that covered Tanya and Verushka's faces. They had been silent for the last four hours. Both snored softly.

He sighed deeply and resisted the temptation to lie down beside them. He was so tired. "Lord, give me the strength to make it through . . ."

His eyes remained closed and he fought the temptation to sleep. He couldn't afford a nap — not tonight when he had to get as far from the front lines as possible if he wanted to make it into Finland safely. He couldn't afford a mistake — like going the wrong direction. Could he risk using a match to look at his compass? Did he have a choice?

Sitting silently, he strained to hear the sounds of human activity in the forest, the crack of a branch, the rustle of leaves. But all was silent. He fingered his compass and took a deep breath.

"Here goes," he whispered.

Light flickered in front of him, and he quickly got his bearings and calculated his direction. If only the sky wasn't so cloudy, he'd be able to use the stars to navigate. But no such luck. Blowing out the match, he stood slowly, bracing himself for another long trek.

"OK, girls," he whispered to Tanya and Verushka. "We're off yet again."

He took off running, praying the dark path would be free of rocks, fallen logs and, worst of all, patrolling soldiers.

# 60

*Somewhere in Karelia*

Dim light filtered through the needles in the trees, sending slivers of light into what was pitch-black forest moments before. Matti yawned. He would have to stop for the day soon — but if he hurried, he could make it another half kilometer or so before he had to hunker down and hide. He trudged on until he could easily see the outlines of trees.

Was there anywhere safe to hide in these forests?

He looked to both sides of the path, seeing swaths of evergreens and nothing else. Which way would provide the best protection? Every direction looked exactly the same.

Flipping a coin in his head, he turned to his left and stumbled two hundred meters from the path to a small clearing shrouded by a pile of rocks. "This is as good as anything," he whispered.

The baby yawned and stretched out her cramped arms just as he dropped his pack. Then she started to cry.

Tanya blinked awake and grabbed Verushka, soothing her with clucks and whispers.

"Are you hungry?" Matti pulled a tin of rations out of his pack. "We have crackers and tinned fish." He snapped open the can and handed it to Tanya, who quickly scooped out some fish to feed to the baby.

He sank down onto the hard ground and ate his own can of fish, fighting to stay awake.

Tanya eyed him warily and ate slowly, clearly relishing every bite.

"Tanya," he started in his broken Russian. "It's really important that we stay silent today. We are still in Russia and Finnish patrols go down that road every hour or so. We must stay low to the ground and out of sight."

Tanya nodded.

"I need to get some sleep. Can you and Verushka stay quiet?"

"I'll do my best, sir."

Matti sank into his parka and curled up. He was asleep in moments but startled awake moments later with the wailing of the baby. He peeked out.

Tanya was desperately trying to calm her. "Shh shh, Ruski. Shh." Tanya whispered, her eyes wide and frantic.

Matti scrambled from his sleeping place and joined Tanya. He reached toward them and tried to pat the baby on the back, not sure what to do.

"I'll take care of her, mister," Tanya said quietly. "You need to rest."

He wanted to — needed to — but how could he rest when even the tiniest noise would draw attention from a passing patrol? *Lord, help her to settle down so that no one hears us . . . and so I can get some rest.* But even has he prayed, his stomach sank at the fact that the baby's wails still echoed through the forest — loud enough for anyone walking by to hear.

The snapping of a twig startled him awake. He jumped to a sitting position and scanned his setting. The baby was squirming her way out of her mother's arms. Panic rose in his chest as he looked at the bright overhead sun. He'd slept for several hours.

*Oh, Lord, protect us.*

As quietly as possible, he searched his surroundings, hoping to gauge what had made that sound. If there was someone in the woods, they were being very, very quiet. Of course, if there was someone sneaking up on him, that's exactly how they would do it. Stealthily.

He listened for a moment. Were there human sounds amongst the chirping birds and rustling of leaves in the wind?

It was faint, but he was almost certain he heard the sound of boot steps. And the cadence of human conversation.

A patrol was coming down the path.

His heart beat frantically, and he looked up at Tanya and held a finger up to his lips. Shhh.

As quietly as possible, he fumbled through the rations, finding one that included dessert. Maybe a sweet snack would keep the baby quiet.

He held out a cookie to Tanya and motioned for her to give it to the baby.

She nodded and handed Verushka the cookie. Then she snuggled her baby on her lap closer to her chest and leaned back against a log just as the Finnish patrol came into view.

Matti leaned back as well, covering his head and praying that he would be calm.

And that Verushka would stay silent.

This time, the rumbling of an engine woke Matti.

Had he fallen asleep again? Blinking quickly, he looked at the darkening sky and jolted upright. What was going on?

Tanya sat next to the log, once again frozen in fear. She pointed toward the road and Matti glanced toward the path. Voices echoing from about twenty meters to his right. His breath hitched in his throat and he quickly flung himself back to the ground. Had they seen them?

The sound of boot steps through the forest told him they had.

After all this, patrol had spotted him because he wasn't calm enough to stay down.

*"Hei,"* A voice called out.

"Hello." Matti motioned for Tanya to stay where she was and then he jumped up and moved toward the soldiers, hoping he could at least keep Tanya and Verushka hidden. How had he let this happen?

The other patrol passed without seeing them, and Matti relaxed and rested as much as he could for what would surely be a long night. Clearly, he had allowed himself to drop his guard because he was about to get caught.

A sick feeling crept into his stomach.

"Company, unit, position, soldier."

"Ma . . . uh . . ." Matti fumbled for the

right words to say.

"Company, unit, position, please." The commanding soldier repeated.

The sound of the baby's wailing drew the men's attention away from Matti.

"What's that?" All of them looked from him to the hedge of birches from where the cries came.

Matti swallowed hard, trying to figure out what to do. He wouldn't get out of this by lying. He glanced in the direction of the cries. Fear crept into his mouth and tasted like bitter tea. "It's a baby. I can explain."

"Go get her." The commander pointed in the direction, his hand on his rifle.

*Oh, Lord, please protect us.* Did they have any hope of getting out of here alive?

He ran to the birch grove and motioned for a terrified Tanya to follow him. He had no choice.

"This . . . is Tanya and Verushka." He stifled the urge to plead with them. "She's . . . we found them in the woods yesterday while on patrol. They were starving. I'm . . . I'm trying to get them into Finland. They'll die out here." Matti said the words that would likely end his military career. And perhaps his life.

The commander stared at him with a frown for several minutes and then his eyes softened. "I have . . . a daughter about that age."

Matti smiled. Was God working another miracle? "I couldn't leave them there to die, sir."

The commander's eyes grew distant. He took several breaths before speaking again. "Let's go."

"Let's go?"

"Yes, I'll take you to Finland. To Helsinki. I've often asked myself what I would do if faced with a Leningrad civilian. Now I know. I won't let an innocent mother and her child die."

"But you — all of us — could be in so much trouble." Matti had known he was putting his own life and career at risk, but he never intended to bring others into it. "I can't allow you to risk your own life to help me."

The commander gave him a crooked smile and looked to each of his men. "I'm all right with a little trouble. You boys can choose to join us or head back to camp and never say a word."

The other two men in his patrol both stepped forward without hesitation. "We're staying, sir!"

Matti closed his eyes. Praise God.

"I'm Ma. . . ." The commander held up

his hand, interrupting him.

"Don't tell me your name. I won't tell you mine. The less we know about each other, the better."

The commander was right.

He was also saving their lives.

God had provided a ride to Helsinki.

Maybe Tanya really would get her miracle.

# 61

Matti held up the slip of paper Takala had given him and read the address aloud.

"All right, let me drop you off here so no one sees us going into a suburban neighborhood. It will just be a quick five-minute walk to that address."

Matti began to collect his things.

"We do this supply route from Helsinki to Kirjasalo every week — on Tuesday nights we drive up here under the cover of night and then drive back down on Wednesday morning. Then, we go again on Friday nights, driving back down on Saturday morning."

Matti mentally calculated the times.

"We pull out at eight. I'll plan on taking the circuitous route on our way out of town for a few weeks, checking this park here around 8:30 in the morning before heading out. If you want to catch a ride back down

413

to Kirjasalo, we'll find you on that park bench."

Matti sat for a moment and tried to figure out his plans. It would take him at least ten hours to drive to Kalajoki, so it would be tight to make it back to Helsinki by Saturday. But waiting until Wednesday could really get Takala into trouble. "I'll try to make it back down here by Saturday. I have to get back to my unit before my commander reports me AWOL."

"Does he know what you're doing?" the commander asked.

"Yes. But no one else in my unit does, so he'll be hard pressed to hold them off. In fact, they are probably organizing search parties to look for me now."

"All right. Well, Godspeed." He pulled over.

Matti stepped out of the truck and turned to help a silent Tanya and Verushka down. They stood in a small park full of towering birch trees.

"Thank you." Matti smiled wearily at the men. "You saved me. And them. You saved our lives."

"And thank you for doing this." The commander pointed at Verushka, a nostalgic look in his eyes. "Take care of that baby."

"Look for me Saturday! And thank you."

And with that, his no-name co-conspirators drove off, leaving him alone on the shadowy street.

It was too early for him to knock on Takala's brother-in-law's door.

Of course, it was also too early for an AWOL soldier, a haggard woman, and a baby to be traipsing through the Helsinki suburbs.

Matti helped Tanya to sit on an icy-cold park bench. He needed to think for a moment to decide what to do. The supply truck had driven through the night, only stopping once at the border for a routine check. Matti, Tanya and Veruskha had hidden under a blanket on the floorboards and no one had looked twice. Thank the Lord.

He had made it, by the grace of God.

Standing up, Matti made the decision to knock. Sure, it was five in the morning, but Tanya and Verushka had been out in the cold for three days. If she woke up, she would attract attention he didn't need.

He pulled the slip of paper out of his hand and carefully followed the commander's directions — down the street and to the left. Ten minutes later, he stepped in front of a small, A-frame house with white shutters and a widow's walk across the second floor.

He lit a match to double check the address and then stepped up to the door and knocked forcefully.

No one answered.

He waited a minute and then tried again. Footsteps sounded inside.

A blonde-haired woman who looked like Takala, only shorter and rounder, peered through the door with a scowl. "Who are you?"

"My name is Matti Ranta. I'm a friend of your brother's. Can I come in?"

"Is Pauli all right?" A dark shadow crossed her eyes.

"Yes, he's fine . . . but . . ."

The woman looked at him skeptically. Then she turned and called into the house. "Aabraham? Aabraham! Come here."

"It's all right. Here." Matti fumbled around in the pockets of his parka for the note that Takala had given him. "Your brother wrote a note for me."

He handed it to her and she read it carefully. Finally, she opened the door a bit further and stepped back to let them edge inside. Just as he stepped in, a man wearing blue and white striped pajamas raced into the room. "What is it, Kerttu?" He stopped short when he saw Matti.

"This . . . man says he knows my brother."

She held out the note to her husband, still eyeing Matti with icy-blue eyes.

"What exactly is this about?"

"Can I come in so I can explain?"

"I suppose." Takala's sister peered sleepily at Tanya and the baby and then stepped back, allowing them to enter a small parlor. He carefully helped Tanya onto the sofa with Verushka on her lap before sitting down beside her.

"What is going on? We don't often get woken up at five in the morning by unexpected visitors." Aabraham sat down on a velvet chair across the room from them.

"Well, I don't often go knocking on stranger's doors at five in the morning either." Matti tried to smile. "Let me tell you what happened."

He told them the story about finding Tanya and Verushka in the woods.

When he finished, their blank, wary looks left him wondering if Takala had been wrong when he'd told them to come here. If they reported him to the war board now, who knew what would happen to him? Or to Tanya and Verushka.

Aabraham pulled the curtain back from the front window and peered out into the street. The lace curtain fell against the sill, blocking his view of the outside. Aabraham

417

cleared his throat.

Had Matti made a mistake in coming here?

# 62

*Helsinki, Finland*
Matti woke up, stretched his arms above his head, and sank into the soft pillow before grabbing his watch off of the bedside table. Three in the afternoon. He had been sleeping for hours.

He flopped his head back on the pillow and relished the feel of real sheets and a real bed. It had been months since he'd enjoyed the luxury of a mattress and now it was hard for him to get up. But he had to get moving. He had to get to Kalajoki.

For the first time, he allowed himself to think of what would happen when he arrived at the Ojala farmhouse. Would Anna already be gone to America? Pain throbbed in his chest. He still loved her. He probably always would. *Lord, I don't think my heart can bear seeing her when she's . . . when she's already let go of me.*

He stood and slipped on a pair of tan

pants and a plaid shirt that Aabraham loaned him last night, carefully lacing up his boots and running his fingers through his hair before making the bed and heading into the kitchen.

Takala's sister was busy kneading dough. "Good morning, sleepy head!"

"Good afternoon is more like it. Thank you for letting me sleep, ma'am."

"Oh, it was no problem. As I said this morning, any friend of my brother's is a friend of mine."

"You sure weren't feeling all friendly-like when I arrived." Matti grinned at her.

"You try getting awakened by a strange man banging on your door at five in the morning."

"I'm sorry about that."

"It's all right. Now that I know your reasoning, I forgive you."

"Where's Tanya and the baby?"

"They're in the living room. Tanya slept well and came into the kitchen and signaled that she wanted to help me a few hours ago. She helped me make this bread dough and then swept the porch. I wish I could speak better Russian so I could communicate with her."

"And how's the baby doing?"

"A sweet one, she is. But boy, does she

have a temper. I grabbed her cup after she finished drinking her milk, and she let me know that she was not finished."

"Yes, I was terrified one of those screaming fits would alert a passing patrol." Matti clenched his teeth as he thought about what had almost happened during his journey out of Karelia.

"So, what are your plans for today, Sergeant Ranta?"

"Call me Matti."

"All right, Matti." Kerttu put her hands on her hips as her husband walked into the kitchen and handed Matti the baby.

"Hello, Tanya. Hi Verushka." Matti smiled softly at Tanya, hoping he could put her at ease. She must be terrified. "I'm hoping to drive up to Kalajoki tonight. It will take ten hours but if I leave soon, we can probably make it by morning. Are you all right with that?" He explained to her in Russian.

He turned to Aabraham. "That is, if it's still all right for me to use your truck?"

"Yes. We'll make it work." Aabraham looked at his wife with a frown.

"Is it too much trouble?"

"I use it to get to work and people will start asking, but I'll tell them it broke down. I'm sure I can get a ride for a few days," he explained.

"Thank you. I figure if I drive through the night tonight, I can arrive by tomorrow morning. That gives me all day tomorrow and part of Friday to stay up there and see my family before I have to leave to drive back down to meet up with the supply truck early Saturday morning."

Aabraham scowled. "That'll be a tight trip. You sure you can make it?"

"I don't really have a choice, do I?"

"I suppose not." Aabraham looked concerned. "Another issue is you might run out of gas. It's strictly rationed these days. I can get you filled up down at the military base. Kerttu's father has all sorts of contacts. But you may struggle to find enough gas to get back once you're in Kalajoki."

Matti hadn't even though of that. "What can I do?"

"Take a few full gas cans with you and bring lots of cash. I heard that in some places they are charging as much as a mark per liter of gasoline."

"That's insane! You could almost buy a new car for that amount."

"I know. Do you have enough cash?"

"I hope so. I had Takala grab everything I had from camp before I left."

"Here, we have a little savings." Aabraham reached into a covered jar on the shelf above his head and pulled out a small stack of marks.

"No, I couldn't take your savings. You have already done enough."

"The alternative is you getting stuck in Kalajoki and my brother getting in trouble. Take the marks. This isn't a time for pride." Kerttu put her hands on her hips leaving no room for argument.

"Whenever you're ready, I'll take you down to the military yard." Aabraham's gaze faded toward the door.

It was a long shot but Matti had to try.

Even if it meant the pain that would surely come when he saw Anna.

# 63

*Kalajoki, Finland*

Anna rubbed her hands together in front of the wood stove, hoping to stir some life into her fingers before she had to help her mother with breakfast. "Just four more days of this," she mumbled to herself, trying to imagine what it would be like to live somewhere warmer.

Hearing her mother clanging pots and pans in the kitchen, she tugged her sweater tighter around her neck and headed in to help.

"Good morning." Anna raked her fingers through her hair, realizing that she must look like a complete mess.

"Hi, Anna." Her mother smiled weakly before handing her a pot. "Can you go to the ice chest and get me some milk for *risi budua*?"

Anna's mouth watered. Her mother's warm rice cereal was one of her favorite breakfasts, even if their rations didn't allow them have sugar or cinnamon to sweeten. "Sure! Yum."

Anna grabbed her parka, not wanting to face the early morning frost without a jacket, and then headed to the ice box on the back porch to grab a jar of yesterday's milk. At least they still had cattle to produce milk. They were the lucky ones.

Leaning into the ice box, the glint of headlights flashed outside in the distance. Who would be up driving around at this time of day? Especially with the snow and ice?

"Crazy person," she muttered and turned back inside. She set the jar of milk on the counter and then added a log to the wood stove before setting a pot on top. She carefully poured the milk and then measured out two heaping spoonfuls of rice to add to the pot.

What was that sound? It sounded like a baby was crying on their front porch.

A knock-knock-knock echoed through the kitchen. Her mother turned to her. "Who would be at the front door at this time of the day?"

Anna swallowed hard. An early morning visit couldn't be good. What if . . . what if something had happened to Matti? Trembling, she hugged her arms to herself and willed herself to take a breath. "Um . . . I . . ."

"Oh, Anna." her mother read her mind. "The war board doesn't send telegrams at 5:00 AM."

Relieved, Anna wiped her hands on her apron and headed to the door. Cracking it open, she saw a man with a heavy parka covering his face standing next to a tightly-bundled woman with a baby locked in her arms. The baby was screaming. "Can I help you?"

"Anna . . ." The man's voice caught, as if he were holding back tears.

"Do I know . . ." Then she saw him. Her pulse raced in her throat. Was she dreaming? "Matti? Is it really you?"

"Anna. Can I come in?"

She backed up against the wall, holding the door open so Matti and the woman could enter the mud room. She closed her eyes, inhaled his scent as he came close. She clenched the folds in her skirt to keep from reaching out to him. No. She must gain control of her spinning emotions.

What was he doing here?

"Anna. I'm sorry to surprise you like this, but I can explain . . ."

Her mother's voice carried through the

426

hallway, interrupting their awkward silence. "Who is here, Anna?"

Her mother turned the corner, her hand flying up to her heart. "Matti?"

"Hello, Mrs. Ojala."

"Anna, run and get Mr. and Mrs. Ranta. Now!"

But Anna's feet felt like two icicles, frozen in place with fear, her heart thumping wildly into her chest.

"Anna? Did you hear me?"

"It's all right, Mrs. Ojala. I'll go get them." Matti turned away from her and she had to force her hands to remain still — the desire to touch his cheek almost magnetizing.

"The baby?" A look of horror crossed her mother's as she looked from Matti to the strange woman and back again. "Is she . . . yours?"

"No. She isn't."

"Then who are they?"

"Can we get my parents first? I'll explain to you all at once." Matti smiled his typical Matti grin, making Anna fear her knees would collapse and she would slide to the cold floor.

"Of course you can. Run and get them and I'll set some extra plates at the breakfast table. You must be starving."

"Yes ma'am. I am." And with that, Matti

427

hesitated for an instant, looking at her and then back at the door before walking into the other room.

Anna turned to the strange woman who still stood in the doorway with wide eyes. "Hello? What's your name?"

The woman just blinked several times with tears running down her face. Then she kissed the baby's head and closed her eyes as if saying a silent prayer.

"Are . . . are you all right?"

The woman stood still, as if she hadn't even heard her.

Anna's mother began to help the strange woman with her coat. She hung the parka on the hooks and then pulled the woman into the kitchen.

Could this woman be his girlfriend? Was she the reason he had broken up with her? Anna's heart started to beat faster. That made sense. He was in love with someone else. Anna swallowed a sob and leaned against the wall.

"Anna, are you all right?" Her mother turned backward to Anna who was still frozen in place by the door.

"I think so. I just . . . I thought I'd never see him again."

Her mother tilted her head and pursed her lips. "You still love him, don't you?"

A hiccup of a sob.

"I'll never stop loving him. I'll never, ever stop."

Matti was having a hard time focusing on the questions that his parents and the Ojalas asked him. He couldn't think of anything except for the green eyes doing everything they could not to look at him. And those rosebud lips that he wanted to kiss more than anything.

And the woman who had broken his heart without even thinking twice.

"Come again?" He looked at his mother who had settled in next to Tanya and kept reaching over to tickle Verushka's chin, willing himself to concentrate on her question.

"You drove all through the night to get here?"

"Yes. I left Helsinki around eight and drove as quickly as I could to get here. I wanted to get here in time for breakfast."

"And do you have to go back?"

Matti bit his lip. Oh, how he wished he didn't. "Right now, I'm AWOL. My unit commander was with me when we found Tanya and the baby, so he's doing his best to hold everyone off, telling them a story that I'm missing in the woods. If I don't get back soon, I may risk military discipline."

Anna blanched. Why did she care about him still?

"When do you have to go?" His mother was relentless.

"There's a supply run going into Karelia on Saturday morning. I'm hoping to catch it out of Helsinki."

"So you can stay for almost two days?" Mrs. Ranta's eyes brightened.

"Yes. As long as no one in town notices I'm here. And no one at this table says anything about it."

Everyone nodded in solemn agreement.

"You'll take care of Tanya and the baby? You know, when I'm gone?" Matti asked his mom, his eyes pleading.

"Of course I will. As though she's my own." Mrs. Ranta turned to Tanya and said in stilted Russian. "We will take care of you. You are safe now."

Tanya nodded, her eyes damp.

"I knew I could count on you, Mama." Matti smiled too. Tanya and Verushka would be in good hands with his mother. And Mrs. Ojala. And Anna. Not Anna. She was leaving. "When are you leaving, Anna?" he asked evenly, willing himself not to reveal the turmoil he felt in his soul.

"Leaving?' Her gaze locked on his.

"For America?"

"How did . . . you know about that?"

"I ran into Johannes. He told me." Matti tried to keep the ice out of his voice, even though every part of him wanted to chastise her for leaving him without so much as a note.

"Oh." Anna looked as if she had been struck by flak from a Russian plane.

Mrs. Ranta looked from Matti to Anna and back again. "You knew she had applied for a visa, Matti?"

"Of course I did. That's why I broke it off with her." The cold words rushed out of his mouth before he was able to rein them in.

"But I . . ." Anna stuttered, tears falling readily down her cheeks. "I wasn't planning on going without you, Matti. I applied without thinking and was going to turn it down if it came in before you got back . . ."

Matti glared at her. Likely story. Why wouldn't she have just told him that instead of keeping it hidden?

Anna let out a moan and turned to her father. "Please excuse me." She ran out of the room, her shoulders shaking with sobs.

Doubt scampered across his heart.

Wasn't she the one who had decided to move to America without him? He shrugged his shoulders, doing his best to hide his own tumultuous emotions from the others at the table.

"You came back just in time, Matti," his mother said. "She's leaving on Monday."

"Just in time for what? You heard that she doesn't love me?"

"Oh, yes, she does."

"Well, even if she does, I don't think I can trust her." Hearing the words made Matti's stomach tighten. Because even if he couldn't trust her, he still loved her. He probably always would.

She would have to talk to him — after all, it wasn't as though she could avoid him for the next two days. He hadn't betrayed her. Instead, she had betrayed him. But what could she say? That she was sorry? That she had never meant to hurt him? That she . . . still loved him? No. It was too late for that. But at least she could do the decent thing and send him back to the front with an explanation.

She couldn't bear the thought of leaving for America while he was so angry. Or of him going back to the front with all of this emotional turmoil surrounding him.

Anna pushed off of her cot and headed into the living room where Matti sat with his parents. She cleared her throat. "Matti?

432

May I talk to you?"

He looked up, a piece of his hair falling over his forehead just above those gorgeous eyes. "I suppose so."

She almost changed her mind, but she had to talk with him one more time. 'Let's go sit in the kitchen." She hoped her eyes convinced him to say yes. She glanced at his parents, who were pretending disinterest.

Matti rose, followed her out to the empty kitchen, hooked his leg over her mother's favorite chair, and slid down into it. He looked at her with narrow eyes.

Could she do this? She focused her gaze on his.

"Kaino saw a letter that the visa office was accepting applications. I had dreamed of going to America for so long that I just applied on a whim." She licked her bottom lip. "I never meant to hurt you."

"But you're going?" Matti glared at her. The kind of glare her father gave when she let the cows out of the pasture by mistake.

"I wasn't going to — at least not without talking to you and seeing if you'd come with me — but then you broke up with me."

"Can you imagine my surprise to find out that you had applied for a visa without telling me?" He drummed his fingers on the tidy, red-checked tablecloth her mother

433

used for every day. She pulled her eyes from his hands. Anna frowned. "I know. I realize now I handled it all wrong. You were gone for so long, and I started to go stir crazy." Her vision blurred. How could she tell him? Would he understand at all? She inhaled the scent of peppermint candles that burned in the window. "I love you. I wouldn't have gone without you."

His fingers stopped their song. His gaze rose to meet hers and softened.

Anna took a step toward the table. "I made a mistake. Can you forgive me?"

"You made me believe you didn't love me."

Her hands fluttered to her chest, hoping to stop the pounding inside. Had she hurt him so much by her thoughtless decision that she might never get to hold him again? No, God wouldn't do that to her. "I was a fool. A fool to reach for something that wasn't real." She tapped her heart. "When I knew what I felt in here."

Tears glimmered in his eyes as his expression changed from angry to sad. He positioned himself inches from her. "Anna," he whispered. "I wanted a life with you. I wanted to marry you. It's hard to stand this close to you and think about what could've been between us."

She closed her eyes. His words were too painful for her heart to handle. Would he ever forgive her?

If only things had been different. If only they hadn't fallen in love in the middle of a terrible war. If only she hadn't applied for that visa. If only Johannes hadn't told Matti.

If only.

# 64

*Kalajoki, Finland*

Tanya sank down beneath the blue flowered quilt and nestled Verushka into the crack between her arm and her torso. Was this really happening? Did she dare believe that she was actually . . . safe?

The last couple of days had been such a blur. The trek out of Leningrad seemed like a distant nightmare — something she remembered as if through a haze. Meeting Matti and Takala in the woods seemed almost surreal. A different kind of dream.

She pinched her leg hard and prayed, "Lord, if this is a dream, help me never to wake up." She stroked Verushka's downy head and relished the feeling of having a full belly and a warm bed. Two standards of her previous life had become the greatest luxuries.

"But, Lord." Her heart rate picked up as she whispered the words. "What if this family in Finland had other plans for her and Veruska? What if they expected her to leave or to work or to . . ."

*Be still, my child.*

The words, whispered to her soul, stopped her spinning thoughts.

*I am here with you.*

Tanya took a deep breath, blew it out, and then whispered her prayer. "Oh, Father, You have given me my miracle. A miracle I never would have imagined possible yet here I am."

And with that, she allowed herself to sleep — the soft breathing of her baby girl bringing comfort, healing to her soul.

# 65

*Kalajoki, Finland*

Kaino burst into Anna's house and ran back to the bedroom carrying a bright red wool sweater in her left hand and a bag of cookies in her right. "Anna! Anna? I came to — oh, what's wrong with you?"

Anna peered at Kaino, tears falling over her cheeks as they had for the past two hours. "Go look in the living room."

Confusion crossed Kaino's face. "Are you all right?'

Anna shook her head.

Kaino placed her hand on Anna's shoulder and squeezed before running toward the living room. A few seconds later she returned, her face sheet-white. "Oh, my. What's he doing here?"

"It's a long story, but the short of it is that he's temporarily AWOL with permission from his commander."

"All right." Kaino narrowed her eyes and

pulled Anna in for a hug.

"Which means I have to sit here and listen to him chatting with his parents while my heart feels as though it's being crushed because he doesn't love me anymore." Anna frantically wiped tears off of her cheeks and pulled Kaino into the room, shutting the door behind them.

"Of all things . . ." Kaino plopped down on the floor. "Matti Ranta comes back to Kalajoki four days before you leave. What impeccable timing."

"Terrible timing, more like it." Anna sighed. "He knew I was going to the United States. Johannes told him."

Kaino's eyes grew wide. "Oh. Oh, no, Anna. I'm so sorry. I shouldn't have said anything."

Anna puffed out her cheeks and then exhaled. "And I shouldn't have applied."

"But you wanted to go, right?"

"I did. I do. But I want to be with Matti more."

"Will you try to patch things up with him?"

"I can't. He doesn't want me anymore. You read the letter. He said I'm not the person I said I was. And he's right. I told him I loved him, and then when he was gone, I went ahead with my own plans without even thinking about what would happen."

"Maybe you could apologize?" Kaino looked hopeful.

"I already tried that. You should've seen the way he looked at me this morning when I tried to talk to him. I apologized, I asked for forgiveness, and he said it made him sad. No proclamation of love. No hope for a future.'

"Do you . . . blame him?" Kaino's eyes pleaded with her.

"What's that supposed to mean? You were the one who told me to apply, weren't you?"

"I was wrong."

Anna blew out an angry breath. "Now you tell me."

"I'm sure you've hurt him deeply, Anna. He was off fighting a war and heard from someone else that you were leaving him . . ."

"When you say it that way, I sound like a horrible person."

"We both know that you're not. But you'll have to figure out how to make it up to him."

"It's too late. He's going back to the front tomorrow and I'm leaving Monday." Anna pulled out her ticket and grimaced at Kaino. "Remember?"

"What if . . . you didn't go?"

"I have to. I spent my entire life's savings on those tickets."

"I'll buy them from you."

Anna stared at her, confused. "What would you do with boat passage to America, Kai? You don't even have a visa. Plus, I thought you were going to marry Johannes and stay here forever."

Kaino blinked several times and then looked up at Anna. "Maybe I've changed my mind."

"What does that mean, Kai?"

"It means Johannes has made it clear he doesn't want to marry me any time soon. There have been several times in the past weeks that I've regretted not applying for that visa when you did. What if . . . I went in your place?"

"But the visa has my name on it, Kai."

"Go get the visa."

Anna raced over to her parent's dresser where she had carefully stowed her travel papers, her mind racing with what Kaino was saying. If she had the chance for a do-over with Matti, would she take it? Would he consider giving her another chance? Did she want one?

"Here it is." Anna shoved the visa and tickets into Kaino's hand.

Kai took a small washcloth, dipped it into

the basin on her parent's dresser and then scrubbed at the *A* in Anna's name. Anna watched, her heart thumping wildly.

"And . . . there . . . we . . . go." Kaino held up the visa, which now said *nna* instead of Anna. "We'll just erase your name and then use my parent's typewriter to retype mine. I was saving up for a wedding, but that won't happen. I'll buy the tickets from you."

Anna's mind raced. Did she want to do this? She looked from her best friend to the door and back to her best friend and took a deep breath. She wanted Matti more than anything. Even America. "I think . . . I want to stay."

Kaino hugged her close. "And know that I want to go, Anna."

"But what if . . . Matti won't take me back?"

"You must try. Otherwise you'll regret it forever."

"Do I just go talk to him . . . tell him I changed my mind?"

"No, I think you need to do something big — something that shows him exactly how much you care. When does he leave?"

"Tomorrow." Anna spun around and listened for Matti's deep voice in the other room. Could she convince him to love her again?

## 66

_Kalajoki, Finland_

"Here goes nothing, Kai." Anna straightened her blue silk dress and set her comb aside after one final check in the mirror.

"No, here goes something. I've seen how he looks at you, Anna. He still loves you."

"I hope so." Anna sighed and then looked toward the hayloft to assess their work. Earlier in the day, Kaino had helped her spread out a woolen blanket on the floor. Around the blanket, they had set dozens of logs upright and on each one sat a tiny wax candle. Now that the candles were lit, the barn flickered with romantic energy.

They didn't have much as far as food was concerned — the entire town of Kalajoki was strictly rationing for the long winter ahead — but Anna had managed to convince her mother to give her a small jar of honey and a pint of flour to make a honey cake. That, with a small tin of pickled herring and some rye crisps, would have to do for their picnic.

"Anna?" Kaino's voice broke into her thoughts.

She turned to her good friend.

"Should I go get him?"

"What if he says no?"

Kaino put her hand on her shoulder. "You'll never know if —"

"— if I don't try." Anna took a deep breath. "All right, go get him, Kai."

Kaino kissed her cheek. "I'll be praying, Anna."

"Kai?"

"Yes?" She turned back.

"Thank you."

The barn door slammed shut, leaving Anna alone in the flickering candlelight. What if he turned around and walked out when he saw her in here? Or worse, what if he laughed at her? Told her that he had never loved her anyway?

"Stop it," she scolded herself.

*Lord, I love him so much. Please give me the words to show him how I feel so that maybe . . . maybe he'll give me another chance.*

Anna's prayer was interrupted by the creaking of the barn door. Her heart jumped into her throat and she quickly pulled her trembling hands to her sides to keep them from shaking. She had planned this entire evening but hadn't thought about what she would say at this moment.

*Just be honest.* Kai's advice from earlier echoed in her heart. *Just tell him the truth.*

"Anna?" Matti's tall frame came into view.

"Matti . . ." His name came out wispy, sticking in her throat as if caught on her overpowering emotions.

Matti's gaze flew to the candles and then back to her and back to the candles, a look of confusion clouding his blue eyes. "What's this, Anna?"

"Matti . . . I. . . . I'm so sorry." Her words began to spill out, unedited. "I never wanted to leave you, and I was so stupid to apply for that visa without telling you first. I'm so sorry."

He pulled his hands from his pants pockets and took her hand. "I told you that I forgive you, Anna. But that doesn't change the fact that you're leaving."

"What if I didn't go?"

His eyes narrowed. "What do you mean?"

"Kaino is going in my place. I want to stay here . . . to see if I can make things work with you." Anna hesitated. For a moment, she saw hope flicker on Matti's face. "I never wanted to hurt you. I have never loved anyone like you before. I missed you so much and got so lonely and I made a huge mistake. I wish I could go back . . ." Anna's words gushed out unfettered in a rush of emotions.

"I believe you, Anna." Matti's eyes reflected the pain in Anna's, showing her that he still carried feelings for her. "But what about the war? What if you get restless again?"

"I'll wait, Matti." She jerked her hands from his and clasped them together. "I'll wait for you as long as it takes."

He pursed his lips and inhaled deeply. Closing his eyes, he blew out a breath and Anna knew he was praying. Then, he opened his eyes. "Anna," he choked out. "I love you. But I don't think I can ever be the man you want. You were born wild at heart. I don't think you'll ever be content with me."

"No!" she cried. "I can be . . . I am . . ."

But Matti pulled her toward him and kissed her gently on the head. He stepped away, shaking his head slowly. "I wish I could say yes, but I can't put my heart through that again."

She swallowed the flurry of hope she had felt all day. Heat rose to her cheeks. He truly didn't love her anymore. Turning to look at the flickering candles, she suddenly felt

447

desperate to escape the barn and go somewhere where her emotions weren't like open wounds.

She looked up at Matti and saw a glistening in his eyes. He too ached for what could've been.

But it was too late.

She turned and raced from the barn, up the path toward the familiar farmhouse where she had grown up. As she took the front stairs two at a time and fell into her mother's waiting arms, she realized for the first time that despite all of her efforts to get away from home, this was the only place where she felt truly safe and loved.

And on a day like today, she needed the refuge of home more than ever before.

## 67

*Kirjasalo, Karelia*

Matti willed his heart to return to its normal pace.

His company mates had assumed he was captured or dead — and had probably spent the last few days facing their own mortality in this war while worrying about his. He hated the lies. But he had also hated the thought of Tanya and Verushka starving. He had done the right thing, hadn't he?

His heart wasn't so sure.

As soon as he had entered his tent, Takala had pounced on him, hugging him tightly, the relief evident. "What happened?"

Matti quickly briefed him on the events of the last few days, giving him a full update on his sister as well as on Tanya and Verushka.

"So everyone is all right?"

"Everyone is great." Matti forced a shaky smile.

"You don't look so thrilled."

"I saw Anna."

Takala bit his lip. "And? It doesn't seem as though it went very well."

Matti looked down at his boot. "It was . . . horrible. She apologized and said she loved me again and cancelled her trip to the United States and I . . . told her I couldn't do it again."

Takala's Adam's apple bobbed. "Why did you do that?"

"Well, because I was scared she'd do it again. You know, leave."

"Oh, man." Takala frowned.

"I regretted it as soon as I had left, but it was too late to go back. I would have missed my ride down here. Do you think I can ask her for a second chance in a letter?"

"Honestly?"

Matti sighed. "I can't stop thinking about her."

Takala exhaled deeply. "I wish I had a woman who made me feel like that, Matti. You are miserable without her."

"I know. And I went and blew it because I couldn't bear to put my ego on the line." Matti swallowed and clenched his fists at his side. "Now there is nothing I can do short of going AWOL again to get her back."

Takala frowned. "Don't even think about

it, Ranta. I'm not going through that again."

"She's probably so angry with me that she wouldn't take me back anyway." Matti wished he believed his own words, but somewhere deep inside he knew Anna was up in Kalajoki feeling as heartsick as he was.

Takala glanced out the window and noticed two of the commanding officers racing toward them. "Hey, ready up. Two officers are on their way in here. They must have heard you were back."

Panic rose and acid surged in his gut.

Takala looked at him with concerned eyes and slapped him on the back. "We'll talk more about this later. Now let's make sure this story sounds right to command. The last thing we need is to get caught now. This is the easy part."

Matti sighed.

"You ready for this?" Takala whispered.

"Ready as I'll ever be." Matti unzipped the tent and zipped his parka, following Takala toward command.

"Oh, and Matti?"

"Yes?"

"Thanks for coming back. It means a lot to me that you did the right thing even when it was so, so hard."

Matti forced another smile.

Takala didn't know the half of it.

# 68

*Kalajoki, Finland*

"I can't believe we're doing this."

"I can't believe you're doing this." Anna stared at her best friend, assessing her emotions.

"I can." Kaino said. "I've spent too much time pining away for Johannes. It's about time I give him a reason to pine." She laughed as she tossed her last few sweaters into her trunk. "Plus, I'm ready for a grand adventure. I need a new start."

Anna choked on a sob.

"I'm sorry, Anna. I am being insensitive. You know that if you still want to go, you still can."

"It's all right . . . I need to stay here, to figure things out before I go running off on some grand adventure."

"I'm sorry things turned out this way. Really, I am." Kaino seemed to know full well that Anna was anything but all right.

"Let's talk about something else," Anna said. "What did your parents say when you told them?"

"They weren't thrilled. But I told them I had made up my mind and they were welcome to visit me."

"Sounds about like my parents' reaction."

"Only yours had more time to get used to the idea. I'm leaving tomorrow."

"And what did Johannes say when you told him?"

"He doesn't know yet. I sent him a letter but he probably won't get it until next week. And I'll already be long gone."

Anna grabbed a hand-knitted sweater and folded it. "So, will you try to get him to follow you to America after the war?"

"We'll see." Kaino shrugged. "At this point, I'm thinking I should just make a clean break."

"But will you miss Finland?"

"Of course. I will especially miss you. But I'm going to America. I'll be doing the whole American-dream thing. You act as if you haven't spent your entire life dreaming of the same thing."

Anna looked at her friend wistfully, wrestling with emotions that were too painful for words.

"Anna, I'm proud of you. You are being so

brave in spite of everything."

"I don't really have a choice, do I?"

"I guess you don't. Still, you're the bravest person I know. And I think God has something in store for you and Matti."

"You sound like my mother. I'm not getting my hopes up."

Kaino held up Anna's old travel documents that now said "Kaino Pajari" in bold letters across the top. They looked slightly worn, but passable. "How do these doctored documents look?"

Anna frowned. It hurt seeing Kaino's name printed across the passport to her dreams.

"Are you having regrets?" Kaino's stare bored into her eyes.

"Yes and no. I don't regret trying with Matti, but I'm sad that it didn't work. Still, God has made it clear that I need to stay here — I never had peace about going anyway."

Kaino pulled her into a hug.

"Will you write?" Anna said, choking on her words.

"Of course I will."

Anna left the room, wishing things had turned out differently. Because while she knew God had kept her in Finland, she was still trying to figure out why.

# 69

*Kalajoki, Finland*

She should be on a train to Hango right now.

Anna sulked into the kitchen and put a kettle on for coffee. She did her best to remain cheerful, but she just wanted to throw a pity party.

Tanya was quietly scrubbing the windows in the dining room while baby Verushka played on the floor.

She shivered. Tanya. How Anna wished she spoke better Russian than the few words she had learned in school so she could communicate with this strange, quiet woman. She needed a friend right now. Someone to talk to. Earlier this morning, she had waved goodbye to her best friend as Kaino pulled out of the train station on the road to living her dream.

She'd sure said a lot of goodbyes lately. To Kaino. To Matti. To her plans. To everything she'd ever wanted. And now — well, now, here she was in the farmhouse where she had lived her entire life with a massive winter storm brewing outside making it all but impossible to leave the house. And the only person to talk to didn't even speak her language.

Watching the young Russian widow wash windows wasn't exactly her idea of a good time.

Why had God left her here? Talk about cabin fever.

*Lord, I know You want me to be here right now, but it's hard. I can feel it in my soul that I made the right choice. But I'm not sure I can stand another winter trapped way up here in Kalajoki with nothing to do but paint and cry.*

Paint.

That's what she could do.

She strode over to the cabinet at the edge of the living room near where Verushka was banging her mother's pan lids together. Anna drew back, the sight of the baby causing her stomach to drop.

Matti had risked everything to save this little girl and her mother.

Yet he wasn't willing to risk anything for Anna.

A lump rose into her throat.

Would she ever be able to accept Tanya

and Verushka as part of her life when they reminded her so much of what she had lost?

She gathered her painting supplies and watched the baby carefully. Bright blue eyes peeked up at her as she raised a spoon into the air and waved it back and forth. She really was a beautiful child. An innocent child.

Anna certainly couldn't blame this baby or even her mother for her own broken heart. Matti had only shown his good heart by saving them.

"*Ga ga gooo.*" The baby beamed, a tiny white tooth showing between pink-tinged lips.

Anna stared at her and sighed. And then she had an idea.

It was almost Christmas. She may not have the capacity to connect with Tanya and Verushka, but she could paint a picture of the baby for her mom. A memento from her time in Finland. Maybe when Tanya went back to Leningrad, she would bring it with her.

Anna scooted her easel to a place near the window where she could see the baby but where it wouldn't be obvious what she was doing.

"*Ba ba baaaa!*" Verushka cooed and Tanya's gaze darted up to stare at her baby girl. She

457

wiped a tear from her face.

Anna's heart dropped. Tanya had been through so much.

*"Ba baaaa!"* Tanya smiled and then turned back to the window.

Anna stared into the baby's crystal blue eyes. Matti had been willing to risk everything — his standing, his freedom, his finances — for this child.

According to the Bible, this child was worth more than rubies or gold. More than Matti's military career. More than . . . her feelings. Maybe this was why God had kept her here. In Kalajoki?

Her paintings were typically filled with distant places and exotic dreams, scenery that only lived in the back of her mind. Whenever she painted something she could see or touch — her father's orchard, her mother's hearth, the eyes of someone she loved — she ended up tearing it up in a fit of emotion. Of indecision.

Suddenly, the idea of painting this baby right there in her own home, with the backdrop of her everyday life behind her felt like a warm breeze on a sultry day.

She pulled out tubes of red, white, and orange paint and began to mix a perfect peachy flesh tone to match Verushka's ruddy skin. Adding a stroke to the blank canvas, she took a step back and assessed whether the color combination was perfect before she began a careful outline of the baby's face.

Two hours later, she stepped back and looked down at the baby, asleep on the floor in a pile of toys. Anna walked over to Verushka and gently stroked her cheek, relishing the smooth feel of supple baby skin.

She glanced at Tanya who was now working on a sewing project nearby. "Can I hold her?" She made a holding motion with her arms.

Tanya nodded.

Anna sat down, pulled the baby onto her lap, and held her before looking back up at her painting.

It looked just like Verushka.

Anna smiled at the image, assessing the sparkle of Veruskha's eyes, the pudgy lines of her knees and even the window she had painted behind the baby's smiling face. A window that showed a backdrop of familiar trees and her family's barn.

She had painted home.

# 70

"Sergeant Ranta! May I have a word?" Takala's voice boomed above the din of the men who were gathered in the mess tent in an effort to stay warm in the middle of the massive winter storm that had blown into Kirjasalo overnight.

Matti shivered as he took a final swig of his bitter coffee and tossed the cup into the mess tray. "Sure. Where to, Takala?"

"Let's go over there." Takala pointed to an empty table in the corner.

"Whatever you say, boss," Matti grumbled. He followed his friend, doing his best to shake the scowl that seemed bent on decorating his expression.

"Ranta, you've been miserable ever since you've gotten back," Takala said sternly.

"I know I have. I apologize, sir!"

"You hate the way you left it with Anna."

"Yes, that about sums it up. I wish I could

460

go back to that night and respond differently."

"I have something that might cheer you up. An early Christmas present of sorts."

Matti looked at his friend, doubting that anything could change his mood.

Takala pulled a folded slip of paper from behind his back and handed it to Matti.

"What's this?"

"Open it."

Matti slowly unfolded it and read the words. "What . . . how?"

"It's two weeks of approved leave for you. I told command that I was worried that the trauma of the past month is getting to you. You need a few weeks of R & R in order to be your best for the spring. You can leave next week."

Matti's lips parted and closed again. "What will I do with two weeks off? Wander around Karelia?"

"Well, that's part two of my little gift." Takala pulled an envelope from under the table. "Train tickets from Helsinki to Kalajoki. You don't have to worry about being sneaky since you won't be AWOL this time."

This time Matti's mouth dropped open. Did he dare show up in the Ojala household after what he'd done to Anna?

"I figure you can catch a ride to Helsinki

on a supply truck," Takala continued, smiling through Matti's fumbling attempts to speak.

"I don't know what to say."

"Say thank you."

"Thank you." He pumped his friend's hand. What a gift. He had an opportunity to make things right with Anna.

"Oh, and this time, you'll marry her. No more of this 'wait for me' and 'maybe soon' stuff. Get down on one knee and make her your bride."

Matti's head jerked to the side. "She'll never marry me after I walked away from her."

"That's why you'll have to do some major groveling."

"Do you think?" An idea started to form in Matti's mind, and he smiled for the first time in weeks. "Do you think she would go for it?"

"I think you'll be miserable and discontent for the rest of your life if you don't try."

"You know me so well," Matti said.

"Spend two weeks with a moping Karelian and you'd do just about anything to escape the doldrums too."

Matti laughed. "If I can make this work, I think I'll need some help."

"At your service." Takala put his hand to

his forehead in mock salute.

Matti explained his plan to his commander, detailing what he needed.

Takala pushed away from the table and headed toward the officer's tent. "I'll send a telegram to Kerttu right now."

Matti smiled. And for the first time in a month, hope flooded his soul.

## 71

*Kalajoki, Finland*

Matti clicked his tongue impatiently at the horse dragging his feet as if he was walking in six inches of snow. Technically, he was, but that didn't mean that Matti could wait for him to dawdle.

He had managed to borrow a horse in Ylivieska after realizing that there wasn't a drop of gasoline in Northern Finland to put into a car. Matti had pounded on the grocer's door and begged him to loan a horse and cart, which the grocer had done begrudgingly after Matti pressed several marks into his hand.

The whole horse fiasco had cost him a precious hour, which now made the journey from Ylivieska to Kalajoki even more painstaking.

"C'mon, boys! Giddyup!" He twitched the reins, checking his pocket for the twentieth time to make sure the tiny blue box was still in there.

It was.

He'd sent a telegram to both his mother and Anna's to make sure she was there when he arrived. Assuming they got the message, everything would be ready.

He huddled into his fur-lined parka and settled into the ride, fidgeting the reins with each slow step. Finally, after an hour, he spotted the lane that led up to the Ojala farmhouse. Matti swallowed impatiently. He could make it faster walking. Or running.

*Lord, I have to get this right today.* Itemizing through a mental checklist, he confirmed that everything was ready. It had taken some finagling — and some major help from Takala's sister in Helsinki — but it seemed that everything was in order.

He only had to convince Anna to say yes.

Taking the steps leading at the farmhouse two at a time, he burst in the door and smiled at Mrs. Ojala, who grinned widely upon seeing him. "Matti!"

He winked and paused for a moment to catch his breath. "Are we all ready?"

She beamed. "About time you got here, Matti. She's been a total mess all week. It was all I could do not to tell her so she'd stop wallowing."

"Let's hope I can help her to snap out of it."

Matti's mother walked into the room, her eyes sparkling. "My boy." She straightened his collar and kissed him on the cheek. "I'm so proud of you."

He smiled back. "Where's Anna?"

"I asked her to work on some mending for me in the living room." Anna's mom said conspiratorially. "Told her if she was to mope away the day, she could do it with busy hands."

Matti turned toward the room. This was it.

He stopped and composed himself before peering in. There she was — his one true love — sitting on the sofa darning a sock while staring out the window into the snowy pasture. The sad look on her face proved to him that her mom had been right about the moping.

Well, not for long. He hoped.

"Anna . . ."

Her gaze shot up, a look of confusion clouding out the sparkling green.

"Matti?" She dropped the sock in her lap and her hands fluttered to her cheeks.

How had he ever told her no? "Anna." He moved to stand in front of her and then bent on one knee. He stroked her bare arm with

466

his hand, marveling at the silkiness of her skin.

"What are you doing here?" She managed. Her voice came out breathless as if she'd been ice skating on the pond in the back field.

Matti choked back the sweet image. Later, there would be time for these thoughts later. "I came to apologize."

She kept his gaze, locking right on as though she didn't believe what she was hearing.

"I never should have walked away from you last time. I regretted it the instant I pulled out of your driveway. I love you Anna — I love everything about you. Even the side of you that wants to go off on some great adventure."

"I don't know what to say."

"Say you'll forgive me. That you'll give me another chance."

Anna hesitated. Would she turn him away? After he'd come so far?

"I still can't believe you are here. Are you, really?" She touched his hair, and it was all he could do not to lean into her hand.

"You said I would hurt you again. That you were afraid I wouldn't be content with you."

"I was wrong." He blinked several times.

"I love you."

"Matti . . ." she finally whispered. "I still love you, too."

"I'm sorry, Anna." He tapped her nose with his finger.

She cocked her head to the side.

It was finally time for that kiss he had dreamt about for so long.

His lips press against her soft ones, and he gave into his desire. He pressed harder, wishing he never had to lift his mouth from hers. A quick sigh came from Anna and she tipped her head back and peered into his eyes. She closed her eyes again and he found her lips a second time, reveling in the peace that came with knowing he was finally exactly where he needed to be.

"You'd better watch yourself, Miss Ojala. Too many more kisses like that and a man will have no choice but to go permanently AWOL."

Anna laughed and pointed toward the window. "Speaking of, are you AWOL again?"

He held a finger to her lips. "We'll discuss that later. For now, I have a more important question."

He reached into his pocket, pulled out the blue box, and returned to his knee. "Anna Ojala, will you marry me?" He opened the box to reveal a small solitaire.

Her mouth dropped open and she sighed deeply, clearly struggling to get a grip on the torrent of emotions.

He took her graceful hand into his and squeezed. "I've loved you for more than a year and I don't know if I can go another day without having you as my wife."

Anna opened her mouth and then shut it again. Finally, after several minutes, a smile crept onto her lips. "Yes! My answer is yes."

"Now that's better." He kissed her hand before standing and pulling her into his arms for a long, slow kiss.

She leaned back, a trembling smile radiating from her face. "It's about time you asked me, Sergeant Ranta."

He grinned at her before planting another kiss on her waiting lips.

She pulled back. "Will you get in trouble for being here?"

"Nope! This time I'm here with full permission of the Finnish Military Commission."

"Is the siege over?" Anna looked at him hopefully.

"I wish. It seems as though it'll be forever. But Takala managed to get me two weeks of leave so I could come up here and have Christmas with my wife."

Anna looked at him and laughed. "We can't get married on Christmas. That's just a week away and I don't have a dress or a cake and we haven't talked to Pastor Laiho or anything!"

"Oh, we're not getting married on Christmas." He kissed her quickly on the lips again as a look of disappointment crossed her face. "We're getting married today."

Her wide eyes registered her disbelief. "And how will you make that happen, soldier boy?"

"I had some help."

Anna's lips parted and then closed again. "But we have so much to talk about . . . to catch up on."

"And we will, my love. But for now, I can't stand the thought of waiting any longer to marry you."

Anna hesitated. "But things are so complicated."

Matti held a finger to her lips. "Shhh, my love. We'll figure it out. Together."

A look of joy crept onto her face. "All right, let's get married, soldier boy."

"I'll head to the church with your father and mine. We'll see you there in an hour."

Anna just sat there, dumbstruck.

"There's a blue box your mother should have put on your bed. That should take care of the dress."

Tears trickled down her face unhindered. "Matti, once again, I don't know what to say."

"You already said it all . . . you said yes."

## 72

*Kalajoki, Finland*

The dress couldn't have been more perfect if she had picked it herself. Anna stood on her tiptoes, and stared at her face in the full-length mirror. It wasn't a traditional wedding dress, but it couldn't have fit her personality more perfectly. Bright emerald satin adorned her bodice, hugging her curves elegantly before flaring at her knees. She twirled, revealing emerald-green heels adorned with tiny white pearls.

"How did he manage to get a dress like this with rations?" She looked up at Mrs. Ranta, wondering who had sacrificed to make her day perfect.

"I guess his commander's dad is pretty high up in the military. His sister Kerttu was able to alter one of her ball gowns to make it just your size."

"It's beautiful." Anna spun around in a twirl, her hands swishing the soft fabric.

"Not as beautiful as you, Anna. Now hold still so I can pin up your hair."

Anna stopped her twirling and sat in front of the mirror, puckering her lips into a kiss as her mom ran fingers through her unruly waves. She twisted the sides to the back and fastened the loose waves at the nape of Anna's neck, pinning it with a beautiful pearl comb that had been Anna's grandmother's.

Every detail of this wedding seemed perfect. And it had all been planned without her even knowing.

Anna smiled. How well Matti understood her.

He'd known that she would've been overwhelmed at the idea of planning a wedding — she would've wanted to just skip the formalities and get to the good part of being his wife.

How perfectly he'd planned everything so she could do just that.

Her mother tucked one last tendril behind her ear and smiled. "You look beautiful, Anna."

"Thank you."

Just then, her father walked in, wearing his best Sunday suit. "You ready to become Mrs. Ranta?"

"I've never been more ready." Her fingers

trembled as she looped them through her father's, not from nervousness but with excitement.

The two of them stepped out into the church lobby where Tanya stood next to Verushka, propped up in a pram wearing a long, pink gown that Anna had worn at her christening.

"You look adorable, Rushkie dear." Anna tickled her chin and kissed her on her downy curls.

Verushka reached into a basket full of rose petals and tossed a handful out of the side of the pram before sticking one into her mouth.

Tanya ran up to the baby and plucked the entire basket out of her reach. "No, no, baby girl," she whispered.

"Who put flowers in her pram anyway?" Anna asked

"I did. I was letting her be the flower girl," Mrs. Ranta chimed in.

"Already spoiling her." Anna chastised her future mother-in-law with a smile, and discreetly handed Verushka a cookie from the table to chew on instead of the flowers. "Here, this will taste better so you can save the flowers for throwing."

The organ music piped up. Anna peered into the sanctuary, which was packed with all of her friends and family members who stared back at her with expectant smiles.

But those smiles blurred as soon as she caught sight of Matti.

The man who still loved her in all of her independence, her flaws, her impulsivity. The man who gave her a reason to breathe, to hope, to dream. The man with whom she would spend the rest of her life.

Tanya pushed Verushka's pram down the aisle and took a seat toward the front.

Anna's father entered the room. He took her arm-in-arm and smiled at her. "Are you ready, my love?"

"Never been more ready." Anna blinked back tears.

He stepped slowly into the aisle, and together they walked to Matti — her groom! Her love. When her father placed her hand in Matti's, he reached down and kissed her hand tenderly, his eyes revealing a hunger that would only be fulfilled by loving her.

"I love you," he whispered, emotion choking his voice.

"I love you too, Matti." She took his other hand into hers and faced him at the altar. At last. All of her hopes, dreams, and plans were finally coming to fruition. Not in the way that she had planned.

No, everything had worked out just as God had planned.

# AUTHOR'S NOTE

There are strands of truth woven into the fiction of this story. My grandmother, Kerttu Ojala, grew up in Kalajoki, Finland during the war. Like Anna's family, her family (of ten!) took in a family of six from Karelia after the Moscow Peace Treaty. They literally split their house in half, dividing their farm, possessions, and their livelihood with a family of strangers. It was incredibly hard — I imagine — but lifelong friendships were forged during those years of poverty, despair, and ultimately, hope.

Several of my great uncles fought in the Finnish army during the war. Many of them participated both in the winter war, and were (somewhat) unwilling participants in the siege of Leningrad. Like most Finns, my relatives desperately wanted to win back Karelia for Finland but were very skeptical of the Nazi partnership and hated the idea of keeping food and supplies out of a city of civilians. In the end, Finland held their lines with the Germans on the outskirts of Leningrad from August 1941 until January 1944, resulting in thousands of civilian deaths as the city nearly starved.

Like Matti, many of my grandmother's Finnish brothers, cousins and uncles were outgoing and passionate, often carrying the emotional side of a relationship, while the women were more analytical. It showed in the way they courted, married, dated, and even in the way they fought.

Like Anna, my grandmother dreamed of going to America. Her older sister Vera applied first and got a visa just after the war, but in a last minute change of plans, my grandmother decided to take her place. She used a washcloth to erase her sister's name and an old typewriter to write her own. It's amazing that it was that simple — but it worked. She came to America in the mid 1940's, married a Finnish lawyer, and raised five children in Oregon. She is now 88 years old and lives right next door to me and my family.

# A DEVOTIONAL MOMENT

Surely your goodness and love will follow
me all the days of my life, and I will dwell
in the house of the Lord forever.
~ Psalm 23:6

God's love endures forever, and Christians
are to emulate it to our best ability. By doing so, we show the love that God has for
us so that others may start a relationship
with God for themselves. People can love
an infinite number of other people — it's
the amazing way God has made us — but
sometimes we experience a once-in-a-
lifetime love which is so deep, that it tran-
scends all other earthly loves. This love is
ever faithful and fulfills the commandment
to love one another fully.

In **Painting Home**, there are two storylines
which intersect, each showing how humans
can do extraordinary things because of the

profound love they have for another. Lives are transformed by that love, and lives are changed in ways they never expected.

Have you ever known someone who was so in love with God that their eyes glimmered with it, their speech resonated with it, their actions proved it? Did you admire them — want what they had — or did you think there was something wrong with them — that their Christianity was too rigid or freakish? We are to love God with such a passion that nothing can usurp it — the same type of sacrificial love He has for us. A love that beckons others towards God. As an extension of that love, we are to love others, also. Even when they are unlovable.

The next time you are tempted to roll your eyes at someone's genuine piety, stay yourself. Ask yourself if it isn't true that deep down you want what they have: that deep relationship with God that surpasses all understanding. If you want it, you can have it! God is waiting. Cultivate the relationship with Him and love will grow by leaps and bounds, and you will be a light to the world.

LORD, KEEP MY HEART, AND HELP ME TO LOVE WISELY SO THAT OTHERS MAY SEE YOUR HEART GLOWING WITHIN MINE. HELP ME TO SHINE THE LOVE YOU HAVE FOR ME TO ALL. IN JESUS' NAME I PRAY, AMEN.

# ABOUT THE AUTHOR

**Erika Jolma** is a staff writer for a major New York advertising agency by day and a Christian novelist by night. She lives in Austin, Texas with her three kids, right next-door to her Finnish grandmother who regales her with stories about life in Finland during the war. This is her first novel.